The Body on Hamilton Reach

Dr Hamish Hart Mysteries - Book Six

Karen Thurecht

Karen Thurecht

Also by Karen Thurecht

Dr Hamish Hart Mysteries

Book 1: Murder at the Dunwich Asylum
Book 2: Plantation Murders
Book 3: Murder at Frog's Hollow
Book 4: Death at Deepwater Point
Book 5: The Blacksmith's Widow

Karen's books are available from: https://karenthurecht.com.au

The author acknowledges the Traditional Owners and Custodians of this land, and pays respect to their Elders, past, present and emerging.

For all those on whose shoulders we stand.

PROLOGUE

Lillian

As Lillian stepped from the Exhibition Hall onto the street a lump settled itself stubbornly in her throat. The night had not gone well. She'd been fully prepared for the likelihood that no one would notice her painting among so many accomplished works. Indeed, she wasn't sure how Miss Langford had convinced her to enter it. But Anne-Marie Langford was everything Lillian was not, a part of the art world, a member of Brisbane society, rich. It was easy for Lillian to believe Anne-Marie when she said the painting was worth showing. It was not. She'd never painted anything before in her life. No one in her family, as far as she was aware, had ever been an artist. It was ridiculous to think she had suddenly taken up a brush and realized some innate talent that had been lying dormant for unknown generations.

Lillian wrapped her arms tightly around herself and threw her head back in a gesture of wrenching humiliation. To hell with the painting, if she hurried, she could still turn her fortunes around.

She was propelled forward by the vision in her mind's eye of dark eyes staring into her own, and the soft sensation of a man's lips against her cheek.

Hope vibrated, intense anticipation rose; she nursed a belief that life could be more than her current experience. A future opened before her, misty and indistinct, but with glimmers of promise, and it swirled before her eyes like an evening fog. An evening that lay somewhere just ahead of her, an evening she had only to step into.

So absorbed was she, in the possibilities of the future, she barely registered the click of horses and the rattle of the carriage pulling alongside.

A shuffle of quick movements followed and something thick came down heavily over her head. Darkness descended and with it a raw, musky aroma. A blanket pulled tight around her neck. She opened her mouth to scream, but woollen fibres caught in her throat and silenced her. She struggled to free herself, but the harder she fought, the tighter the hold became around her neck. Suddenly, she felt herself leave the ground, lifted like a sack of flour upward, her arms held firmly against her body, her legs flailing wildly unable to find ground to gain purchase. Darkness swallowed her and it was impossible to tell whether her eyes were open or closed.

A final lurch told her she was being thrown into a vehicle. She landed on the floor, stuck between what must have been the seat and the front panel below where the driver sat. A smell of leather and horses mixed with the oil from the wool left her gasping for air. One of her captors leapt over her to place his boots firmly down on her curled body, pinning her in place.

Trembling and cold, despite the heavy blanket and the confined space, she tried to tease her mind into making sense of the situation. She was vaguely aware of the need to summon her wits, to divine a purpose, to derive an escape plan. But beyond the foggy sense that this was essential to her survival she couldn't drive her will forward. Nausea and the urgent need to breathe consumed her. It occurred to her that if she were to vomit, she would choke. Encouraged by that single coherent thought she poured all her effort into not yielding to the nausea.

The vehicle staggered into life and pitched forward. As it listed from side to side her body shifted with it. But the confined space kept the movements small, and she felt her body bruising with every bump against the wall of the vehicle. The bone of her ankle had been smacked against the door as they bundled her inside and a thunderous throbbing ran in waves from her ankle to her brain. The heavy boots of her captor pressed down on her sending daggers through her shoulder blades. Shock and pain consumed her for those first few moments. Then she sensed the horses find their stride and gather speed - she knew she needed to regain some form of internal control before her senses descended into chaos.

Curled in a foetal position, Lillian knew, if only she could think clearly, she should be able to imagine the direction they were travelling. She tried to visualize the familiar buildings racing past, the bends, the corners. As they rattled over a different ground, she wondered if it was a bridge. It felt like a bridge. But the blanket absorbed much of the sensation and her body felt heavy and full of pain. She thought they might have rounded a curve and were travelling straight again. But how could she tell? A straight road. She was almost certain they had been travelling on a straight road for some time. But how long? Was it twenty minutes? Or three hours?

What if she could push the door open with her feet? Would she be able to roll herself out? Would she die in the attempt? But her knees were tucked tightly against her chest and her ankle ached. Her brain sent signals to her feet directing them to push, but the force of the confined space pressed back, and pain shot like lightning through her ankle. Trapped between two opposing forces, she remained still and helpless.

With her knees pressed hard against her rib cage, it was difficult to achieve the outward expansion required to breathe. Lack of oxygen was beginning to take its toll. Suddenly, there was a jolt, and her body was forced to one side, pressed tightly against the wall. At the same time, her captor was dislodged from his seat and thrown against the door of the cab lifting his feet from her body for less than a second. She drew on all her energy and attempted to free herself from the blanket, but the space was too tight, and she couldn't achieve momentum. Soon her captor had righted himself and now had his arms around her like a vice.

The rock of the carriage changed to a slow plough, as the horses struggled, finding the going difficult. She was sure they'd left the road.

What is that smell? The air had changed. A pungent, organic odour of decaying vegetation, and...fish...

At last, movement ceased with a sluggish dragging sound. The vice around her was released, the blanket loosened. She breathed deeply, grateful to fill her lungs with fetid air.

The blanket fell away as large hands tossed her from the vehicle like so much rubbish and she sunk, face up, into mud and brackish water. Her hair floated around her face thick and grey with sludge. She wanted to haul herself from the mud and run, but all her body would do was lay limp, while she stared at the stars. The shape of two figures loomed over her, bodies silhouetted against the sky. It was easy to see they were men, but impossible to distinguish any features. If she tried to run, they would instantly grab her and truss her up in that blanket again. She wondered why she wasn't crying. There was rage and fear and confusion. Certainly shock. But no tears.

What's happening? Who would do this? With all Mamma went through, was it ever as bad as this?

One of the men rolled her over so she was face down in the mud. Instinctively she turned her face to one side to breathe. But not before she tasted the slightly salty, greenish slime of the riverbed. She thought she was screaming but only a gurgling sound came out as the river water frothed in her mouth. A shock of pain and she felt herself being pumped into the mud from behind. All promise for the future was leeched from her and dissipated into the swirling waters. Something was wrapped around her neck.

Her stocking?

It drew tighter and tighter. She was being absorbed into the river. Or was she absorbing the murky brackish waters herself. Was she becoming the river?

CHAPTER ONE

"Art is the child of nature – Longfellow" Art whether poetical or pictorial, is of slow growth in young countries. Not until there is a class so far removed from the struggle for daily bread as to have time for the cultivation of the mind and taste, and sufficient means to gratify the desires which spring there from, can we expect art to be cultivated and artists encouraged. **Australian Town and Country Journal 28 January 1888**

***

Rita sat with her legs sprawled across his favourite blue velvet settee. Lovely as her ankles were, tucked into soft leather boots, Hamish couldn't see why they needed to be on his furniture.

"But why won't you accompany me?"

Rita flicked a paper fan open and closed, while Hamish tried to catch the flamingo dancer's scarlet gown flickering between the folds. Dots appeared on the insides of his eyelids, and he felt a headache forming.

"I don't want to be stuck in a corner with some insufferable art critic while you hone your seduction skills on the luscious Spanish Countess."

Rita swung her boots onto the floor and sat up.

"You agree she is beautiful then?"

Hamish's sandy fringe flopped down over his face in the usual manner, so Rita didn't see him roll his eyes.

"Devastatingly so."

"Then join me at the exhibition. You can admire her from afar."

Rita's eyes narrowed. "As long as it is from afar."

Hamish lit up a cigarette. "I have no interest in your Spanish Countess. I have it on good authority that her romantic interests lay more in your court than mine, anyway."

While he was talking, the doctor walked a few steps to bring himself behind the settee and closer to the bay window where he took in a long draw of his cigarette and let the smoke escape slowly from between his lips. "I'm more interested in art than I am in Spanish nobility," he said, "and I'm not terribly interested in art."

He blew a ring of smoke toward the window.

Rita jumped up over the back of the settee and wound her arms around him from behind placing her chin on his shoulder.

"You need to socialize more," she whispered into his ear.

Hamish felt his resistance weakening.

"Since you took up the post as medical examiner, you have done nothing but work."

Hamish inhaled the calming effects of tobacco. She was right. He had thrown himself into organ the autopsy room to his liking and examining the few corpses that had come before him with meticulous thoroughness. Much more than was needed, as the causes of death were both routine and obvious. It was not for the want of trying that Hamish was unable to find evidence of more obscure causes for demise. If he was honest with himself, he was bored. Before taking on the role of medical examiner, he had only been invited to become involved in an autopsy when a death was interesting. He enjoyed a puzzle; he enjoyed investigating unusual deaths. Most of all, he enjoyed murder.

He drew in another breathe of tobacco and felt the warmth catch in his throat. It occurred to him that the last thought was very bleak.

"I'll come," he said.

He unlocked Rita's grip around his hips and turned to face her.

"Really?" Her eyes glowed.

"Really."

He instantly regretted the decision. But there was no backing out now.

The sweet tang of honey approached as a stocky, older man with wisps of ginger hair beginning at his ears and hanging low on his shoulders, brought in a plate of steaming crumpets and a pot of fresh local honey.

The intrusion was welcome.

"Thank-you Wallace, this will sustain us nicely until dinner. We're going out, apparently."

Rita's face stretched into her most charming smile. "We are going to the first exhibition of the Queensland Art Society," she said.

Wallace looked sideways at Hamish.

Hamish knew the old cook was mocking him. He knew as well as anyone that Rita would always persuade him to do whatever she wanted him to do.

"Good for you, you need to get out more."

"Why is everyone saying that?"

Wallace helped himself to a crumpet and spooned a lavish amount of honey on top with a decorative silver spoon. The old man's role in the household was blurry. He was servant, friend and mentor to Hamish.

"Come with us," said the young doctor.

Wallace stopped, crumpet mid-air on its way to his lips. Piercing eyes twinkled in the sun hardened face.

"I'm not one for the arts," he said, "although as a sailor I appreciate a well rendered nautical scene."

"Walter Isaac Jenner will be there," said Rita enthusiastically.

Hamish stared at her.

"He paints nautical scenes. Ships and seascapes."

Hamish wondered if it would be undignified to beg his man-Friday and friend to accompany them to the art exhibition.

"Even so," said Wallace, "Red and I are looking forward to a quiet night in. A shot of brandy and early to bed."

Red, the copper-coloured wiry terrier appeared on cue and made his way directly to his master's plate dripping as it was with delicious honey. He slipped out his tongue and began to lick.

"Red! Stop," cried three voices in unison.

The terrier glanced up at them with a look of pure innocence, then sat at Wallace's feet licking the honey from his whiskers.

Hamish had come to Brisbane four years earlier to establish a medical practice. He was young and eager to make his mark in family medicine. But he found he needed more stimulation than could be provided by seeing to the ailments of Brisbane's growing middle-classes. He was interested in the new public health, disease histories, the spread of infectious diseases, vaccines, clean water and sanitation. He was interested in how individuals die from unnatural causes, and why. His curiosity was too broad for the confines of family practice. And he lacked the discipline and focus to build up a sustainable business.

He stumbled into forensics by accident when he was visiting Stradbroke Island in Moreton Bay four years earlier. He was there conducting research at the Benevolent Asylum when he became embroiled in a murder investigation. Through that experience he met Wallace, who was working as a cook at the asylum and ultimately Sergeant James Bellamy who took charge of the case, once they delivered the culprit to the mainland.

Since then, he had become increasingly involved in investigations into the suspicious deaths of the citizens of Moreton Bay and its surrounds. When the role of Police Medical Examiner came available, Bellamy offered him the opportunity to put his investigating on a more formal standing. He wasn't a coroner or a trained pathologist, but the sergeant convinced him that his experience outweighed the benefits of a qualification.

Hamish had been more invested in chasing killers than he had been in general practice, so he decided to accept the offer. But he didn't imagine he would spend the rest of his life as a medical examiner either. He didn't know what direction his life would take. Life seemed to spread before him like a puzzle, one he chipped away at daily, but for which he had no final solution.

One of the first friendships he made as a young doctor was with Rita Cartwright. Rita was a doctor herself, having graduated from the London School of Medicine, but as a woman, she was unable to register as a doctor in Australia, so she worked as a chemist at the Lady Bowen Lying-In Hospital. A shared sense of being 'outsiders' in the medical establishment brought them together. Hamish didn't come from 'old money' like most doctors, and Rita enjoyed flouting her preference for the company of ladies over men. Hamish and Rita complemented one another, but if Hamish was honest with himself, his feelings for Rita went deeper than friendship. Still, he was rarely honest with himself on that score preferring to wonder hopelessly why he was unable to form a serious relationship with other women.

Fortified by Wallace's fresh crumpets and Rita's cheerful disposition, Hamish allowed himself to look forward to an evening out of the house. Regardless of his lukewarm interest in Brisbane's art crowd, he would be with Rita and that was all he needed to have a pleasant evening. He committed himself to supporting an interest of hers, and learning something about art.

They strolled down the hill from Wickham Terrace into town and on to Ann Street. It was a pleasant evening in late October, and the pretty signs of Spring were all around them. The native golden wattle contrasted with purple Jacaranda imported from South America, in the front gardens of Brisbane's finest houses and the relentless sub-tropical greenery fought and almost won the battle over British styled order and control. A yellowish light flooded the gleaming sandstone buildings and reminded everyone that the heat of summer would soon make the pretty town intolerable at this time of the afternoon. For now, the yellow light was mild and offset by a cool breeze that wound its way along the river and through the town.

Hamish and Rita stopped before the newly established Masonic Temple.

"Impressive," said Hamish. "Sandstone, in the Renaissance style."

Rita, used to his interest in architecture that bordered on the obsessive, gazed up without commenting.

"You see the columned balcony," he pointed to the central portion of the building that projected outward.

"I do see," she said.

It was clear from her tone that she was feigning interest, but that act alone stood as a testament to their friendship and he was grateful for it. He told himself he would return the favour by showing interest in the paintings on display at the exhibition.

As they stood observing the building, a flow of Brisbane's citizens stepped by them to enter. Hamish watched the women pass, wearing their finest gowns, mostly slender to the figure with angular bustles and high shoulders descending into impossibly tight sleeves. All the fashionable colours could be seen, though light pastels and newly available prints heralded in the warmer months. Every public event in a frontier town such as Brisbane brought with it the excuse to show off one's very best. That a woman could access the finest silks or satins meant much more than the fact that she could afford them, in a town where ships took many weeks or even months to travel from Britain or Europe. And most of the goods were offloaded in Sydney, Melbourne and Adelaide. The men in frock coats, cut away at the front with striped trousers, made Hamish think about how art, surely timeless, existed hand in hand with the more transient pursuit of fashion.

He and Rita joined the flow, ascended the stairs and entered the hall with the crowd of eager art lovers. He scanned the walls to gain an immediate impression and concluded that while the southern states may already have a plethora of well-established artists and dedicated galleries to display their works, Brisbane was still yearning for self-awareness.

"Do we have sufficient artists of merit in Brisbane to warrant an exhibition of this size?" he wondered aloud.

Rita put up a gloved hand to stabilize her hat.

"You are such a philistine," she said. "We have excellent artists. There are over 200 paintings on display at this exhibition."

They entered the banquet hall and Hamish took a more considered look around the walls. The range of paintings was extensive in both size and quality, but they didn't appear to be catalogued into any system he could discern.

"Most of these seem to be of English scenes," he said. "Are there no scenes of note in Brisbane to record?"

"You're right," agreed Rita. "There are too few paintings that depict local scenes. Keep in mind that artists learn by copying old masters, so there are plenty of copies on the walls as well."

Hamish wrinkled his nose.

"I'm not sure that an exhibition is warranted if the artists are students and copyists. Maybe they should have waited until there were more works of note of local interest."

Rita rolled her eyes.

"There are some skilfully depicted scenes here."

Hamish looked doubtful.

Rita's eyes lit up with an idea.

"I know what will interest you."

She took his arm and guided him to the work of Mr C.M. Friström. Hamish stood before a portrait of an Aboriginal man painted in oils against a background of neutrally tinged columns of the Classical Greek style. As the dusky figure in tattered shirt and trousers stared back at Hamish, he recognized a character who was well-known around Brisbane, holding a boomerang in his right hand.

"You are right, this is interesting," he said squinting at the painting. "There's a juxtaposition here, I can see what the artist intended. There's a blankness captured in the subject's eyes. It's as though he's not truly present."

Rita read the engraving on the frame,

"King Sandy," she whispered.

Hamish sighed.

"Yes. I've seen him around. He sells fish in the streets. He once said that the British took his land and gave him a neck plate that reads 'King Sandy', in return."

Rita examined the painting silently.

"I don't know how I feel about it," said Hamish.

"The Painting or the King Plate?"

"Both. They're the same thing, aren't they?'

Rita seemed puzzled, and sad.

Hamish realized he was spoiling her evening when he had promised to be supportive.

"There is resilience in the portrait," he said with a note of appreciation.

"I believe there is a similar work on view at the studio of Oscar Friström in Adelaide Street," said Rita. "There's also a bust of King Sandy's granddaughter, Sarah. Some of Friström's paintings will go to Melbourne to be displayed temporarily."

Hamish stared at the painting for a moment longer.

What is it about the objectification of this subject that I find so disturbing? Is it the interpretation of one culture by another? Is it the oppression made so overt by the King Plate? The not-so-subtle nod to Europeanisation in the Greek columns?

Rita urged Hamish forward past the image of King Sandy.

"There are some adequate copies," she said hurrying Hamish past some reproductions of famous Rembrandt paintings, but I agree, they seem out of place in the exhibition.

"Look," this is local," she pointed to a landscape in oil.

"A view on the Brisbane River," read Hamish.

He saw that a gum tree stood tall in the foreground dominating the space while an old sugar mill languished in the background. But it was the winding river that was central to the painting and carried his eye. The river brought life, trade, industry, and progress. The river wound its way to the horizon and beyond the scope of the image, moving progress deeper into the country, opening the way for new settlements, forcing back the forests and the people like King Sandy.

Hamish felt a little dizzy as he peered into the painting. Why did he have to be so cynical? Why couldn't he simply enjoy the aesthetics of the paintings?

He picked his words carefully, to convey a more positive appreciation.

"The colours are well chosen," he began. "They capture a melancholy of the Australian bush that resonates with my experience."

Hamish noted that most of the paintings depicting local scenery were muted and sad. Whenever people were present in bush scenes, the insignificance of the people was emphasized. The environment was always expansive, while the people and buildings were small. The artists instinctively portrayed a sense of feeling overwhelmed by the environment, a sensation that the colonialists might not admit to, but existed, nonetheless. Even as the pioneers charged forward with the project of progress, in their hearts they knew that it was the vastness of this land that terrified them.

"This is the artist I mentioned to Wallace," said Rita.

Hamish stood before a series of seascapes with fragile ships tossed in rolling grey seas.

"Walter Isaac Jenner," she said. "He's here somewhere."

She looked around to see if she could point the artist out. But the crowd had thickened, and she couldn't catch sight of him.

"He's painted some lovely pictures depicting Moreton Bay beneath the sunset, and look, here - Hamilton Reach."

Hamish followed her gloved finger with his eyes. The painting again captured the grandeur of the river. It was easy to see how large a part the river held in the psyche of the residents of Moreton Bay. It featured in almost every local landscape.

They were about to enter one of the rooms jutting from the hall when Hamish spotted a still life in oil. It caught his eye because it differed so vividly from the long line of landscapes and seascapes that lead to it. It showed a blue vase with flowers, a fruit bowl and an open box with trinkets spilling onto a tablecloth.

He didn't think it was well-executed, but he was willing to concede he didn't know the rules of execution involved in producing an admirable still-life painting. He was preparing to have a closer look when a murmur meandered through the crowd behind them. Rita squeezed his arm, and they both looked back, abandoning their departure from the main hall. Everyone stood still and all eyes were turned toward the entrance as a collective sense of awe hung over the crowd.

CHAPTER TWO

A lecture on 'Australian Art' was delivered at the Oddfellows Hall in Williamstown on Monday evening by Dr. Mclerney. The doctor proceeded to say that every man is influenced by his surroundings. Contrasting the climate in Australia with that of Great Britain he said we have lighter air and a purer atmosphere here. On bright sunny days the sky appears a great distance away; in Great Britain it is possible to contemplate the clouds falling over on the observer. While we might not know it, we are influenced by this.

The doctor gave an example of the Australian forest, and said language was insufficient to convey its wild, silent majesty. It's influence, he said, is seen in the brown, well-tanned faces of the bushmen. He described the Australian gum tree as shadowless, while the English Oak has a broad leaf forming thick shade. The leaves of the gum are vertical enabling sunshine to pass through them. Then there is not the moisture in the trees here that is to be found in the old country. There is no moisture in the air or in the men of Australia.

In Australian art we see the jagged edges of the leaves, the dead timber, the dry leaflets, the weird surroundings, the sad look of the lost traveller. The works not only represent the Australian forest, but also the amount of energy and suffering required to make it habitable. **Williamstown Advertiser Saturday 8 September 1888.**

***

Hamish turned to see the guests' part as a breathtaking vision of elegance glided through the crowd. A young woman, no more than twenty years, with raven black tresses cascading over her shoulders and dark almond shaped eyes swept through the guests with the majesty of a ship parting water. An elaborate beaded gown danced as she moved. Her porcelain skin bore a delicate radiance that screamed aristocrat.

Accompanying her was a dashing nobleman, no older than she, the epitome of masculine charm. Black curls framed his face with a touch of rebellious allure and deep-set eyes sparkled like stars. Impeccably tailored and exuding effortless refinement, he carried himself with the confidant grace of one who knew his place in the aristocratic hierarchy. He appeared to represent the perfect balance between aristocratic poise and spirited passion.

Anne-Marie, a member of the organizing committee for the exhibition and a friend of Rita's, skipped like a labrador puppy a couple of feet ahead of the Spanish guests. When they reached Hamish and Rita she was grinning from ear to ear.

"May I present the Countess Isabella de la Vega," she said breathlessly. "And her companion Don Alejandro Ramirez."

Hamish noticed the blush on Rita's skin deepen. "Drs Hamish Hart and Rita Cartwright," said Anne-Marie.

Hamish was taking a moment to catch his breath. The young couple commanded an inspiring presence.

"My pleasure," said Rita holding out an elegant hand to the countess.

Isabella smiled disarmingly. Hamish wondered for a moment if the warmth in the smile was genuine, but he chastised himself for the umpteenth time this evening, for his negative thoughts.

The countess took Rita's hand and held it gently in her own. When she released it, she turned to Hamish with the same gloved hand, and he touched her fingers lightly with his lips. Their eyes met briefly, and Hamish noticed a spark that confused him. He greeted her a little clumsily as a result.

Hamish realized that every guest had stopped chatting to watch them meet the Spanish nobles. Anne-Marie winked at Hamish as she slid one hand through Rita's arm and the other behind the elbow of the countess. She gently guided them toward a quiet corner of the hall while at the same time directing a waiter to bring them drinks. Anne-Marie left the countess and Rita alone to become acquainted while Hamish was left standing with Don Alejandro.

"How are you enjoying your visit to our small colony?" began Hamish, unsure what else to say.

The young man displayed none of the warmth of the countess, contrived or otherwise.

"It's lovely, I'm sure," he said, "though provincial."

His eyes were searching the crowd for his companion. She and Rita had disappeared through a door onto the balcony.

Hamish tried again. "I believe you and your...."

"Cousin," supplied Don Alejandro."

"Cousin... are staying with the Governor and Lady Musgrave?"

Don Alejandro blinked slowly. "That is correct."

Hamish glanced around the walls at the array of paintings, large and small. Watercolours hung alongside oils, portraits alongside landscapes, copies and amateur works alongside more accomplished pieces. "Have you had an opportunity to view the exhibits?" he asked.

The young nobleman snorted loudly and waved his hand dismissively around the room. His eyes were cold, and he avoided directing them at Hamish. "I'm afraid the only piece worthy of examination is the Sorella," he said. "It's lost amongst a sea of works of little note, I'm afraid. Though my countryman is a world class artist. It comes from the private collection of your Governor. I will be sure to view it before I leave this evening."

"Splendid," said Hamish, suspecting that while a little ingenuous, his observation was probably true. Hamish thought the Friström well executed, but a little disturbing, though he couldn't put his finger on why. He did think the works of Jenner may be world class. Still, he was the first to admit he had no experience of European art on which to base a comparison. He made a mental note to look out for the Sorrel, if Rita ever returned to rescue him.

Don Alejandro stood firm by his side showing no interest in mingling with the crowd, despite the admiring glances that were shooting his way from every woman in the hall. Perhaps because of them.

Hamish tried to think of a new line of conversation.

"Have you always had an interest in visiting the colonies?"

The Spanish nobleman snorted his distaste once again. His moustache, still sparse in his youth, twitched upward on one side. "We are here at the request of Count de la Vega, Isabella's father. It is a business arrangement of sorts. He has business with a large shipping company based in Sydney. Our trip to Moreton Bay was undertaken in response to a whim of the countess'. She met Lady Musgrave at a ball in New South Wales and was intrigued by her stories of the north. She accepted the good Lady's invitation to stay with her for a week, and I had no option but to accompany her."

"She is young to be travelling alone," said Hamish.

Alejandro sighed. "That is precisely why I am obliged to escort her. Tiresome, though it is."

Hamish was at a loss to find any new topic of conversation that might interest the Spaniard. He was clearly bored, not only with the exhibition, but with his entire mission travelling the colony with his young cousin. When Hamish thought he could stand the strained silence between himself and Alejandro no longer, Rita and the countess finally rejoined them.

"Shall we take a closer look at the works in here?" Rita said as she took Hamish's left arm. The countess took his right, and they guided him playfully into the adjoining room, while Alejandro followed reluctantly.

Stopping before the small still life that Hamish had seen from the entrance, he noticed for the first time the detail in the trinkets spilling from a silver embossed box. The box and the beads were well-articulated with careful manipulation of light and shadow capturing each facet. In contrast, the flowers in the vase behind the box lacked vibrancy. The colours were dull and flat and the proportions seemed slightly off. Overall, the composition had a disjointed and unbalanced feel.

Hamish was trying to come to terms with the painting when he noticed the countess become rigid beside him. Her eyes grew wide, and the blood appeared to visibly drain from her face.

"What is it?" asked Rita. "Are you unwell?"

Hamish felt the weight of the countess on his arm as she leant into him for support.

"Perhaps we should get out of here," suggested Rita. To Hamish she said, "The countess and I are going to take a walk down to the river, it's so stuffy in here and Isabella needs air."

Hamish leant past her to see if Alejandro had heard. The Spaniard leant forward to steady his cousin, though she was already well supported between Rita and Hamish. Alejandro's face was anxious, but he nodded slowly.

The countess allowed herself to be guided away from the small room and back into the main hall. Seemingly unaware of her surroundings for a few moments, once away from the cramped space of the anteroom she threw back her head and took a deep breath.

"I'm sorry," she smiled. "I felt feint for a moment, but I am not unwell. I agree that fresh air is required."

"Alejandro, please ask Mateo to meet me at the door with my shawl. I would like to have a quick word with him."

Alejandro bowed.

"The doctor and I will follow you," he said. He looked to Hamish, "If that is acceptable to you."

Hamish raised his eyebrows. Following Rita around was not something he was used to. She was the most capable and independent woman he knew.

"Certainly," he said, glancing at Rita.

She smiled.

Alejandro left them to fetch the footman, and the shawl.

Lady Musgrave had finished her speech, officially opening the first exhibition of the Queensland Art Society and the attention of the guests shifted to the lesser officials who took up the task of ongoing formalities.

The countess received a silk shawl with magnificent embroidery from her young footman and whispered a few words in his ear. He bowed deeply and left the hall to return to the waiting coach.

The party then departed onto the street and headed for the river, Rita and Isabella walking arm in arm, chatting, while Hamish and Alejandro strolled behind them. There was no sign that the countess had suffered a shock or been unwell only minutes earlier.

The river shivered with moonlight as a light breeze gently skipped across the water to kiss their skin. Hamish watched Rita snuggle close to Countess Isabella as they talked.

As pleasant as he found the night air, he was aware they could only afford to be away a short time before the absence of the countess would cause concern. For many of the guests, the primary motivation in attending the exhibition was to catch a glimpse of the exotic Spanish Countess, not to view the paintings.

Hamish and Alejandro walked in silence until they caught up with the women.

"I feel I can breathe at last," Isabella was saying. "That room was suffocating me, so small and so many people."

"And so many ordinary paintings," added her cousin.

Again, Hamish felt strangely insulted and then chided himself for being irrational.

"This new colony does not have access to two thousand years of art and culture such as we enjoy in Europe," said Isabella. "You are spoiled."

"You are right," he agreed. "I wish nothing more than to return to my homeland and wallow in timeless accumulated treasures."

The countess threw him an irritated glance.

"I was obligated to create new networks for my father's business in the colony," she said. "I have met my obligations in Sydney, so our visit here is for pleasure. I wanted to experience the colony of Moreton Bay, it's remoteness and untamed beauty."

"What do you think now you are here?" asked Rita.

The exotic beauty looked thoughtful. "I am surprised by the spirit of optimism and opportunity that permeates the place. There are both difficulties and hope."

Alejandro straightened his cravat.

"My hope is for a speedy departure from here."

A smile tickled at the edges of Isabella's bow shaped lips and her tone softened.

"Only a few more days until we sail," she said. "You will survive."

She turned to Hamish and Rita with a smile.

"Our parents forced him to accompany me, he will never forgive them – or me."

Rita and Isabella laughed.

Hamish caught a quick and nervous glance from Alejandro. For all her charm, he wasn't convinced the countess was genuine. There was a tension that shifted between her and her cousin that Hamish found difficult to ascribe wholly to family affiliations and responsibilities. An energy rattled between them that unnerved him.

When they stepped back into the light of the Masonic Hall, they found the bulk of the guests gathered around the entrance to the smaller anteroom that held the still life. Nervous excitement radiated from the group. Hamish and Rita left the countess and Alejandro in the hall entrance and pushed their way to the front of the crowd.

"What's going on?" Rita asked her friend.

Anne-Marie turned to her in wide-eyed shock.

"A painting has been stolen," she said.

"Which painting?" asked Hamish.

She pointed to an empty spot on the wall. "The still life."

"Are you sure the artist didn't take it down for some reason?" asked Rita.

"That's the artist over there." Anne-Marie pointed to a slender girl, no older than twenty-one, seated at a bench against the wall, crying into her handkerchief.

Hamish went to speak with her. "Here, here," he said, replacing the wet handkerchief with one of his own. "What's your name?"

"Lillian," sniffed the girl.

"I'm sure the painting will turn up. Afterall, where could it go?"

The girl looked up at him with reddened eyes.

"I don't want it back," she sobbed.

"Why?"

A loud choking sound escaped from the girl.

"The painting's rubbish and not worth stealing," she said. "I'm so embarrassed. I don't know why anyone would take my painting. People are saying they can't understand why the thief wouldn't have taken the Spanish painting, or one of the Fistrom works, or even a Jenner. And it's true. Why take my painting?"

She blew her nose into Hamish's handkerchief.

He had to admit to himself he'd thought the same thing, although he would not have voiced the thought in earshot of the artist.

Lillian held Hamish's crushed, wet handkerchief out for him to take. He hesitated as he watched it lay limp in her hand then he gestured for her to keep it. Just then Alejandro approached them.

"Good God, there is a Sorrel on the wall right there!" he cried. "It must be worth four thousand pounds. Why on earth...?"

Hamish shot him a warning glance, and he stopped.

"Do you have any idea who might have taken your painting?" asked Hamish.

The girl shook her head furiously.

CHAPTER THREE

One evening, some months ago, a bush chum was in Brisbane and proposed a drive to the Hamilton and along the riverbank. I agreed and we set off, both prepared to enjoy the glorious freshness of a cool summer Queensland night. When we had driven some distance past the Hamilton and were going toward the flats, our attendee was attracted by the lights of a cab which had evidently been brought to a standstill, and by loud remonstrances in a troubled girlish voice. Our cab carried no lights, it being a moonlit night.

Thinking an accident had occurred, we proceeded to the stand still cab. The absence of lights on our vehicle, the noiseless revolution of the wheels, and the clamour of the altercation prevented the parties from noticing our approach. We alighted and proceeded on foot to the rescue.

We saw a cabman trying to force a girl out of his cab, evidently to her great terror and objection. Of course, he desisted immediately we called to him, while the girl shrunk back into the cab so as to hide her features from inspection.

Upon demanding an explanation the cabman, with indistinct innuendoes told a rambling story and unintelligible yarn and tried to pass off the affair as a joke.

The girl, still cowering back in the deepest shadow of the cab, for the better concealment of her identity, sobbed out a very different story. She said she was in domestic service in Bowen Terrace, and that she had set out to walk to town. The cabman had driven alongside, asked her where she was going, said he was also going to town and would give her a lift for nothing. She had foolishly accepted what she considered was a generous offer and stepped into the cab. Whereupon the cabbie had whipped up his horse so furiously that such a speed was attained as prevented her from identifying the route, until the well-known features of the Hamilton Hotel were passed.

Of course, my chum and I gave credence to the girl's story in preference to the yarn told by the cabbie, and by threats of physical and legal punishment compelled him to drive back towards town just in front of our own vehicle. At the convent gates in Ann Street Fortitude Valley, the girl requested the cab man stop. She alighted when he did so, still studiously concealing her features and flew rather than ran in the direction of Bowen Terrace. **Queensland Figaro and Punch 25 September 1886.**

***

Saturday morning brought with it a delicate yellow haze that, like a fine mist, blurred the edges of distant hills and added a quality of stillness to the town. The gentle light wrapped the town's inhabitants in a comforting embrace, softening edges, slowing movement and dulling sounds. The light reminded Hamish of the painting he had seen at the exhibition the night before. He wondered if it was seeing the light in the paintings that had made him see it so clearly this morning. The golden light was as familiar as the sandstone buildings and the drab olive trees that surrounded his home, but so familiar, he mostly forgot to notice it. He marvelled at the impact the art from the exhibition had had on him. He was seeing his hometown differently through the lens of the artists. He had always relied on science as an appropriate lens through which to view the world, but perhaps he should make more effort to appreciate the influence of the arts.

When he arrived at the police station, there was a note directing him to the hospital morgue. A corpse had been delivered there in the early hours. He looked around for Sergeant Bellamy to find out more about the incident and the deceased, but the sergeant wasn't to be found. He couldn't even find young Constable Pennyweather. There was nothing for it but to walk to the hospital and find out more there.

As he entered the morgue, he saw that his laboratory assistant Jan was already attending to a body. A young woman Hamish estimated to be between eighteen and twenty lay on the autopsy table looking as vulnerable in death as she had proven to be in life.

Hamish blinked at the sight of the body. The young woman's face was swollen and bruised, but he had the impression he had seen her before. He let the thought go and prepared himself for the objectification of her corpse that his investigation required. His vision narrowed to the minutia of skin, bones, organs and particulates.

Jan had only just finished removing her clothes and laying her out ready for him. Born of Dutch parents in Brisbane Jan wasn't much older than the woman on the table. He was a medical student who had run out of funds in his second year and was working in whatever position he could to save up money for the continuance of his studies. There was not yet a medical school in Brisbane, so he needed sufficient funds to accommodate himself in Melbourne in addition to his tuition fees. While autopsy assistant seemed a morbid job for someone so young, Hamish found him competent and respectful. And quiet. He spoke only when something needed to be said, consequently avoiding any unnecessary interruptions. Hamish appreciated the space the assistant's silence afforded him to process his thoughts.

Jan was tall for his age, wiry in build with a shock of white-blonde hair and eyes as clear as ice. Having grown up in Brisbane, he had an odd accent that combined a hint of Dutch from his parents with a broad Queensland drawl. It was an unusual mix that invited awkward pauses while people tried to make out what he was saying. This may be one reason the lad limited his speaking to only what was essential to say. He was both physically and socially awkward. Hamish wondered at his potential as a medical doctor and thought him more well suited to medical research. The insulation of the morgue was a perfect fit in the meantime.

"She was discovered on the mudflat this morning," Jan said.

"Why didn't they call me?"

Hamish was adamant that he needed to see the body in situ in cases of unusual death. Time and again he tried to ram home to the constables the importance of calling him, even during the night, when a body was found.

"A couple of men on an early morning ride found her," said Jan. "They brought her in. They didn't want the tide to take the body."

Hamish swallowed his anger. The public were not to know any better. And they were probably right. When the tide came in it would have destroyed any evidence at the site anyway. He forced his attention onto the corpse before him.

It always rocked Hamish to face the body of a young person who had apparently been in perfect health prior to death. He wondered about the life that had now been extinguished. The joys and heartbreak, the children that would never be conceived, the dreams that would never come to fruition.

He placed his palm on her cold forehead. He told himself he had a job to do, a process to follow. He would honour her by using his training and his skill to determine how and why her life had been stolen. And by whom. He allowed the objectivity of science to take over.

Hamish spoke aloud as Jan wrote notes. "Evidence of ligature marks consistent with manual strangulation observed around the neck," he began. "The marks indicate forceful compression by something thick, a scarf or perhaps a stocking, leading to asphyxiation."

Hamish looked down the length of the corpse.

"Pronounced lividity observed in dependent areas of the body, indicating the postmortem interval and positioning."

He turned to the assistant. "Found on the mudflats you say? Where?"

Jan looked up from his notebook. "Hamilton Reach," he said.

"She wasn't there long," said Hamish. "Five or six hours at most. I would put the time of death at between eleven and midnight. What would a young woman be doing out there at that time of night?"

Jan continued to stare at him, his pencil poised to take notes.

Hamish returned his attention to the corpse.

"Multiple contusions and abrasions noted on various parts of the body, suggestive of struggle or physical altercation prior to death."

He held up the woman's fingers. Her neatly cut nails were torn.

"She's tried to grasp at the ligature."

He glanced across at Jan to make sure he was writing. When he was satisfied the lad was getting down each point, he scanned the corpse, once more from head to toe.

"Extensive deposition of mud and debris covering the body, indicative of exposure to the elements."

Hamish stretched upright and threw his shoulders backward in a circular motion to loosen his muscles which had clenched tight from crouching over the corpse. He looked back down at the young woman.

"She was lying on the mudflats waiting for the river to take her for hours," he whispered.

Hamish remained still for a few moments before taking up his knife in readiness for the internal examination.

"Evidence of hyoid bone fracture and haemorrhage in the soft tissues of the neck," he said. "Consistent with manual strangulation."

He moved on to the chest cavity.

"Internal organs show signs of congestion and petechial haemorrhages, consistent with asphyxiation. Congestion and oedema present in the lungs, indicative of compromised respiratory function prior to death."

He placed his hands on the table to support himself and let his chin fall to his chest.

What has this girl suffered in the last moments of her life?

"Please pass me the lamp," he said.

Jan brought over a cylindrical device with a chamber constructed after the fashion of a coach lamp. He lengthened the handle like a pocket telescope. Within the chamber, Jan had ignited a flame that flickered within a glass cylinder and gave out light through the front wall of the lamp. Hamish inserted a slightly crooked glass piece that reflected the light on an angle.

Shivering, he turned his attention to the lower portion of the corpse and positioned the lamp so that he could examine the area of the vagina carefully. He found extensive bruising to the girl's labia and inner thighs. Samples of bodily fluid were taken to place under his microscope, though he knew already that the fluid was semen. There was ample evidence of sexual penetration. He looked up at Jan, whose face was devoid of expression. The lad had had a reservoir of objectivity that Hamish lacked at certain moments.

Hamish breathed deeply to calm himself then restored the body to its previous state. What terror consumed this woman before her death? He tried to imagine her fear, but he couldn't. His body only shuddered with the shame of what men could do. Stories conjure swirling images of devilish creatures and monsters; but these were only men. The only true monsters live in our own hearts, he thought with a knot in his throat.

Some time was spent scrubbing his hands and arms all the way past his elbows as though he could scrub away the filth of the world as easily as he could the germs that threatened his sanitary autopsy room.

Throughout this process, Jan stood patiently, pencil at the ready. At last Hamish turned to him with his conclusions.

"Based on the findings of external and internal examination," he said, "the cause of death is determined to be asphyxia due to manual strangulation. The manner of death is deemed to be homicide, given the presence of ligature marks and evidence of struggle."

He turned his face away.

"And she has been sexually violated," he added. Another breath and he went on, "Further investigation into the circumstances surrounding the deceased's demise is warranted."

Jan copied the words quickly into his notebook in his usual impassive way. He knew those particular words signified the completion of the forensic examination, and the beginning of the broader investigation. It was his job to clean the body and dress her ready for seeing into the next world. He got onto it without delay.

"As soon as you're finished here, get the notes to Sergeant Bellamy," said Hamish. "He'll want to act quickly on this one. I'll write a full report and complete the Certificate of Particulars when we have more information."

CHAPTER FOUR

The incident relates to the arrival on 20 January, 1849 of the "Fortitude". The first of the vessels sent out with immigrants by the Reverand John Dunmore Lang. It was known in advance of her arrival that there was some controversy between Lang and the English Land and Immigration authorities regarding these immigrants and their "land orders" Captain J.C. Wickham and Dr Ballow realized the delicacy of the situation and the value of delay until the will of the Governor in Sydney could be ascertained. In those days it was simplicity itself to find an excuse for quarantining any vessel – "ship fever" (typhus) was ever present – and as there had been a few cases (far below the usual average) during the voyage of the "Fortitude" she was ordered into quarantine.

When the governor's orders came, they were devastating: the land orders were to be ignored or repudiated, and the immigrants themselves were to be refused assistance and admission to the town and thrust out beyond Boundary Street to the edge of the official settlement. They established themselves not far from a point near the black's camp and fighting ground at York's Hollow (the present Exhibition Grounds). They set up makeshift shanties in what was soon called "Fortitude Valley". **Medicine in Queensland, Part 1. Sir Raphael Cilento in an address to the Royal Historical Society, Thursday 27 July 1961.**

***

Hamish retreated to the small office where he kept a kettle simmering on an iron stove. It was a luxury he insisted upon. The aroma of fresh scones told him Wallace had called in while he was working. He wondered again how the man managed to anticipate his every need.

Wesley Wallace had travelled the world as a ship's cook until he settled at Dunwich where he worked at the asylum. Wallace had been favoured by his ship's captain as a lad. The captain schooled him in music, poetry, history and science throughout his youth. Because of this relationship and his extensive travels, Wallace was both intelligent and wise in ways that separated him from most of his contemporaries. In the four years Wallace had worked for Hamish, he had become a father figure. Hamish held a respect for him he had never held for his own father. Where Wesley Wallace fed Hamish's confidence, his real father gnawed away at it until only fragments remained. Hamish came to depend on his cook, not only for his culinary skills, but also as a sounding board and a calming influence.

While Hamish applied liberal pats of butter to a fluffy scone, a voice startled him.

"You're finished then?"

Hamish turned to see Sergeant James Bellamy in the doorway. "You know when to arrive," he said pushing the platter toward him.

"What's the time of death?" asked the sergeant.

"About midnight. Perhaps slightly earlier."

Bellamy chose a particularly large scone and took the knife from Hamish. He dissected it and popped half in his mouth in one movement.

"Jan will deliver the notes to you," said Hamish.

Bellamy swallowed. "I'm in a hurry," he said.

Hamish watched as Bellamy wiped crumbs from his mouth and at that moment Jan entered with a folder, handing it to Bellamy without even a sideways glance at the plate of scones.

Bellamy wiped his hands on his trousers and took the folder. Jan immediately disappeared into the autopsy area.

"Who is she?" asked Hamish.

Bellamy skimmed the file. "Her name is Lillian Murphy," he murmured, "we found her purse with her name in it on the mudflat. It's a miracle we found anything because the tide has been in and out since she was killed. Luckily, it's a low tide this week and the water line didn't quite reach the body."

"Lillian?" Hamish said. A wave of recognition descended, but he kept it to himself for a moment to get his head around the implications. "Have her parents been notified?" he asked.

"We have notified her mother and sister. They live alone in a cottage in Bowen Hills. The sister works for a friend of yours, I believe."

Hamish's eyes narrowed. "What friend?"

"Anne-Marie Langford. The girl's sister is Miss Langford's Lady's Maid."

Hamish brushed his fringe away from his face. He wore his hair long to hide a scar on his left cheek, the result of an accident when he was a child. The scar made him self-conscious but whenever he was troubled, he pushed his hair away exposing it, leaving his rationale for growing it long in the first place redundant.

"Anne-Marie is more of a friend to Rita," he said. "I've only met her a few times." He raised his eyebrows. "I saw her last night though. We both did. She was at the art exhibition."

"The theft of that little painting was curious. I'm guessing you heard about that since you were there."

"Indeed," Hamish said quietly. "I'll tell you what is even more curious. This girl on the table painted the little oil that was stolen."

Bellamy almost dropped the mug of tea he'd been holding. Fortunately, he had emptied its contents, or it would have been all over Hamish's trousers.

"Wait a minute," said Bellamy. "We know the murdered girl was sister to Anne-Marie Langford's maid. But now you're telling me she was also the painter of the oil that was stolen last night?"

"Exactly."

"That's quite a coincidence."

Hamish ran his hands threw his hair again. "I spoke to her after the painting was taken. She was distraught."

Bellamy pursed his lips.

"I suppose she was."

Hamish shook his head. "She wasn't upset about the theft. She was embarrassed because everyone was expressing shock that the thief stole such an unexpected piece."

Bellamy raised his eyebrows.

"Was the painting worth stealing?"

"It was not," said Hamish. "Not at face value anyway. It wasn't worth any money, there must have been an alternative reason for taking it."

"Fascinating," said Bellamy.

He stared at a blank page in his notebook.

"Did you happen to notice the artist leaving the exhibition?"

Hamish rubbed his chin. "No, we left soon after the painting was stolen. Lillian was still there when we left."

"What time was that?"

Hamish looked to the ceiling for inspiration. "I can't give you a specific time. But it was ten-thirty when I arrived home. The clock upstairs was striking the half hour as I entered."

"Is your house about twenty minutes ride from the exhibition?"

Hamish tilted his head to one side. "I'd say it took longer. I dropped Rita off at her place on the way. More like thirty minutes."

"Right. We need to interview everyone at the exhibition last night and find out what time the girl left the hall. How on earth did she end up on the mudflats at Hamilton?"

"I can make a list of those I know attended," suggested Hamish.

"Don't worry, I have a guest list from the organizers. They had people sign a ledger on entry, a Visitor's Book.

"Oh yes, so they did."

Bellamy's eyes narrowed to a squint, and he clasped his jaw with his right hand to look up at Hamish.

"Let's start with your friend Anne-Marie Langford," he said. "She may know what time the girl left the exhibition. And we'll check her sister's lodgings as well while we're there. The sister's name is Delia, I believe."

"Rita's friend," Hamish corrected him while putting on his coat.

"Who is?" Confusion drew Bellamy's brows downward.

Hamish stared at him. "Anne-Marie," he said irritably. "Anne-Marie is a friend of Rita's. I hardly know the woman."

Half an hour later Hamish and Bellamy stood before the Langford home on Bowen Terrace, situated on the hillside of an expansive estate.

"About forty acres," said Bellamy whistling through his teeth. "The stone for the house was taken from the Petrie's quarry in Albion."

Hamish gave an appreciative nod and cranked his neck to take in the full extent of the estate. Beyond the impressive main house were several outbuildings, including a detached kitchen and servant's quarters to the side, and a two-story coach house and stable at the back. There were acres of planted gardens and fruit trees, and three large water tanks.

They entered through a grand stone gateway on the edge of the hillside and followed a gravel path to the door.

Bellamy knocked twice before the door opened revealing a stern woman on the wrong side of middle-age. He introduced himself and Dr Hamish Hart.

"We would like to speak with Mrs Langford if we may, and her daughter Anne-Marie Langford," he said.

The woman stared unmoved.

"Mrs Langford is indisposed. She's not taking visitors today," she said as she began closing the door.

Bellamy placed his foot forward to block it.

"I realize that Mrs Langford and her daughter have suffered a shock this morning," he said quickly. "Indeed, that's why we're here. It's incredibly important we talk to the family as soon as possible so we can build our investigation and ensure justice is done."

The woman hesitated a moment, her grip still firmly on the door. Bellamy's foot the only obstacle to her slamming it in their faces.

Hamish engaged her eyes and smiled. "Miss Langford is a close friend. I hope to call upon her and offer my condolences."

Bellamy shot him a startled glance, which he ignored. Not once shifting his attention from the housekeeper.

Gradually her grey eyes softened, and she stepped aside to let them in, guiding them to a pleasant room with plenty of natural light, a bay window, and a smattering of smart mahogany furniture. A grand piano watched over the room from the corner. The housekeeper left them alone without another word.

"Close friend?" whispered Bellamy. "A moment ago, you barely knew Miss Langford."

Hamish shot him a sideways glance as they settled themselves on a chintz covered settee.

Soon a woman in her early thirties entered the room.

"My mother is unwell," she said. "But it is me you need to speak with in any case."

Hamish and Bellamy stood.

She held out her hand to Hamish first.

"Dr Hart," she said as he took her hand in his. "I'm so glad to see you."

Hamish placed his left hand over his right holding her small white hand protectively within his.

"Anne-Marie," he said.

Bellamy rolled his eyes, then held out his own hand in greeting. Anne-Marie's attention shifted from Hamish to the sergeant.

"Please sit down," she said. "Would you like tea?"

They both declined while Anne-Marie sat opposite them, adjusting her skirt as she did so.

"You were at the exhibition last night I take it?" Bellamy said, notebook open and pencil at the ready.

"Oh yes, I was one of the organizers." She smiled broadly at Hamish. "Did you and Dr Cartwright enjoy the exhibition?"

"Indeed, we did - an admirable display of talent," he said, wondering if his cheeks were burning from the lie.

Bellamy raised his eyebrows at him.

"Somewhat marred by theft and murder," he said drily.

"Yes," agreed Hamish quietly. "It is a great shame."

"Did you stay until all the guests had left?" asked Bellamy.

"I did."

"What time was it that Lillian left the hall?" he said hopefully.

Anne-Marie studied her fine long fingers and took in a deep breath.

"I'm afraid I didn't see her leave," she said. "There was chaos when the discovery of the theft was made, and people were all milling about. I know Lillian was upset."

Miss Langford looked across at Hamish. "I saw you talking to her," she said.

Hamish nodded.

"Then I was caught up with people saying their good buys. I didn't see her go. She must have slipped out of the hall at some stage because later only the organizers remained. She was gone."

"What time did you leave the hall?" asked Bellamy.

"Eleven," she said. "I can be certain of that because we had to be out by that time, and I was keeping an eye on it, with all the confusion I thought we might run overtime."

Hamish made a note in his mind. Lillian must have left the hall sometime between ten, when he left and eleven, when Anne-Marie noticed she was missing. It was probably closer to ten, while chaos reigned, because after that as people started leaving, Anne-Marie would have been seen Lillian if she were there.

Bellamy's voice was steady, though there was a softness to his tone as he approached a delicate matter. "Did any of the guests see the theft?"

Anne-Marie, still clutching a handkerchief, sighed deeply, her voice fragile. "No." Her eyes flitted toward the window, as though searching for the stolen painting there. "No one saw anything, to my knowledge. It seems the painting was there one minute and... gone the next."

Bellamy leaned forward slightly, catching the subtle shift in her expression—a flicker of doubt or fear, perhaps. "Did you notice anyone paying particular attention to the painting?"

She blinked, her brow furrowing as if sifting through memories. "It's difficult to say..." Anne-Marie's fingers toyed with the lace on her cuffs, the action almost unconscious. "People were looking at all the paintings, commenting, admiring... But I didn't see anyone focused on the still life." Her lips twitched into a bitter smile. "If anything, people passed over it to view the works by the better-known artists."

Bellamy, sensing her discomfort, shifted the conversation gently. "What can you tell me about your maid, Delia?"

A moment of hesitation hung between them, and Anne-Marie's gaze dropped to her lap. "I don't know what to tell you, she's been with us for about six months. It is her first position..." Her voice grew tight, and she looked up, her eyes seeking understanding.

"I know it's unusual for a girl so young to be hired as a lady's maid," she continued, her words rushed now, as if trying to justify the unspoken. "But it's been difficult of late, to find servants of... suitable background, you understand."

Bellamy watched her closely, his face unreadable. "And is she? Of suitable background?"

Anne-Marie's head jerked up at the question, her expression defensive. "Oh yes, she is a good girl." Her voice wavered, and she paused. "Young, you understand. But a good girl." She swallowed hard. "She lives with her mother and sister...well...her mother... in a cottage just down the hill." Her words stumbled as though saying them aloud made them more real. She opened her mouth to continue, but paused, gathering herself before going on in a strained voice. "Her father passed a few years ago, and they managed to hold on to the cottage. Of course, Delia stayed with us during the week, but she always spoke of the cottage as home." Anne-Marie's voice faltered, and she glanced at Hamish, her eyes pleading for reassurance.

Hamish offered her a small nod, though he, too, seemed uncertain.

Bellamy pressed on gently. "I believe you were very well acquainted with your maid's sister."

Anne-Marie's breath caught. She began to fidget with her lace again, twisting it between her fingers. "Yes... Lillian. She... wanted to be an artist." There was a vulnerability in her voice now, as though admitting this was somehow dangerous. "I have a studio at the back of the house, and I invited her to use it..." Her eyes darted to Hamish again, searching for words.

This time, Hamish could only listen, his brow furrowed with the same helplessness.

Anne-Marie's voice grew quicker, the need for validation evident in her tone. "Many artists come and go. I wanted to encourage her. I thought... I thought it might help."

Bellamy, his tone soft, nodded, though Anne-Marie's breath was still shallow. She bit her lip, tears beginning to well in her eyes. She stared at the ground, her body trembling with the weight of the young woman's death.

Hamish, unable to watch her fall apart any longer, reached for her hand and gave it a gentle squeeze.

"Anyway, I invited Lillian to use the studio. It has excellent light, and many artists come and go." She hurried on as though further justification were needed. "I wanted to encourage her, you see."

"That's very generous of you," said Hamish.

Anne-Marie's eyes shone, and her cheeks reddened.

"I was the one who insisted she enter that little painting in the exhibition," she said. "I hoped it would build her confidence, but I'm afraid the experience was rather traumatic for her instead."

Anne-Marie's eyes seemed to change in an instant from sparkling with the praise Hamish had offered, to moist with tears of remorse.

"And now...with her death..."

"Have you spoken with Delia or her mother this morning?" asked Hamish. He found himself feeling protective of Anne-Marie. It was clear she was deeply affected by the young woman's death.

"I sent Delia home first thing to be with her mother. I sent a note offering the woman my deepest condolences, but I didn't wish to intrude any further."

"Tell us what happened yesterday," said Bellamy.

Anne-Marie looked around the room.

"I don't know what happened," she said. "Delia had the evening off. I was going to the exhibition, as you know," she nodded to Hamish. "She lay out my outfit and assisted me to dress, then she was free to do as she pleased. She left the house before I did. I saw her walking down to the gate at five. I imagine she was walking into town."

"Is that the last time you saw her?"

"Yes, apart from when the police arrived with the news this morning. At that point I woke her and sent her home to her mother."

"We may need to speak with the other servants, but I want to talk to Delia and her mother first. I also need to interview the guests at the exhibition," said Bellamy in an official tone.

Anne-Marie nodded.

"May we see the studio now? And then we'd like to see Delia's room," he reminded her.

Anne-Marie stood, her movements deliberate as she smoothed the fabric of her skirt, each gesture controlled, almost practiced. Her attire was modest, a plain linen skirt paired with a simple white blouse, not unlike the kind of outfits Rita favoured. There was a quiet unassuming quality to her, something that blended into the background like shadow at dusk. She seemed the perfect friend for Rita, a kind soul, humble, perhaps even forgettable at first glance. Yet, something about her tugged at the edges of Hamish's mind.

He sensed the sorrow beneath her calm exterior, the grief over Lillian's death. It was genuine, of that he had no doubt. She had been close to Lillian, Delia, and, of course, Rita. But there was something else, something unsaid lingering between them. Her eyes darted, betraying a nervousness that seemed out of place. Was it the typical unease of someone caught in the aftermath of a brutal murder? Or was it something deeper?

Hamish couldn't shake the feeling that Anne-Marie was hiding something. He felt it as surely as he knew the theft and the murder were linked. And one thing was becoming clearer with each passing moment. Anne-Marie was the thread connecting them both.

She led them to the studio, a converted conservatory at the back of the main house. Light flooded the room through three glass walls and a glass panelled roof. Easels, paintboxes, brushes, turpentine and linseed oil bottles were scattered around on old tables and trestles while canvases and half-painted boards leant against the one solid wall. Everything was as expected for a space used by several artists.

"Lillian worked here, in this corner."

Anne-Marie stood alongside a large easel with the bar adjusted to take a small canvas. Used oil paints and brushes soaking in spirits rested on the easel, but nothing that could be considered a clue to either the theft or the murder.

They followed Anne-Marie upstairs to the attic and entered a small clean room with minimal furniture including a bed, a bedstand and a closet. The bed was neatly made with a hand sewn patchwork cover and a single pillow with a yellowed case. The bedstand held a washbasin and jug and there was a small wooden cross hanging over the bed.

Hamish opened the closet and noted two neatly folded black skirts and two white cotton blouses, he supposed to be Dehlia's uniforms. Other than that, there was a brown day dress.

"Delia has no other personal possessions?" he asked her employer.

"Her mother and sister live nearby, as I have said. All her possessions would be there. She brought with her only what you see."

Hamish opened a small drawer in the bedside table and a glint of metal caught his eye. He picked up a small silver badge in the shape of an A within a circle. He squinted. He had seen the shape before, but he couldn't place where he had seen it.

Hamish passed the badge to Bellamy.

"Have you seen this?" he asked Anne-Marie.

She looked at it for a moment.

"No," she said, but her eyes said something different. Hamish found himself intrigued. The woman's eyes gave her away.

"You don't know where Delia got it?" pressed Hamish.

Anne-Marie shook her head vigorously, but she continued to eye the badge as Bellamy put it in his pocket.

Hamish watched her carefully while she avoided looking directly at him. He sensed she wanted to tell them something. But the moment passed, and she remained silent.

Bellamy was also watching her closely. He looked as though he might press her about the badge, then he must have changed his mind.

Hamish was surprised when he ended the interview abruptly.

"Thank-you for your time," he said. "We'll leave you to your day."

When they were clear of the house, Hamish asked Bellamy about the badge.

"I think she has seen it before, don't you?"

Bellamy sniffed. "Absolutely," he said. "The question is, why isn't she telling us?"

CHAPTER FIVE

The rain had come so suddenly that the countess could not possibly, even by putting spur to the horses, reach the castle before she was wet through. So, her groom drew in under the portico of a dilapidated building that seemed uninhabited. The countess sprang from her carriage shouting, "Here there is shelter at least. Is not this one of my farmhouses? Put up the horses and we will wait in one of the rooms for the storm to pass."

"Your Ladyship forgets..."

"What? Are the rooms all shut up?"

"Not shut up, but your Ladyship knows that a regiment was stationed here after battle last week and you gave them your farmhouse for quarters."

"Oh, is that this one?" she laughed knocking on the door with her riding crop.

The door opened and an officer stepped out. He was tall, slender, yet strongly built. He was in a dishevelled state, yet his beauty was singular. "Pardon me," he cried.

"We have come to beg for shelter from this storm."

He stepped aside and she found herself in a room hung with damaged uniforms. There was a table with a chaos of books, letters, cravats, ink stains and small change. He swept the table clear, and she seated herself looking through the windows at the howling storm.

He bowed politely, but with slight indifference, almost mechanically. In everything that he did, there was something measured, almost soulless. For the first time they looked each other in the face, and she marked his youth, his exceeding beauty and his unnatural pallor, and shivered as if suddenly cold. And as his eyes rested on hers, he seemed to fear her, lovely as she was. **The Telegraph Saturday 12 September 1885.**

***

Isabella de la Vega

The day before the first exhibition of the Queensland Art Society...

Countess Isabella de la Vega slumped onto the silk opulence of the daybed in her suite at the Governor's mansion. She could tolerate no more platitudes from the citizenry of this remote colony.

Since her arrival she had been surrounded by the intolerable middle-classes with their mundane obsessions and inconsequential lives. None of it mattered.

The only reason she had accepted Lady Musgrave's invitation was to seek out the one man who brought meaning to her life. A fire ignited within her when he spoke, when he was close enough for her to feel his breath on her cheek. His fervour, his passion was contagious. He challenged her to question her life and break free from the constraints of her privileged upbringing. But most of all, he challenged her to feel. She wondered whether, before meeting him, she had ever really felt anything at all.

Discrete queries in Sydney revealed he had travelled to Brisbane by steamer some weeks earlier. When she was in Sydney this news left her clenching her jaw so tightly the muscles in her neck became rigid and painful. It was unthinkable to find that now that she was in this godforsaken colony at the very edge of the world, he was even further away from her.

When the invitation came from Lady Musgrave to visit the colony at Moreton Bay, it was like a gift from heaven, a sign that she was destined to catch up with him at last. What barrier could stand between them once the tyranny of distance had been vanquished? This lawless and uncivilized colony would scarcely have the power or the motivation to keep them apart.

Of course, she knew Alejandro would protest. He had no reason to support her desire to travel to Brisbane to meet the schooner there, when they could more easily board from the port in Sydney. But she also knew that in the end he had no choice but to follow her wherever she was determined to go. Her cousin's life revolved around the single task of keeping her from harm.

She smiled to herself. Though it was the only thing expected of him, he wasn't particularly good at it. She led a secretive life, that Alejandro not only allowed, but at times facilitated. He was the only person who knew about her affair with the anarchist Perez. Excluding Mateo, but as a servant, he didn't matter. And Alejandro knew the anarchist had fled to Australia to escape the Spanish authorities.

What he didn't know was that Perez had travelled further north after a short stay in Sydney. Nor did he know she had sent Mateo north ahead of their party to seek out the anarchist. He had done more than find Carlos Perez, he had arranged a meeting between herself and the anarchist when she was settled into the Governor's mansion in Brisbane.

The time agreed upon for the meeting was now less than an hour distant.

Isabella slipped from the daybed and paced the elegantly furnished chambers, her heart pounding with anticipation. The scent of jasmine wafted through the window beckoning her with the delicate fragrance of secret trysts, of love and desire.

She peered through the window, the light of the chamber at her back and the dim glow of the moonlight ahead. Every rustle of leaves, every distant footstep thrilled her. Was he, even now, out there in the darkness waiting for her? Was he as full of anticipation as she?

With one eye on the carriage clock by her bed, she resumed pacing. Every effort went into slowing her breathing to keep time with the click of the hands. If she couldn't still her nerves she would be sweating and flushed by the time they met. She forced herself to sit, but she couldn't stop herself from watching the clock.

Finally, it was time. She peered from the door to her chamber and saw that the house was quiet. She crept down the corridor to the large staircase and placed each foot softly onto the stair to avoid making any sound. When she finally placed her foot on the marble floor below, she took the first breath she had taken since she left her room. A wave of relief washed over her. From here she only needed to make her way across the hall to the French doors at the back of the house and let herself out.

The sight of a dim light emanating from a room to her left stopped her for a moment, her ears straining for the sound of life. But there was none. Perhaps someone had left a candle alight. It was too dim to be one of the new electric lights recently installed in the mansion. She hesitated for a few moments to be sure there was no sign of movement in the room. She proceeded slowly until she reached the door then she quietly opened it, just enough to slip through. With a deep breath she realized she was out of the house and on her way across the lawn toward the river. A wide strip of silver showed her which direction to take. Wild exhilaration swept her forward, her slippered feet hardly touching the ground.

When she reached their agreed meeting spot at the riverbank, she gripped the back of the cast iron bench and forced herself to slow her breathing. Her heart continued to pound in her chest. What would she do if he didn't come? A wave of nausea hit her, and her legs buckled. It was the shock of the run, she told herself. She lifted her shoulders and focused on her breathing. What a mess she must look. Her eyes peered into the darkness for any sign of him.

Only a moment passed before she glimpsed the silhouette of a man approaching. The shape of him, the liquidity of his movements filled her with longing. She steadied herself by leaning against the back of the bench. Knowing it was him long before she could see him properly was easy. His image was impressed into her memory, recalled time after time over their many months of separation.

He took her arm, and the warmth of his touch sent electricity through her body. The air crackled with unspoken words and unfulfilled promises. A flame ignited in her soul and as his lips met hers the world melted away. There was nothing but his skin on hers, the weight of the time they had spent apart and the cool breeze that wafted along the river to gently caress them both.

An intense twist of agony and ecstasy wrung at her as she drank in every moment knowing it may be the last for some time. He whispered that he had longed for her, that she was his only love, and she breathed in his words, committing them to her heart as if they were scratched into her very soul.

CHAPTER SIX

Sir, there is an outcry of discontent among the residents of the Hamilton district about the disgraceful state of the road between the Hamilton Hotel and the new Breakfast Creek bridge. I have resided in this district for two-and-one-half years, and nothing has been done to this road, while the road around Nundah and other parts of the division are well looked after. At present, after the rain, the road is barely passable. The other morning the omnibus stuck and a number of well-known residents had to get out and walk through mud a foot deep to the tram car.

As this road is used as a pleasure drive perhaps more than any other in Brisbane it ought to be kept in a reasonable state of repair. It would be well for the Brisbane Municipality to contribute to its maintenance as the racecourse traffic alone is enormous. At present residents cannot go to any evening entertainment as it is both dangerous and disagreeable in the extreme to drive through the quagmire unaided by light of day. **The Brisbane Courier 3 September 1889.**

***

It didn't take Hamish and Bellamy long to arrive at the worker's cottage where Delia lived with her mother. It was a short ride down the hill from the Langford home.

Hamish knew it would be difficult talking to the women so soon after their loss. But it was important to find out as much about Lillian as they could as soon as they could. At this point they had no witnesses to her killing, or even to the moments directly before it. In lieu of this, they could only make assumptions about who may have wanted her dead. If this turned out to be a senseless abduction of a young woman for the purpose of rape and sadistic murder, they may never find the culprit at all. This possibility clawed at Hamish's nerves.

As they climbed down from the buggy Hamish and Bellamy noted the simplicity of the building and its slightly unkempt appearance. The grass was high between the roughly hewn timber fence and the veranda, and the house itself, a timber structure with a gabled roof of corrugated iron was in sore need of painting. It was a house that struggled to maintain what was once a respectable, if working-class presence. Delia's mother met them at the door, her face puffed and red from weeping.

Bellamy introduced himself and Hamish, in a grim but determined tone and the grieving mother stood aside to allow them to enter. They were led into the first room to the left of the hall where a younger woman, who they assumed to be Delia, was curled up in a worn armchair in the far corner. The furniture was scant and functional without unnecessary adornment, but cleanliness was an obvious priority.

Hamish was struck by the physical similarity between Delia and her sister Lillian. They appeared to be close in age, and had the same small frame, mousy brown hair and pale skin. Delia, who was the younger of the two girls, looked slightly sturdier in build than her sister. But Hamish acknowledged to himself that he wasn't seeing either girl at their best. Lillian had turned up dead on his autopsy table and Delia was curled up in a ball suffering palpable grief.

"We're terribly sorry to intrude at such a time," began Bellamy, "but it is imperative that we act quickly if we are to achieve justice for Lillian."

Mrs Murphy invited them to sit, and Delia nodded through her tears.

"When did you last see Lillian?" Bellamy began.

Mrs Murphy answered promptly.

"Not at all yesterday."

She looked to Delia who nodded without speaking.

"The day before she called in briefly to tell us that her painting would be on display at the exhibition. Anne-Marie Langford had been encouraging her to exhibit for weeks, though Lillian was reluctant. Delia and I couldn't understand it. We thought she'd be pleased. She kept saying the painting wasn't any good. But if Miss Langford thought it was…"

She glanced at Delia.

"Well, we didn't understand. Anyway, at the last-minute Miss Langford made sure the painting was included."

Hamish took down notes in his notepad while the sergeant continued with his questions.

"I take it Lillian had Miss Langford's permission to use her studio to paint?"

Mrs Murphy rushed to answer.

"Yes, of course she had permission. Miss Langford was very generous in her encouragement of our Lillian. As you can see, we have neither the light nor the space to paint here."

Hamish looked around the small room, probably the largest in the house and had to agree.

"It was Friday yesterday," said Bellamy, "You would have expected Lillian home after the exhibition, but was Dehlia expected home?"

"Dehlia works until two o'clock on Saturdays. "I expected her to sleep in her room in the servant's quarters at the Langford's."

"So, Lillian would not have expected a ride home with her sister?"

Mrs Murphy flashed a peek at her daughter, still curled up in the armchair. The girl shook her head slowly.

"How was Lillian intending to travel home from the exhibition?"

"She would usually take the tram, or walk," said Mrs Murphy. "But I cannot say for certain what her intention was last night.

"Would she catch a cab?" asked Bellamy.

Mrs Murphy looked shocked.

"She couldn't afford to pay for cabs," she said. "Definitely not."

Bellamy hesitated.

Hamish wondered if he should share with the woman the fact that they had found wheel marks near the murder site. He decided the level of detail wasn't necessary and could only serve to upset the two women.

"There were tracks in the mud, probably from a cab," Bellamy said. "Not many as the tide had come in and gone out, but some were found where the cab would have veered off the road onto the mud."

Blood drained from Mrs Murphy's face.

Hamish pursed his lips. He wondered if his Sergeant had any sensitivity at all.

In response to Mrs Murphy's reaction, Bellamy had the decency to pause his questions for a moment while the colour returned.

"Did Lillian have any friends she might have gone to meet? Perhaps a male friend?"

Hamish noticed Delia's eyes open wide at the question.

"Certainly not," cried her mother. She looked to Delia for confirmation, but her daughter remained silent and avoided her eyes.

Hamish knew immediately there was more Delia could tell them on that score, but Bellamy seemed determined to forge ahead without exploring the question further.

"Where were you both last night?" he asked.

Both women appeared startled by the question.

"I was here, at home, of course," said Mrs Murphy.

Bellamy turned to Delia and waited.

She squirmed in the chair and her face reddened so her mother answered on her behalf.

"Delia walked into town to meet with friends, other girls in service."

Hamish and Bellamy both stared silently at Delia knowing there was more to it than that.

"Where did you meet your friends?" prompted Bellamy.

Delia looked up under wet lashes.

"The Oddfellows Hall in Charlotte Street," she said in little more than a whisper.

Hamish's eyes widened and his eyebrows shot up.

"May I ask why a group of young ladies would be meeting at the Oddfellows establishment?" Bellamy asked.

Delia's face reddened to a deep fuchsia.

"It wasn't only ladies," she said continuing to avoid her mother's eye. "It's more of a worker's meeting. A group of people in service meet fortnightly to discuss working conditions."

It was Mrs Murphy's turn to raise her eyebrows and blink rapidly.

Delia began to sob again.

"Lillian would have been there, but she went to see her painting on display at that stupid exhibition."

"But Lillian was not in service, was she?" asked Hamish.

Bellamy glanced at him startled by the suddenness of the question.

"Lillian was keener than I was, actually," said Delia. Her shoulders curved forward and her head drooped. She avoided eye contact with anyone in the room, staring instead at the worn rug as she spoke. She was more interested in…politics."

Hamish wasn't convinced and he could see that Delia was aware of it. Why would a young woman who had never worked outside her own home be interested in a meeting about labour conditions?

"What time did the meeting end?"

"About a quarter past ten, I think. I wasn't the last to leave, though," Delia sniffed.

"And how did you travel home, Miss Murphy? Surely, you didn't walk from town to Bowen Hills on your own at that time of night?" Bellamy spoke as if implying such a thing was incredulous.

"I did not," said Delia defiantly. One of the male attendees accompanied me. He usually walks both Lillian and I home after the meetings."

She took a breath and sighed.

"He is in service at the Langford's, as a matter of fact."

She sat back in the armchair and stared sideways at her mother, defying her to challenge her. Hamish watched the older woman's mouth drop open. It was clearly the first time she was hearing of this man.

Bellamy's interest was piqued.

"What is his name?"

Delia blinked before answering. Hamish could almost hear her whisper, 'in for a penny, in for a pound,' before she volunteered his name.

"George," she said quietly. "George Prentice."

The girl's face reddened to her ears and her mother's lips pursed.

An awkward silence followed while everyone processed this new information. Hamish was the first to break the silence.

"Could Lillian have headed to Charlotte Street after she left the exhibition?" he said. "Could she have been meeting someone?"

Delia's face contorted.

Hamish knew immediately they would need to separate the two women, if they were to hear the truth from Delia.

"I hate to ask," said Hamish directly to Mrs Murphy," but could the sergeant and I trouble you for a cup of tea?"

Mrs Murphy nodded and sprang to life as though she had been reticent in leaving them for so long without the offer of a drink.

"I apologize," she said, and hurried from the room to the back of the house.

Hamish and Bellamy watched Delia carefully until her mother was out of earshot.

"We need your help to find out who did this terrible thing to your sister," said Bellamy.

Hamish held his breath while the girl chewed her lip.

"Lillian may have liked the fellow who runs the meetings," she said quietly.

"What is this man's name?" asked Hamish.

"Carlos. I don't know his surname. He is very charismatic... talks about the importance of us workers knowing our value. That sort of thing."

"Could Lillian have been hoping to meet this man after the exhibition?"

"I don't know," she said. "Lillian is...was stubborn. I don't know," she repeated, tears welling in her eyes again.

"Do you know where we can find him?" asked Bellamy.

Hamish and Bellamy heard footsteps in the corridor as her mother returned with tea.

Delia lowered her eyes and said "No."

Hamish and Bellamy thanked Mrs Murphy for the tea, drank it quickly, then said their goodbyes. There was little point continuing the interview with Mrs Murphy present. They had two men to follow up on now. And time was critical.

"We need to speak with George Prentice," said Bellamy as soon as they were out of the house. "I wouldn't mind betting there's a serious courtship between the lad and Delia Murphy of which the mother is unaware. And I'm anxious to catch up with this fellow Carlos."

"It will be interesting to learn if Lillian made it to the Oddfellows Hall," said Hamish.

"This man Carlos may not want to tell us, even if she did," suggested the Sergeant.

Hamish nodded.

"The administrators responsible for hiring out the hall should have an address for him."

They settled into the police buggy.

"Do you think we could collect Rita on the way?" asked Hamish. "I promised I would pick her up from the Lady Bowen. She finishes at one o'clock on Saturdays, and it's almost that now."

"Do you want Rita to join in the interview at Charlotte Street?"

"No. I was hoping you could drop us both at my home in Wickham Terrace and go back to Charlotte Street alone."

"Good grief, man, that's quite a round trip." Bellamy rolled his eyes. "As you wish." He gave the instructions to the driver with a frustrated sigh.

"Why don't you join us for dinner tonight? We can go over ideas about the case. Bring Agatha with you."

Bellamy's face hardened. "Mrs Bellamy is in Toowoomba visiting her sister," he said blandly.

"What, again?" said Hamish.

Bellamy flashed him a look that could freeze water.

CHAPTER SEVEN

Sir, not only is there no bus service between the hours of seven p.m. and nine p.m. as stated, but during the running hours of the morning and toward evening, unless one is very fortunate, there is no possibility of getting a seat, even at the excessive fare of six shillings. I think there is a splendid opening on this line for a bus to dart from the tram terminus at Breakfast Creek and running to the Hamilton Hotel and to Eagle Farm arranging so that the last bus could meet the theatre tram.

At present there is only one bus at eleven p.m. and the fare is to the Hamilton Hotel. Anyone who misses this single bus from the Town Hall has to walk from the creek the rest of the way. The Hamilton district is rapidly growing, and it goes without saying that no working man can afford to pay six shillings for bus fares. **The Brisbane Courier 3 December 1888.**

***

Hamish and Rita were settled into Hamish's smart townhouse with the general practice on the ground floor and living quarters above. Hamish had wondered about converting the rooms below now that he was no longer running the practice. He didn't need two fully equipped practice rooms, and he could use more space for entertaining. He didn't have a dedicated dining room for a start, only a foldaway table in the sitting room upstairs. He regularly daydreamed about how he might furnish the downstairs area, but he hadn't acted on the idea.

Again, on this occasion he put the idea aside thinking he might return to it later. The idea of the practice was a backstop. Whenever he felt unsure in his current role as medical examiner he drew confidence from the existence of the two rooms, fully equipped, and ready for him to return to general practice. Not that he had been satisfied in his work in family medicine either. If he had enjoyed it, he would have put more energy into establishing the business. The truth was, he preferred the forensic work. Still, there were parts of that he found unsatisfactory as well.

The tedium of sitting in an office every day, when there was often nothing productive for him to do was one thing. Then when there was a death, nine times out of ten, the cause was plainly obvious. It necessitated only the completion of a superfluous number of forms. Inexplicably, when a suspicious death occurred and he was intent on investigating it, the administration complained that it was taking him too long.

Hamish had invited Rita to dinner so he could fill her in on the details of the case. She worked with Bellamy and himself on previous cases, and she always offered a unique perspective. In this case, with her friend Anne-Marie, at least indirectly involved, he thought she may have valuable insights.

Rita listened carefully to his account.

"Let me know if I have this right - Anne-Marie's maid Delia's, sister Lillian, had her painting stolen from the exhibition, and the following morning she was found dead on the mudflats at Hamilton Reach."

"Exactly," said Hamish.

"And Delia claims Lillian had a crush on the leader of the worker's group they belonged to, so you are assuming she may have gone to meet him after she left the exhibit."

"Right, you are," said Hamish.

What time did Lillian leave the art show?"

"Anne-Marie says about ten o'clock."

"And Delia left Charlotte Street about one quarter past ten?"

Rita wrinkled her nose.

"What else do you have?"

Hamish thought about it.

"Nothing, really."

Then he remembered the small silver badge he found in Delia's bedside table. After slipping a notepad and pencil from his jacket pocket he drew a likeness of the A with the circle around it and showed it to Rita.

Her eyebrows arched and she gasped.

"What's that doing in a lady's maid's bedside table?"

Hamish turned the badge over in his fingers.

"Why? What is it?"

"I might be mistaken, but I've seen a photograph of a group of men all wearing berets with this badge. It was in a pamphlet discussing the Spanish Anarchists. I believe it's their symbol."

"Spanish Anarchists?" repeated Hamish. "What on earth would that be doing in Delia's drawer?"

"I don't know," said Rita.

Hamish pushed back his fringe.

"I wonder how Bellamy fared with tracking down this man leading the labour meetings. It would be interesting to know what he thinks of the badge. Do you think he might be an anarchist?"

"He might be. It doesn't necessarily follow that a man advocating for fair treatment for workers is an anarchist. But the badge is suggestive."

Wallace came in with a silver tray balancing two wine glasses and a crystal decanter glistening with dark liquid.

"What's this about anarchists?" he asked.

Hamish took a glass from the tray and Wallace poured him a drink. He then made sure that Rita also had a full glass of red wine before sitting down to his own. In addition to the wine, the tray held a selection of light sandwiches.

"I fear neither of you have eaten lunch," Wallace said. "This will see you through."

Rita tucked into a tiny triangle of fresh bread with butter and cheese, while Hamish explained about the badge.

"The Spanish Anarchists are a dangerous lot," said Wallace. "The Palace in Madrid was bombed last year, and this group were suspected."

"Goodness," cried Rita. "Was the Royal family harmed?"

"No. But they were shaken up and there was terrible damage to the Palace. The bomb was placed on the internal staircase, apparently. It is pure luck no one was hurt."

Rita placed her glass down on the table with such force it made Hamish jump. Her eyes sparkled with the seeds of an idea.

"Do you think the countess would know about this group?"

Hamish tilted his head to one side.

"She might."

Wallace took a sandwich from the tray and popped it into his mouth whole.

"She would certainly know of them," he said. "The Royal family and nobility in Spain are anxious about the rise of these groups. They're acutely aware of their activities."

Hamish took an egg and lettuce sandwich and tried to imagine how a Lady's maid had come by a symbol of Spanish anarchists. Surely there had to be a connection with this fellow who lectured at the Oddfellow's Hall.

The doorbell rang as he was about to speak, and Wallace disappeared beyond the banister as he hurried downstairs to answer the call. Hamish and Rita were both surprised when he returned with Sergeant Bellamy, whose dishevelled appearance reflected the long day he'd had, since the discovery of the body at five that morning.

Wallace made sure he was seated comfortably with a drink in one hand and a tiny sandwich in the other while Hamish and Rita peppered him with questions.

"Did you find out about this man, Carlos?" asked Hamish.

"Do you have a surname and an address for him?" asked Rita.

Wallace gestured at them to stop. "Leave the man to catch his breath."

Bellamy smiled gratefully at him.

He was not able to focus on their questions until he had swallowed a long draught of wine and taken a sandwich.

"The administrator at the Oddfellows had scant records. They told me they allowed community groups to use the hall for meetings for a small fee and that a Spanish fellow of about thirty years had arranged the hall for the workers in service to meet fortnightly. As long as they left the place tidy, no one was too bothered by them. The person responsible for the hiring is usually asked to leave his full name and address, but in this case the clerk was unable to find any such record."

Hamish and Rita both sat back in their chairs with a collective groan.

"We know no more about him then," said Rita.

"That's not true," Bellamy went on. "While there is no written record, the man remembered that his name was Perez, Carlos Perez."

"Well, that's something," said Hamish. "We have the connection with Spain. Perhaps this man is associated with the anarchists."

"Anarchists?" asked Bellamy puzzled.

Rita looked thoughtful.

"I think we should ask the countess about him."

"Why?" said Bellamy. "Why would a Spanish Countess know of a labour organizer operating in a remote colony in Australia?"

"Because we think he may be a member of the Spanish Anarchist Society," said Hamish.

"Why?"

Hamish reminded the sergeant of the badge they'd found in Dehlia's bedside table and Bellamy placed his hand in his pocket.

"Can I see it?" asked Rita.

He held it out and handed it to her. She turned it over.

"It's definitely the symbol of the Spanish Anarchist Society," she said.

"We think Carlos may be a member and he's either gifted the badge to the girls, or they've taken it as a souvenir, without his knowledge."

"It's unlikely he'd give it away. It incriminates him."

Wallace came into the room with a steaming tureen of his famous lamb stew.

"I assume the sergeant is staying," he said, laying out clean white China on the table in the drawing room. Hamish thought about how almost half his premises was currently underused and resolved to do something about. He must take the time to rearrange things. He would attend to it when this case was solved.

"You're right," he said. "It could be quite damning for this Perez, if the badge links him to this group considered responsible for the bombing of the palace in Madrid."

"Even so," began Bellamy, "Just because they are both Spanish, there is no reason to suspect that the countess knows this fellow, or where we might find him."

"True," agreed Rita, "but it is worth asking what she knows about the group. She may not know of individuals involved in the organisation being in the colony, but I imagine she would be interested."

They all moved to the table without any interruption in the conversation.

"Do we have any other leads?" asked Hamish as he served liberal portions of Wallace's famous lamb stew onto his plate.

Bellamy broke a piece of fresh bread and dipped it into his gravy.

"Not as such. What I don't understand is why the painting was stolen and the girl killed on the same evening. There has to be a connection between the two events."

Bellamy held a chunk of bread dripping in lamb gravy to his lips and hesitated. "What do you know about Anne-Marie Langford?" he asked Rita.

"Anne-Marie?" Rita nearly choked on her mouthful of stew. "Surely you can't suspect Anne-Marie of being involved in this thing?"

Hamish watched them both.

"I'm not sure I suspect anyone yet," he said. "I'm simply making enquiries."

"Really?" said Rita. "I've been involved in too many of your investigations to be fooled, remember? Why would Anne-Marie steal her maid's painting, at the exhibition no less, and then have her killed? It doesn't make any sense."

Bellamy pushed back in his chair until only the back legs were on the ground and the back of the chair leant against the wall.

Hamish instinctively put out his hand to steady the chair. The sergeant's habit of tipping chairs onto their back legs was one thing in his office, but these spindle-legged dining chairs might not take the abuse.

"You're right," said Bellamy. "It doesn't make sense that she would steal the painting at the exhibition after several people had already seen it. Afterall, she could have stolen it at any time, if there was something she didn't want seen. She does seem relevant to the case, though I'm not sure how exactly."

The central figure is this Carlos Perez," said Hamish carefully eyeing his dining chair.

"I'm going to see the countess tomorrow," announced Rita. "We arranged a meeting when we were at the exhibition. Isabella will be at the fountain in the gardens at two o'clock. Will you join us, Hamish? Alejandro will be there of course. We can ask her about Carlos Perez and the Spanish Anarchists."

"You didn't tell me you were meeting the countess." Hamish tried not to sound put out.

"I was going to."

Rita watched him from the corner of her eye as she took a sip of wine.

"Really, I intended to invite you," she said.

"You need to be careful," Bellamy cut in before Hamish could respond. "The death of Lillian Murphy was violent, and we don't yet know who was involved."

Hamish thought about the sergeant's warning.

"It's a stroll in the gardens in broad daylight with a countess and her cousin," he said. "I doubt we can come to any harm. Still, it will be interesting to know if Isabella has heard of this Perez fellow."

The meal was completed in companionable conversation then Bellamy and Rita left early enough to ensure a decent night's sleep. Bellamy dropped Rita off at her flat before riding home himself in the police cab.

The following day, summer appeared to overtake spring and hold her hostage. Usually, the heat at this time of year was gentle, tinged with a light breeze and energizing. But on this day, as Hamish and Rita stood in front of the cast iron gates peering toward George Street, it was exhausting. There was a sting in the sun that seemed to leech energy. Whether or not it was the heat that was affecting him, Hamish had become sceptical that meeting the countess would help them in the investigation. Nonetheless, Rita was determined to meet with her and ask her about Perez. Hamish had long ago learned there was no point arguing with Rita when she set her mind to an idea. He had hoped it would at least be a pleasant way to spend a Sunday afternoon. Now the heat made him wonder if even that were likely.

"What time did you say the countess would meet us?" he asked.

"Two o'clock."

Hamish checked his pocket watch again.

"It's already twenty minutes past. Do you think she is still coming?"

Rita sighed.

"She had to attend a formal luncheon with the Governor and his wife after church. These things can go on longer than expected. I'm sure she'll come when she can."

Hamish wiped away the beads of sweat forming on his brow.

"That looks like her coach now," said Rita, a clip of excitement in her voice.

"Why is she in a coach? Government House is right there," he nodded toward the mansion leaning over the gardens.

Hamish looked to his left and saw an elaborate coach turning into Alice Street.

"The luncheon was in Toowong," she said.

The coach stopped at the elegant iron entrance gate and Rita's face flushed as the Countess Isabella de la Vega stepped out. She was in a violet organza gown that made her olive skin glow. The gown shimmered in the sunlight.

Hamish wondered at how the woman appeared to float when she walked and carried with her a presence that set her apart from everyone around her.

The footman, Mateo, who had fetched her shawl at the art exhibition, assisted her from the carriage. Alejandro stepped down after her looking equally as ethereal as the countess in a gold embroidered vest, black jodhpurs and white stockings. As a couple, they were vision enough to take a person's breath away.

The countess held a gloved hand out to Hamish, and he kissed it gently. Alejandro held Rita's fingers in his own lightly, almost not touching them and made the gesture of lowering his lips without quite touching the back of her hand.

"I'm afraid I only have an hour," said the countess apologetically. The luncheon went on far too long and I need to be back at the Governor's residence for another gathering by four o'clock."

"How was the luncheon?" asked Hamish.

Alejandro rolled his eyes slowly. "Insufferable," he said. "Incredibly boring."

The countess almost smiled, but not quite. "Such bad manners," she chastised her cousin.

The four of them strolled toward the fountain. As on any Sunday afternoon there were numerous couples promenading across the gardens in their finest attire. Every one of them turned to watch and whisper as the Spanish nobles passed. When they reached the fountain, Rita turned to the countess. "As your time is limited," she said, "what would you like to see most?"

"Cricket," said the countess.

Hamish's eyebrows shot up under his fringe. "Cricket?" he repeated.

The countess turned to him fluttering her impossibly long dark eyelashes. "The sport fascinates me," she said. The Governor speaks of nothing else."

Rita nodded.

"We shall see cricket in play, then."

They strolled across the gardens toward Queens Park where a crowd had gathered around a sizeable oval. Women were seated comfortably in garden chairs while men cheered on the players. The countess watched as a particularly tall man sent a ball spinning toward the batsman with a flourish of arm and leg movements something akin to a dance. The bat hit the ball with a crack and sent it skyward in an arc that continued over the heads of the screaming crowd. The batsman and his partner at the other end of the wicket didn't bother moving as the crowd shouted "Six" in unison.

"Your men are strong," said the countess in a deep throated voice that led Rita to suspect she had been mistaken about the Spanish noblewoman's preferences.

"That they are," she said watching Isabella's face carefully.

The ball whizzed back onto the field, caught by a fieldsman and dispatched once more, hurtling on to the next man until it was back in the hands of the bowler. Another flourish of arms and legs and the ball was spinning once more toward the batsman. This time it made direct impact with his shin pads. The player threw his bat into the air as the crowd erupted in a collective groan.

"Is he injured?" asked the countess.

"No," said Hamish. "He is out."

They watched the man retrieve his bat and stride from the wicket.

"A new batsman will take over," explained Hamish.

Alejandro was staring into space away from the game.

"Does sport not interest you?" asked Hamish.

"It does not."

Hamish wondered what did interest him.

"We should probably walk back," suggested Rita. "Since you only have a short time."

Countess Isabella turned away from the game reluctantly and they began the slow walk back to the carriage waiting at the gate.

Rita took the opportunity to get to the question of Carlos Perez.

"I read of an awful event in your homeland," she began. "The bombing at the Palace in Madrid. Is this something that had an impact on you?"

The countess turned to Rita frowning. "You have read deeply on the politics in my country?"

"No. I simply came across the article and wondered if it had an impact on you."

The countess spoke carefully.

"It did not affect me directly. I am, of course, a member of the royal family and I have visited the Palace in Madrid on occasion. We all detest the violence perpetrated by these radical groups. And fear them."

"Do you mean the Spanish Anarchists?" asked Rita.

The countess seemed to miss a step.

"Yes, them and others," she said. "What do you know about them?"

"Not much. I know of them."

They walked in silence for a moment.

"Have you heard of a man who goes by the name, Carlos Perez?"

The countess stopped and Hamish, who was following them, almost bumped into her. The colour drained from her face and she looked as though she might feint. Alejandro rushed forward in time to take her arm and steady her.

"I feel quite unwell," she breathed.

"Please, take her other arm," Alejandro said to Hamish.

He supported the countess by taking her left arm and between them they assisted her to stumble toward the waiting carriage. The footman saw them approaching and ran out to meet them. He placed his arm around his mistress's waist and replaced Hamish as he and Alejandro led her back to the coach. The footman lifted her into her seat. Hamish tried to help, but the footmen guarded his mistress carefully.

Isabella leant into his shoulder. "Thank-you, Mateo," she said quietly.

"Don't worry," said Alejandro over his shoulder. "Mateo has been her protector since she was a child. He is a bully, but she trusts him."

Hamish took a few steps back and watched as Mateo and Alejandro fussed over Isabella. When she was finally comfortable, the carriage lurched forward on the short trip to Government House.

Hamish joined Rita.

"She's heard of him, then," he said.

"That's the same reaction she had when she saw the painting," Rita pointed out.

"Let's take a walk to the Police Station and talk to Bellamy."

"It's Sunday," said Rita. "Will he be there?"

Hamish snorted. "Agatha is away. Of course, he'll be there."

They found Bellamy in his office with paperwork piled high on his desk as always. "The amount of official documentation needed every time someone gets themselves killed is ridiculous," he said. "Have you completed the Certificate of Particulars yet?"

Hamish stopped short of the desk.

"What no greeting when friends drop in?"

Bellamy glared at him.

Rita tucked her skirt behind her legs and sat down.

"Not completely," said Hamish, "We know where the body was found and when, and I have completed the cause of death section. But we don't yet know the last person in whose company she was seen."

"Write down Anne-Marie Langford. I need the form."

"But Anne-Marie may not be the last person to see her. We need to find out if she went to Charlotte Street to the Oddfellow's Hall. And we haven't yet interviewed the other guests at the exhibition. Maybe one of them saw her?"

"It doesn't matter at this stage. I need the form completed to send to the Undersecretary of Justice along with these notes. I'm aiming to get them away this afternoon."

"But why the rush? Surely it would be better to wait until we have more accurate information."

"The Undersecretary wants the documentation on his desk by morning. The powers that be are pushing for a fast result on this one. Apparently, there's a financial review going on. Resources are tight."

"Tight?" gasped Hamish. "Surely an investigation takes as long as it takes and costs what it costs to be carried out properly."

The sergeant looked up at him, pencil in mid-air. "They are suggesting costs have risen since you took over the role of medical examiner. Every case doesn't need to be investigated to the nth degree."

Hamish was taken aback. "What about the expectation that a post-mortem will be carried out if there is the slightest suspicion that death was due to foul play?"

"Yes, but there is also a requirement that any such investigation will be frugal."

Hamish shook his head. "Noted," he said. "But surely there's no argument against this death being suspicious and in need of our closest examination."

Bellamy threw back his head and stared at the ceiling. "Fill in the form," he said. "You can do it now since you're here. That will keep the administrators happy, and we can get on with the investigation."

Hamish went to open his mouth, but Rita's eyes caught his and he decided better of it. He went into the adjoining office and wrote "Anne-Marie Langford" under "Person last seen in company of deceased." It went against the grain to do so.

"When he returned to Bellamy's office and handed him the document, Rita gave him a smile of approval. He sat grumpily in the simple wooden chair opposite Bellamy. The sergeant piled the forms and report together and tapped them on his desk.

"Done," he said. "Pennyweather comes on at four, it must be nearly that now. He can run them over to the Government Offices and drop them in the box."

"Surely, Jan could take them first thing in the morning," suggested Hamish.

Bellamy glared at him.

"Pennyweather will take them."

Hamish was no longer in the mood to talk about the meeting with the countess.

"I found someone who saw Lillian walking toward the Oddfellow's, as it happens," said Bellamy.

"That person is the last one to see Lillian then," he cried. He was ready to grab back the form from Bellamy's desk.

"Settle down," said the sergeant, "The fellow doesn't want to be named, he was up to no good, leaving the opium den in Albert Street. We need these people on the streets at night to trust us. They need to know that if they come forward with information it won't get them into any unnecessary trouble."

"What if he's the killer?" said Hamish, not thinking for one minute that he was, but determined to make a point.

Rita stifled a laugh in her handkerchief.

"He's not the killer," said Bellamy. "For one thing he was so out of it he could barely stand, let alone drive a buggy. Anyway, he says he not only saw her, he also saw a cab turn the corner soon after her."

Hamish raised his eyebrows.

"Did he see how many people were in it?"

"He thinks one man plus the driver – but he couldn't be sure."

"Did he recognize either man?"

Bellamy smiled like he was enjoying himself.

"He says he might, if he saw them again."

Hamish felt his spirits rise. A witness would make all the difference. If they could identify suspects, this might be the only way of bringing the killer to justice.

Hamish settled down and let the information sink in.

"We can be reasonably sure she went to the Oddfellows Hall, then. Was she hoping to meet with her sister? Or was she wanting to see Mr Perez?"

"It is also reasonable to assume that Carlos Perez is connected to the Spanish Anarchists in some way, given the presence of the silver badge."

"It may be why he's in Australia," said Rita, "laying low after the bombings in Madrid."

Bellamy nodded and chewed the end of his pencil.

Hamish caught Rita's eye. He knew she was bursting with the news of their encounter with the countess. He shot her a silent warning not to share their news so easily.

Then she spoke, "We talked to the countess this afternoon," she said.

Hamish drew his lips tight.

Rita glanced at him from the side of her eye and shrugged. "Don't be petulant," she said. Then turning back to Bellamy, "When I mentioned Carlos Perez, Isabella was visibly shaken."

"She looked like she was going to feint," Hamish added reluctantly.

Rita bit on her bottom lip. "I've been wondering why the countess is in Brisbane," she said slowly. "It seems odd that she would travel this far to such a small colony. I know Lady Musgrave offered the invitation, but still..."

"You think her visit is linked to this Perez fellow, don't you?" asked Hamish.

Rita shrugged again.

"We need to find him," said Bellamy. "That much is clear."

CHAPTER EIGHT

None of the official statistics available give a correct idea of the work done by the Criminal Investigation Department. The returns contained in the annual statistical register are of a general nature, comprising the work of the whole police force in every department of crime, down to the most trivial of offences. The statistical register showing the number of undetected crimes does not draw any distinction between the work of the uniform branch and the plain clothes branch. If the returns for the detective force alone were given, it would show an even worse condition of things than has been described. Instead of one offence in every two reported being undetected, it is no exaggeration to say that out of every dozen cases the detective branch addresses, not more than one is cleared up. Therefore, it may be asserted that even in the class of work which it undertakes to do (and much of which we say should not be given to the detective force at all) it fails to satisfy public requirements.

If the stolen property list supplied to the pawnshops is taken as a guide to the success of the department in this class of crime the result is far from satisfactory. These lists are published twice a week and at the foot is mentioned the articles recovered, but the latter do not average more than about three percent of the whole. It might be said that the value of the articles recovered would barely cover the cost of printing the list.

With such a force as is regularly maintained by the Criminal Investigation Department, the daily life of every criminal of any consequence should be an open book to the police authorities. There should be a complete system of surveillance under which regular returns should be prepared dealing with the movements of all dangerous criminals and suspected persons.

For every person put under arrest by the Criminal Investigation branch the public pays a very large sum. But it is not to the cost of the department that exception should be taken; the public will not object to paying seven thousand pounds or more, for proper security against dangerous criminals; it is the paying for that which they do not get that they object to.

The blame for this inefficiency of the force may be divided. To the unsuitableness of the bulk of men employed for detective work must be added those official shortcomings and errors in administration. Good men cannot make a success of a bad system, and however efficient members of the force might be, an inadequate system under which they are employed will not admit of the best results being achieved. **The Argus Melbourne Tuesday 28 June 1898.**

***

Hamish returned home from the police station more optimistic than he had earlier been about his and Bellamy's chances of identifying the attackers of Lillian Murphy. The potential of having a witness, who could identify the individuals in the cab that was spotted near the area where the girl disappeared, was at least hopeful. If they could ferret out suspects, they might be able to place them at the right place at the right time. Even so, it could be a difficult case to argue without any discernible motive. Just because any such suspects were in Charlotte Street on the night in question didn't prove they killed anyone.

Hamish settled comfortably in his favourite chair with a glass of his best sherry, still wondering if they would be able to get justice for Lillian. He was slightly irritated that the administrators thought he was spending too much money on investigations. It was important to examine every possibility when an unusual death occurred. Guesswork was no longer sufficient in the new policing, rigorous methods of investigation were required, providing evidence, not supposition. Forensic investigation was a matter of scientific enquiry. It took time.

In the long run what they needed were systems. Every medical examiner in the country should eventually be following the same processes, taking the same steps, as they progress toward a conclusion. Every suspicious death was a learning opportunity to gain new skills and share them for the benefit of the discipline.

Hamish was developing processes that could be followed, should be followed, by any medical examiner, to ensure consistent practice. It might take longer as the new methods were tried and tested, but it would save time and money in the future as new medical examiners were trained in consistent and effective methods. But while Bellamy understood his passion, and gave him his head to a certain extent, the powers over the sergeant's head were not obliged to do so. Hamish was feeling underappreciated when he heard a knock at the door downstairs.

Who would be calling at this hour on a Sunday evening?

Moments later Wallace appeared at the top of the stairs with a slim young man of impeccable appearance.

"Alejandro!" cried Hamish. "Good evening."

The Spanish nobleman held out his hand. Hamish took it in his own and gestured for him to sit.

"More sherry, Wallace," he said as Alejandro perched himself on the edge of the blue settee.

"I apologise for the late hour," said Alejandro. "My purpose is somewhat sensitive." His usual cool demeanour had been displaced. He wrung his hands nervously.

"Have a sip of this sherry, I'm sure it will fortify you."

Alejandro swallowed the whole measure and held his glass out for more.

Wallace poured. He showed no inclination to leave the room, fascinated by the appearance of this attractive young man in the house at this hour.

Hamish rolled his eyes at the old cook and nodded to a vacant chair. "Sit down and have a drink, if you're staying," he said.

"Thank you, sir. Don't mind if I do." Wallace sat.

Alejandro appeared unphased by the presence of a servant joining them for drinks.

Hamish wondered if the serving classes were indeed invisible to the truly rich.

"I have come about Isabella," he began. "You must have noticed how distressed she was at the mention of Carlos Perez this afternoon."

"I did notice."

Alejandro took a deep breath.

"She is obsessed with the fellow."

Hamish opened his eyes wider.

"They met in Madrid, the circumstances don't matter, but from the moment of their meeting she could think of nothing but that man. She would sneak out to meet him in smoky coffee shops, in disguise of course. No one could know she was the Countess Isabella de la Vega. But he knew, the blackguard. I suspect he wanted to use her to get information on the activities of the royal family. Perhaps even access to places of importance."

Hamish and Wallace were spellbound. They said nothing for fear anything they said may cause the Spanish man to stop talking.

"It was like Isabella was in a dream. She was smiling all the time, humming beneath her breath. Whenever she was not with him, she was plotting their next meeting, what she would wear, what elaborate story she would tell her parents to cover her absences."

He looked up at Hamish with impossibly dark eyes. "I tried to talk to her. I was the only one who knew what she was up to, apart from Mateo, of course. She used me to create diversions and to lie for her. The family have always expected me to chaperone her everywhere. Keep her from danger. I'm afraid, in this, I have let everyone down. Most particularly Isabella. Her passion for this man is like a train I cannot stop."

Hamish was confused. "I've heard...we thought...the rumours..."

Alejandro shook his head. "I know, there is no need to say it. There are rumours about a liaison with a French actress. The countess fostered and perpetuated those rumours to keep the public from the real truth – that she was hopelessly entwined with an anarchist."

Hamish and Wallace exchanged glances.

Rita will be surprised to hear this.

"Is that why Countess Isabella accepted the invitation to come to Brisbane?" asked Hamish. "Did she find out that Carlos Perez was here?"

Alejandro nodded.

"Yes. I didn't know it at the time, but now I realise it is so. When Lady Musgrave offered her kind invitation it was impossible for Isabella to turn it down. She had to find him."

"Why did Perez leave Spain?" Hamish was almost sorry he asked, afraid of what the answer might reveal.

"After the bombing at the Palace the Police became more aggressive toward the anarchists. I don't know if Perez was directly involved, but he certainly would know who was. Anyway, he must have decided to get out of the country as quickly as possible. He simply disappeared. Isabella had no note from him. Nothing. She was miserable."

"And you were relieved, no doubt, to see the end of it," said Hamish.

"If only it were the end. Isabella could not leave the matter rest. She tried having people ask around about him within his networks, but no one would speak. It is a time when such people have closed ranks in my country. Isabella represents the enemy of the people in the eyes of some."

"Yes, I see. It is an unlikely match for sure. Couldn't your cousin see there could be no future in it?"

Alejandro shook his head. "She could see nothing. Her heart beats only to find him."

Hamish brushed his fringe from his face with both hands while Alejandro continued.

"We heard nothing of Perez until a casual conversation in Sydney revealed he was in the colony. Isabella tracked him to Moreton Bay. Now that she is aware you have some knowledge of him, she will try to find out where he is through you and your friend. She is obsessed with this man and will not let this lead go."

Hamish blew air through pursed lips forcing a long, slow whistle. "What do you want us to do?"

"She must not see this man again. He is like poison to her. He will destroy her." Alejandro was more passionate than Hamish had ever seen him. "I implore you, if you know where this man is, you must not tell Isabella."

Hamish took a long sip of his drink. "I have no idea where Mr Perez is," said Hamish. "But we are looking for him, in relation to the death of a young woman."

"Ha!" cried Alejandro. "I know this man is diablo himself! I wish you luck with your search. Be wary of him. We only have a couple of days left on our visit here. I will try to keep Isabella away from you until we leave."

Alejandro stood, thanked them for the drink and bid goodnight. He resumed his formal stature, back straight, aristocratic nose held high while Wallace led him back down the stairs to the door.

"Well, that's a turn up," said Hamish when Wallace returned.

"When will you bring Dr Cartwright up to date?" A small smirk tugged at the corner of the older man's lips.

"In the morning. Rita doesn't work tomorrow so I'll have all day to enjoy her reaction."

Moments later, Hamish was preparing for bed while thinking about Isabella driven half-mad with her longing for the anarchist. How could such a match ever work? Would she renounce her family? Would he live contrary to his ideals? Would he still be the man she had loved if he did? There was no way to twist fate that offered a happy ending in this situation.

Hamish slept fitfully with images of a demon, complete with horns and tail, dressed in impeccable silk clothing, and sporting a thin moustache, slipped in and out of shadows beneath the buildings of Brisbane. He passed below the streetlamps at the entrance gates to the Botanic Gardens and disappeared into the black foliage. Hamish was pursuing the demon, although he couldn't remember why.

The following morning, he woke up groggy. It was partly the dream that disturbed him, he felt as though he had been running half the night, and it was partly a sensation of dissatisfaction with his work as a medical examiner. Bellamy's comment about overspending had rattled him. He suddenly realized that his excitement about the development of a forensic discipline that could be taught and followed by all medical examiners, might be his idea alone. He considered it a given that everyone from the Governor and the Chief Magistrate down would see it as essential, but perhaps he was wrong. Perhaps the job really was about completing the appropriate documents as quickly as possible and ensuing someone goes to goal so the citizens can feel safe.

Hamish was still sipping his morning tea and perusing the newspaper when Rita arrived on her bicycle, sporting her fashionable split skirt and a crisp white blouse with mutton sleeves. She bounded upstairs with all the energy of a gazelle. He looked up lazily. Rita was glowing, even after her ride in the morning heat.

"How do you display such energy in the mornings?"

Her bountiful health irritated him.

Rita laughed and threw herself across his velvet settee, legs over the arm.

"I can't get away from thinking about that painting," she said plucking her gloves and removing them one by one to reveal slender white fingers. "We have been distracted by this Perez fellow, but I can't help thinking the key to this puzzle is in that painting. Why would someone steal it?"

Hamish folded his newspaper neatly and placed it on the table as Wallace walked in with steaming crumpets and local honey. "Have you eaten?" he asked Rita.

"Of course she hasn't," said Hamish. "She never eats breakfast left to her own devices. I don't know how she hasn't faded away to nothing by now."

"She looks good to me," smiled Wallace.

He placed the crumpets and a cup before her then retrieved the teapot from the table and poured her tea.

Rita tucked into a warm crumpet dripping with honey.

"I had a strange visitor last night," said Hamish.

"Oh really? Who was that? Bellamy can't sleep again with his wife away?" She smiled.

"No," Hamish went on. Alejandro called in."

Rita stopped chewing.

"What?"

Hamish tapped his fingers on the table. He was enjoying having information that Rita did not. He wasn't sure whether it was useful to the investigation or whether it counted as nothing more than gossip. But either way he was sure she wanted to know.

"He came to enlist our assistance with something."

"What could Alejandro possibly want from us?"

"He told me that Isabella had an obsessive love affair with Carlos Perez in Madrid and the real reason she came to Moreton Bay was because she heard news that he was here."

"You can't be serious?"

Rita's eyes were as wide as saucers as she sat up straight on the settee and placed her boots on the floor. Her lips glistened with honey.

"It seems she is attracted to men, after all. Albeit inappropriate ones."

Rita leant back against the settee.

"Oh, I realized that" she said. "She showed no romantic interest in me at all."

Hamish laughed. "Do you think the fact she showed no romantic interest in you evidence that she prefers men?"

Rita put her nose in the air. "Yes, in fact, I do." Her eyes twinkled. "It is a revelation that she is in love with Carlos Perez though. That couldn't be a welcome relationship as far as her parents are concerned."

"It wouldn't be, if they knew," said Hamish.

"Oh dear!" cried Rita.

"It sounds more like an obsession than a relationship," said Hamish. "Alejandro says the countess is quite out of her mind where the anarchist is concerned. He wants us to help keep her from meeting with him for the next couple of days until they depart for Spain."

"We need to find him first," said Rita.

"Bellamy is working on it. I suppose we need to share Alejandro's visit with him."

"I have an idea first…"

Hamish was eager to hear it.

"I propose we pay Anne-Marie a visit and ask her to help us recreate the still life that Lillian painted. All the items must be in the studio or around the house. I'm sure Anne-Marie will remember the subject of the painting. She saw it every day."

"Sounds reasonable," said Hamish. "Is Anne-Marie taking visitors this morning?"

"She will if she knows you're coming," said Rita looking at him knowingly.

Hamish stopped with only one arm in his coat.

"What does that mean?"

Rita fluttered her eyelids in a way that unsettled him.

"What's that supposed to mean with the eye fluttering?"

She turned away from him and shrugged.

Hamish struggled into his coat finding it difficult to get both arms in the correct holes.

"Anne-Marie likes you," said Rita.

"I like..." His eyebrows shot up. "Oh!"

Hamish felt the flush moving up from his neck to his cheeks.

"You make things up," he said, his coat finally sitting firmly across his shoulders and the sleeves neatly down over his shirt cuffs.

"Please yourself," said Rita, as she closed the door behind them.

When they arrived at the Bowen Terrace mansion, they were met with a stern greeting by the housekeeper, but the voices of Anne-Marie and her mother could be heard chattering in the entrance hall. Anne-Marie was thrilled to see them, just as Rita had promised. She laughed when Rita told her they were longer than expected because Hamish couldn't get into his coat. Hamish felt his cheeks becoming hot once again, but he liked the sound of her laugh and the way her dark eyes shone.

Anne-Marie agreed that recreating the still life was an excellent idea.

Morning light flooded the studio making the canvases pop. Most of the items they needed to recreate the painting were still in the studio. Anne-Marie gathered them together and arranged them in the exact spot they had been for the painting. Anne-Marie, Hamish and Rita stood back and stared at the little group of objects. There was the vase of flowers, not the same flowers as they had withered, but a similar fresh arrangement from the dining room, a bowl of fruit, the silver trinket box and the contents of glass beads spilling out onto the tablecloth.

"There's something missing," said Rita.

Hamish rubbed his chin.

Anne-Marie glanced at Rita and looked away again.

Hamish caught the flicker in her eyes, but he didn't know what it meant.

All at once, Rita called out, "It's the badge, the silver badge you found in her bedside table." She smiled triumphantly at Hamish and Anne-Marie.

"So it is," agreed Hamish. "That's exactly what's missing."

Rita nodded. "Yes, that's definitely it."

They both looked at Anne-Marie, but her face had become pale. "Where is it now?" she asked quietly.

"Bellamy has it," said Hamish from beneath furrowed brows.

"Do you think the badge has something to do with the painting being stolen?" Rita asked.

Hamish shifted his gaze from Anne-Marie still unsure about her reaction while he brushed his fringe from his face.

"I think it's likely," he said. "It is the one thing that identifies Carlos Perez as an anarchist. If he's hiding in the colony after some unpleasantness in Madrid, he wouldn't want people to know about his connection."

"All roads lead back to Carlos Perez," said Rita. They all nodded lightly in agreement, but Hamish noticed Anne-Marie biting her lip.

"Is everything alright?" he asked.

There was a troubled look in her eyes, as though she was trying to piece something together. "Yes," she said at last. "Everything's fine."

She smiled broadly at Hamish, making him blush. He wished Rita hadn't told him about Anne-Marie's interest in him until after the investigation. It was going to be irritating to feel the flush race up his neck and into his cheeks every time he spoke with her. And technically speaking, there was nothing to discount her as a suspect, not of the rape and murder, but of being involved in some way. Even as he thought it, he realized how ridiculous it sounded in his mind. But he was certain of one thing, there was something she was not telling them.

"We need to talk to Bellamy," said Rita, cutting into Hamish's thoughts.

"Take my buggy," offered Anne-Marie quickly. "Mother and I have no need of it today."

She caught Hamish's eyes and held them, eager to be seen as helpful. The tension between her eagerness to help and the sense she was holding something important back, confused him. Nonetheless, they could get around much more quickly without having to either walk or call on cabs. He thanked her for her kindness and accepted the loan of the vehicle for the day. She smiled broadly. It was a genuine open smile.

As soon as they were alone in the Langford's buggy, Hamish debated with himself on whether to voice his suspicion that Anne-Marie was hiding something from them. After running a scenario through his mind in which Rita chastised him for being paranoid, he decided to jump in anyway.

"I think Anne-Marie knows more than she is telling us."

Rita turned to face him. They were only inches apart and he saw the tiny wrinkle appear between her eyebrows.

"What makes you say that?"

Hamish struggled to organize his impressions into coherent thoughts under her gaze.

"She was nervous when Bellamy and I interviewed her yesterday and just now, she seemed...puzzled."

"Of course, she's anxious and confused, her maid's sister, her friend, has been murdered."

Hamish shook his head slowly.

"I said nervous, not anxious. It was like she was careful to answer our questions without revealing too much."

"Like what?" Rita demand to know.

"I don't know," said Hamish feebly.

Rita clucked and they continued the remainder of the journey in silence.

By the time they arrived at the police depot they were both eager to speak with Bellamy about Alejandro's visit. They found Constable Pennyweather at the front desk and saw past him through the open door to Bellamy's office. The sergeant wasn't inside.

"The sergeant is out of the office," said Pennyweather without looking up.

Hamish scanned his eyes across the tangle of tiny metal springs and wires sprawled across the counter.

"When will he be back?" asked Hamish as he tried to work out what the miscellaneous pieces on the desk added up to.

"He said by lunchtime."

The skinny young constable was struggling to hold a tiny spring with one hand while fitting it into a larger component with the other. The pieces were too small for his fingers and the spring kept unloading itself and flicking across the desk.

"What are you doing?"

"It's an electric pen," mumbled the constable, his lips stretched into a straight line as he struggled to trap another spring between two pins.

Hamish recognized a pen-like structure among the items on the counter and picked it up.

"Don't touch it," snapped Pennyweather snatching it back. "Sir," he added catching himself.

Hamish peered at the pen carefully and placed it back on the counter. There was a tiny motor attached to it and an electrical wire that went to a small battery. Beside the pen there was a flatbed press, of some sort.

"There," said Pennyweather, pleased with the result of his fiddling. He placed a sheet of blotting paper flat, flicked the battery and began writing with the pen. He held the result up for Hamish and Rita to see. They both peered in and witnessed light shining through tiny perforations in the paper.

"There's a needle in the tip that makes the perforations as you write,"

Pennyweather couldn't keep the excitement from his voice.

"You can make as many copies as you like using the press. The ink is forced through the holes. See?"

He demonstrated the process and handed Rita a perfect copy of his own signature.

"That's marvellous," she said, showing the paper to Hamish.

"How many copies can it make?"

Hamish took up the pen to examine its tip more closely.

"Three thousand or more, they say."

Both Hamish and Rita were still mesmerized by the electric pen when Bellamy walked in.

"Does Pennyweather have his new toy out again?" he said.

The young constable gathered up the various parts of the electric pen and ink block and cleared the desk.

"My office," said Bellamy.

Hamish and Rita followed him.

"We have news," said Hamish.

"As have I," said the sergeant, but you go first."

Hamish relayed the information gained from Alejandro's late-night visit and then told him about their re-creation of the painting.

"We think it was the inclusion of the anarchist symbol in the painting that caused it to be stolen," said Hamish.

"I think that is a likely scenario," agreed Bellamy. "Even more reason to find Perez and question him."

"If only we could find him," said Rita.

Bellamy leant back in his chair and waved his pencil about triumphantly.

"I know where to find him."

Both Hamish and Rita sat forward.

"I've discovered he's working as a short-term labourer on the construction of the new Aquarium at Hemmant."

"Brilliant," said Hamish. "We should go there right away."

"I'm afraid he's not on site today. I am informed he is to work Tuesday until Saturday. I've no home address for him. As he's not a permanent employee, the owners of the Aquarium have scant records."

Hamish felt his shoulders slump.

"Tomorrow, then," he said.

Rita was glowing with excitement.

"I've been keen to visit the aquarium, this will make the perfect excuse."

CHAPTER NINE

Brisbane holiday makers have now another place of resort when pleasure days come round, a place which is quite safe to say will ultimately become very popular. The Queensport Aquarium is situated on the bank of the river, behind Gibson Island about two miles below the Queensport Meat Works at Hemmant and can be reached by steamer in about three quarters of an hour.

Landing at the wharf and entering the grounds the first object that arrests the attention of the visitor is the main building – a two-story structure of wood and iron, 100 feet by 30 feet; surrounded by a 12 foot veranda. Entering from the riverside, the first curiosities are the fish tanks in which every species of sea creature swims in an endless circuit.

At the other end are the refreshment bars, at which almost everything except fermented and spiritous liquors are purchasable. In the centre is a fountain with three basins, the top of which rises to the upper floor. Passing on the right, the fernery is the next object of scrutiny. This is 90 feet in length, by 70 feet in width, and though in a pristine condition now, it will, with the progress of time become beautiful to behold.

Retracing his steps and ascending one of the broad flights of stairs, the visitor reaches the upper story and enters a room which will seat about 1,300 persons, in which entertainments can be given or dancing parties held. At one end there is a stage, 36 feet by 14 feet, with two dressing rooms, the whole neatly fitted up. In one corner near the stage stands an electric pipe organ, the only one of its kind in the colonies. In the opposite corner stands a piano.

The hall which is furnished with Australian bentwood chairs is delightfully cool. In the grounds the great attractions include the seal tank where four of these slimy, footless creatures delight to show visitors how to dive and swim. The shark tank is yet to be erected.

Looking around visitors will be struck with a number of summerhouses for picnics. Some half a dozen swings have also been erected and a merry-go-round for the young at heart. **The Telegraph Thursday 8 August 1889.**

***

Tuesday again dawned with uncharacteristic warmth for the time of the year and progressed as it began. A dazzling blue sky cast an inviting glow on the river, which in its turn shimmered with anticipation. As Hamish, Rita and Bellamy stood on Campbell's wharf waiting for the ferry to take them to Queensport Aquarium they were filled with cheerful excitement about the day ahead. There were a dozen others also watching for the ferry and smouldering with the same enthusiasm.

"I wouldn't have expected so many visitors to the Aquarium on a Tuesday," said Hamish.

Rita scanned the faces of her fellow tourists. Everyone was smiling broadly.

"I read in the paper the people of Brisbane are flocking to the new attraction every day. It is, by all accounts, a huge success," she said.

At that moment Rita caught sight of the Natone ambling down the river toward them, churning up water in its wake. She called out in delight as though greeting an old friend. This was the same ferry that had taken them to Deepwater Point at Southport on a previous adventure.

"Why would they use the Natone for this short journey downriver?" said Hamish to no one in particular.

"They use the Natone on busy days, or when the usual ferry is out of service," a well-dressed man in a top hat answered him.

Hamish swept his eyes across the people on the pier. While there were more than he might have expected on a weekday, there didn't seem to be the kind of numbers that would have warranted use of the large steamer.

"The usual ferry must be out of service, then," he said.

The man in the top hat didn't hear him. He was busy shuffling his wife toward the end of the jetty where they would board.

As soon as the vessel rattled to a halt, and the gangplank was firmly secured, the man and his wife rushed aboard. Hamish, Bellamy and Rita followed closely after them. They chose to stand outside where they could enjoy the sunshine and the light breeze that skipped off the river. They gripped the railing and immersed themselves in the scenery as the riverbank moved slowly in the opposite direction.

Rita removed her hat and threw back her head to feel the breeze in her hair.

"We're not setting off on a holiday," Hamish reminded her.

"On the contrary, the day might be tense," Bellamy said. "Perez may try to run if he finds out we're looking for him. I've asked the manager to meet as at the wharf, but I have sworn him to secrecy about our intent to speak with Mr Perez. Still, one never knows, secrets are not always kept."

Rita's enthusiasm wasn't dimmed.

"I've been looking forward to visiting the aquarium and I'm going to enjoy it, regardless of Mr Perez."

Hamish relaxed slightly when Rita took his arm.

Meanwhile the Natone chugged slowly down the middle of the river without any sense of urgency. It was a large vessel taking an easy journey and the captain had no reason to hurry. They passed two impressive steamers loading in front of the brick woolsheds at Teneriffe, then they rounded the bed at Newstead where the magnificent Newstead House watched them from its perch above acres of gardens. Next Breakfast Creek snaked off to the west where construction was well underway on the new Breakfast Creek Hotel. Hamish wondered at the size of the building tucked into the fork between the river and the creek. How quickly this northern shore was developing.

Soon the lush green tapestry of the rainforest was marching all the way down the hillside to touch the river. Towering trees, ancient and tangled in rich velvet vines filtered the sun and created a canopy of dappled light that reached out over the river's edge. The hum and splash of the steamer excited the birds as it passed sending them squawking and chattering into the sky.

A fork in the river created by Gibson Island saw them veer to the right. They had been on the ferry about forty minutes when they disembarked.

James Fitzpatrick, a distinguished gentleman in his late forties with a well-groomed moustache and greying temples, was waiting for them on the wharf. He wore a tailored suit with a maroon velvet waistcoat, gold pocket watch and chain; A showy man, well placed to promote Brisbane's exciting new attraction. There was warmth in his smile, but Hamish noticed the same warmth was not reflected in his eyes. He wondered if this was a man to be trusted.

Greetings were made, and Hamish, Bellamy and Rita followed the other visitors who had arrived on the Natone into the two-story wooden and iron structure that served as the main building. The group stopped to look around and there was a collective hush as they each took in a single breath. Surrounding the ground floor were six large fish tanks. Hamish calculated them at about thirteen feet long, four feet wide and four feet in depth. Each was fronted with glass an inch thick and filled with several tons of water. Fish of all shapes and sizes darted back and forth in the tanks.

As Rita pressed her face close to the window a stingray glided by, its long wings gently touching the glass as it passed. Seconds later an enormous cod swam casually close to the glass as if to greet them. Rita looked directly into the cod's eye.

"It can see me," she said with awe. "There's recognition there," she remained spellbound as the fish turned and sailed on.

Hamish joined her, marvelling at the array of fish on display. From vibrant tropical fish with bold colours and striking patterns to sleek silver-bodied creatures swimming in synchronized units. He wondered if they were distressed in the confined space when they previously had the world's seas to explore. He studied their eyes, and decided they simply looked bored. Did fish even have complex emotions? He struggled between his undeniable enjoyment at viewing the creatures up close and sadness that they had been captured and confined in this way for his enjoyment.

They moved on to the seal tank where a pavilion surrounded the pool, so that visitors could see both under the water and above. Four black seals with glistening eyes and whiskers like large cats, ducked and dived in the water. This was a display he could watch without guilt. The animals seemed to thoroughly enjoy entertaining their guests. The amusement in their antics seemed almost perverse, as if the visitors were really there to entertain them.

"We have crowds gathered around this tank on the weekends," said Mr Fitzpatrick proudly. "The seal tank is our most popular exhibit. Of course, the sharks have not arrived yet. Once the shark tank opens it will garner some excitement, I expect. We'll have a fellow in a diving suit go in to feed them once a day."

Rita's mouth formed an 'O'.

"How will the beasts not tear the diver apart?" asked Hamish, watching a seal leap onto the edge of the pool to accept a dead fish from the handler.

"They'll be too well fed for that. They'll be full and sedate. Well-fed long before the diver goes in. It's just for show."

"Still, a braver man than me," said Hamish.

The seal had slipped easily back into the pool and was circling underwater.

Mr Fitzpatrick guided them away from the tanks to a three-tiered fountain at the centre of the main building. The top of the fountain reached the upper floor. To the right of the fountain Hamish admired a fernery displaying a rich tapestry of exotic ferns.

"These ferns will be magnificent when they've settled," said Hamish.

"Yes, the planting is new at the moment, but a year from now they'll have grown huge in this humidity."

They followed Mr Fitzpatrick upstairs to a room that appeared large enough to seat over one thousand guests. "Dancing parties and other entertainments are held here," he said. Hamish walked to the corner of the stage to take a closer look at a massive electric pipe organ.

"It is the only one of its kind in the colonies," said Mr Fitzpatrick. Hamish imagined the depth of sound, the colour and gaiety of the space filled with a thousand guests dancing and conversing. It would truly be a spectacle. He made up his mind to bring Rita back to enjoy it.

Next, Fitzpatrick led them downstairs and beyond the main building. Acres of grounds were arranged with picnic areas and amusements, including merry-go-rounds and swings. There was even an enclosure with wild cats.

"Tigers," breathed Rita heading for the enclosures.

She peered at the great cats through bars as they paced back and forth within the confines of their enclosure. Hamish felt the sharpness of his own shame as he watched. Every muscle in the animal's bodies was tensed. They were wound tight ready to spring. Their eyes were agitated and self-aware. They understood themselves to be constrained. Hamish turned away unable to witness the humiliation, then Mr Fitzpatrick, his voice loud and confident, and completely ignorant of Hamish's discomfort, announced they would soon complete similar enclosures for other large cats, monkeys and reptiles.

They continued across a playing field with several summerhouses dotted around the edges. A couple of them held families enjoying a picnic. At last, they reached the edge of the vast property.

"This is the area where Perez is supposed to be working," Fitzpatrick said.

Shovels and fencing wire lay abandoned on the ground.

"Where are the men?" asked Rita looking around.

Mr Fitzpatrick checked his watch. "Ah," he said, "It's lunchtime. The men will be at the Queensport Hotel. It's down the road, not far. Why don't you have lunch in our dining room, back in the main building. They won't be long."

Bellamy looked about at the tools abandoned on the grass and at the half-complete structures at the other end of the field. There wasn't a workman in sight.

"No," he said. "Thank-you, but I think we'll go to the Queensport Hotel and meet Mr Perez there."

The aquarium manager looked bewildered, but he pointed along a road that ran horizontal to the river.

"As you wish," he said. "You can't miss it. It is before the Queensport Meatworks."

They made their way back to the entrance and Hamish looked down the road in the direction the manager had indicated. He could see the hotel from where they stood. It was a two-storey building with a wide veranda on two sides at the second level. He, Bellamy and Rita strolled the short distance to the hotel enjoying the warmth of the sun on their backs.

When they entered a group of men each with a meat pie and tall glass of beer before him on the bench, looked up.

"It's no doubt unusual for strangers to appear at this hotel during weekdays," said Hamish quietly.

He scanned the faces of the men. "I think that's him," he said quietly.

"Long dark hair, olive skin," said Bellamy. The man was speaking loudly to the men accompanying him in a distinctly Spanish accent.

They made their way over to the table while the five men crammed around it continued to glare at them. Only the foreigner concentrated on his meal in a show of indifference.

"Carlos Perez?" Sergeant Bellamy's voice cut through the low murmur of the bar as they neared the table.

The man lifted his gaze slowly, his dark eyes locking onto Bellamy with a piercing calm. Hamish noticed that Perez, while fixated on the sergeant, subtly assessed his surroundings from the corner of his eye, as though mapping every possible escape route.

"We only wish to talk to you, Mr. Perez," Bellamy said, his tone steady but firm. "We believe you are acquainted with a young woman named Lillian Murphy."

The tension in Perez's posture melted slightly, a flicker of relief in his eyes. Hamish sensed the man had braced himself for an entirely different line of questioning—likely about his ties to the anarchists.

Perez's mouth curved into a charismatic smile, one that seemed honed to win hearts and deflect suspicion.

"Ah, yes, Miss Murphy," he replied smoothly, glancing around the table with a wink that drew a few chuckles from his companions.

"Are you aware that Miss Murphy's body was found on the mudflats on Hamilton Reach this past Saturday morning?" Bellamy continued, an edge to his voice.

Perez blinked and the humour vanished from his face. Hamish scrutinized the man's reaction, noting the subtle shift in his expression. There was no hint of foreknowledge, but then, Hamish reasoned, a man like Perez, an activist, constantly dodging the law, would be a skilled liar.

"No," Perez said at last, his voice low and measured. "I was not."

"We believe she was on her way to the Oddfellow's Hall on Friday night, intending to meet with you," Bellamy pressed.

Perez's posture stiffened. He ran a hand over his glass, tracing patterns with his fingers as he spoke.

"I did attend a meeting that night," he conceded, his voice taking on a defensive edge. "But Miss Murphy was not there. Her sister, Delia, however...she was. Perhaps you should speak with her."

"We already have," Bellamy replied, scanning the room as though seeking a more private space. "Is there somewhere quieter where we could speak with you, Mr. Perez?"

Perez's eyes darkened, a silent battle waging within them. After a pause, he rose and called out to the barman, "Could I trouble you for use of the dining room to chat with these... fine people?"

The barman cast a wary glance at Bellamy, Hamish, and Rita, then nodded, retrieving a key and leading them through a set of French doors into a more formal dining room, the table laid with a pristine cloth and silver cutlery.

Once seated, Bellamy wasted no time. "Were you in a relationship with Miss Murphy?" he asked bluntly.

Perez stroked his chin, his fingers grazing the light stubble along his jawline. Hamish couldn't deny the man had a certain rugged appeal, a quality that hinted at charm and danger in equal measure.

"Which one?" he asked, arching a brow with a hint of mischief.

"The deceased one," Bellamy said, his patience wearing thin.

Perez shrugged nonchalantly. "I wouldn't say that."

"Would Miss Murphy have said that?" Bellamy shot back.

Perez hesitated, his bravado faltering. "She might," he admitted, finally.

Bellamy reached into his coat and withdrew a small badge, holding it out just far enough for Perez to see. The effect was instantaneous. Perez's eyes widened, a fleeting flash of alarm crossing his face. His body tensed as though he might leap from his chair, grab the badge, and bolt. But, under the watchful eyes of Bellamy, Hamish, and Rita, he seemed to reconsider, sinking back into his seat.

"Where did you get that?" he asked, his voice hoarse.

Bellamy leaned forward. "Have you seen it before?"

Perez's jaw clenched, the muscles working beneath his tanned skin. Hamish could tell there was no hiding the truth now; the badge held an undeniable pull over him, something almost visceral.

"Yes," Perez said quietly, the words barely a whisper.

Bellamy's expression turned almost cheerful, a glint of triumph in his eyes. "Wonderful. Then we'll know who to return it to after the investigation." He slipped the badge back into his coat pocket with a flourish.

Perez's face darkened, his fists clenching as he stared at Bellamy with barely concealed resentment. "Where did you find it?"

"In Miss Delia Murphy's bedside drawer," Bellamy replied smoothly. "Care to explain how it ended up there?"

Perez dropped his gaze, his face clouded with frustration. "So, that's where it went. I had no idea anyone had taken it."

He lifted his head, meeting Bellamy's gaze with a look that suggested there was more he wanted to say but didn't dare.

Bellamy, sensing his reluctance, shifted his line of questioning. "Do you own a cab?"

Perez's lips twisted into a sneer. "No, I don't have a buggy. I'm not Lord bloody Muck!"

Bellamy held his gaze, waiting. Perez let out a sigh, his annoyance barely concealed.

"I walk," he said, his tone heavy with disdain. "I stay two miles back, on a farm. They let me board in exchange for helping with the land, but it's been slow out there. I took on this job for extra cash. I walk into town when I need to. Plenty of folks around here have seen me."

Bellamy breathed slowly and sighed.

Hamish was waiting for the sergeant to say, 'Now that wasn't so hard, was it?' But he didn't need to say it aloud.

"Did you walk home after the meeting at the Oddfellows Hall on Friday night?"

"Yes."

There it was. He was placed at the likely scene of Lillian's abduction, albeit without evidence of the cab.

"And you didn't see Miss Murphy?"

"Not Lillian Murphy, no. Her sister Delia was at the meeting as I said."

Why had neither Perez nor Delia run into Lillian? She was seen passing the corner at around the time they were leaving the club. It didn't make sense, unless someone was lying. Or some unknown party abducted her during the few moments between when she was seen and when they were on the street.

Hamish was keen to know more about the Spaniard.

"When did you come to Moreton Bay, Mr Perez?" he asked.

"Six weeks back. I travelled from my homeland to Sydney town, then caught a steamer up the coast to Brisbane. I thought it more likely I could find work in the north."

"Why did you leave your homeland?"

Carlos Perez stared long and hard at him. "Adventure," he said at last with a crooked grin.

Bellamy's head tilted back, as he looked up at the ceiling. Hamish knew he was impatient, anxious to get to the point. On the other hand, Hamish was interested in placing context around their suspect. He couldn't help wondering: Who is this man and why would he want to abduct and kill a local woman barely known to him?

"I think you need to describe your relationship with Miss Lillian Murphy in full," said Bellamy in a measured tone. "From beginning to end."

As Carlos Perez began, Hamish and Rita exchanged glances and settled in, ready to soak up every word and nuanced change in facial expression.

"I started holding these sessions at the Oddfellows Hall for workers," he said. "I had a lot of men in service coming along. While other trades have secured eight-hour days and paid leave, the service industry has lagged behind. Those in service are beginning at last to understand their value to their fat and spoiled employers."

Hamish shuffled uncomfortably in his chair.

"Anyway, Delia Murphy appeared at one meeting. I think she was brought along by one of the men. She seemed interested, but I suspect she only came as an excuse to be with her man."

"Who is this man?" asked Hamish.

"He works for the Langford's, same as Delia, I think he's in charge of the stables, horses, something like that."

"Then after a couple of weeks, Lillian began turning up. She was passionate." The Spaniard laughed. "Ironically, she doesn't work in service. Unless you count waiting hand and foot on the mother for nothing," he added.

"Go on," urged Bellamy.

"She's an attractive girl, one thing led to another," he continued.

"What led to what, exactly?"

Perez looked offended. "A couple of drinks after the meetings," he said. "With both of them...sometimes."

"And sometimes Miss Lillian Murphy alone?"

"I might have sweet-talked her a bit," he admitted. "It was all in fun."

"Did Lillian take you seriously?" asked Hamish.

"She might have done," he held the doctor's stare.

Rita huffed and turned her head away.

"What of it?" Perez demanded. "She was willing, I can tell you."

Rita's lips were pursed, and Hamish knew the Spaniard was in trouble if they continued in this vein.

"Do you know the Countess Isabella de la Vega?" asked Bellamy quietly.

Hamish and Rita caught their breath as they examined the man's face.

He paled slightly, but there was no other sign of discomfort.

"I know of her," he said. "Anyone from my country would know of her." His eyes flicked from one to the other of his interrogators daring them to call him out.

Hamish was terrified the sergeant was going to inform him of the countess's presence in Brisbane. It seemed unlikely he didn't already know, but Hamish didn't want them to be the ones to break it to him.

"Are you a member of the Spanish Anarchists?" Bellamy asked the question for which they had all been waiting.

Perez's eyes narrowed. "I have certain affiliations," he said.

"Is it the trouble in Madrid that led to your fleeing Europe?"

"No!" he cried. "I had nothing to do with what happened at the Palace." His face was fierce.

Bellamy loosened the tension in his voice. He would let the fellow stew on the fact that they knew about the bombing.

"And you have no explanation as to why Delia Murphy had your badge in her possession?" he said.

"None."

"Don't leave town, Mr Perez," went on Bellamy. "We may need to speak to you again."

Hamish and Rita took the cue to stand, and they followed Bellamy from the room. But not without Hamish taking note of the Spaniard's thunderous look as he watched them leave.

They had already informed Mr Fitzpatrick they would leave directly after speaking with the Spaniard, so they used the steady walk back to the ferry to turn over thoughts about the interview in their own minds. They each nursed their own considerations as the sun beat down on them stinging their shoulders.

Hamish wondered about the Spaniard with his dark eyes and his crooked grin. Did he appear guilty? Perez was flippant, but not funny. There was a cynicism to him. Hamish didn't like him. But was he guilty of killing Lillian? For all the indicators that he might have done so, Hamish couldn't see it. He didn't appear to take the girl seriously at all.

Hamish decided to let the interview sit for a while, often his perceptions became clearer after he stopped focusing on them. Instead, he looked around at the expanse of gravel that stretched from the road to the river. Where there must have been scruffy gums tipping their foliage over the water, the space was now open and bare. The sun beat down on the gravel burning the stones and scorching the sandy soil. The bush was retreating backward away from the shore, to make way for human development, but the river glimmered along in the sun oblivious to the progress of estates and tourist attractions.

As they approached the wharf, they each remarked on how quiet it was. The tourists were still lunching at the Aquarium's buffet, and the workers were still at the Queensport Hotel fortifying themselves for an afternoon of labour. Still, there wasn't long to wait for the steamer. It wasn't the Natone this time, but one of the smaller steamers that frequented the journey from the city centre to the Aquarium and back during quieter times.

Once settled on the boat, grateful for the light breeze that swept up the river, they were finally ready to share their thoughts.

Bellamy was the first to break the silence, his voice a low murmur. "What do you make of him, really?"

Rita's gaze was unwavering, her expression cool. "I think he's a scoundrel. But he's a clever one."

Hamish brushed his fringe away, but the breeze thwarted his efforts, blowing it back over his eyes. "He is, indeed. But did he kill Lillian? What would his motive be?"

Bellamy frowned, pondering. "Maybe Lillian cared for him more deeply than he did for her. Perhaps that imbalance was dangerous."

Hamish scoffed softly. "Seems like that's his pattern, charming young women, then moving on."

Rita nodded. Her eyes narrowed as if she was peering through Perez's facade. "But what still puzzles me is why Delia, not Lillian, had that badge. It makes no sense."

Hamish's brow furrowed. "You don't think he was stringing Delia along, too?"

Bellamy shook his head. "No. If he were, he wouldn't have hesitated to admit it. My guess? Delia wasn't there for Perez. She was probably attending those meetings for someone else, maybe the stableman from the Langford's. What was his name?"

"George Prentice," Rita replied, her voice tinged with suspicion.

Bellamy's expression hardened. "We need to speak with him. And quickly."

Rita glanced at Bellamy. "And what about Perez? Now that he knows we're onto him, do you think he'll stay put? The warning about not leaving the area might not mean much to him."

A sly smile crept onto Bellamy's face. "Once we're back at the station, I'll have Pennyweather tail him. He can follow Perez home and keep an eye on him for a few days. See if he tries to slip away."

Hamish chuckled dryly. "You'd better hope you can pry Pennyweather away from his latest obsession with that electric pen. You know how he gets when he's fixated on something."

Bellamy's grin widened. "Oh, he'll be up for it. Nothing stirs Pennyweather quite like a good chase."

CHAPTER TEN

"Oh, yes! Low to my heart love sang, his old sweet song. There are few women who have not at one time, or another listened to love's pleading."

"And yet you are sceptical as to the reality of the tender passion."

"It is simply an exquisite fairy tale in which we believe while young and silly. Experience dispels the illusion." **Gippsland Mercury Saturday 23 November 1889.**

***

Isabella de la Vega

Isabella hurried through the gardens until she was standing with her back to the elaborate fountain where they'd agreed to meet. She concentrated on slowing her breath while she scanned her surroundings. The garden was cloaked in moonlight casting long shadows through the trees and over the cobbles. Her arms picked up fragments of light as she folded them across her body to keep from trembling. A gentle breeze rustled through the leaves in a soothing whisper, and she drew in a single long breath of orange jasmine. How long had it taken her to reach the fountain? The clock in the great hall had sounded the quarter hour as she slipped into the garden. It could only have taken her five minutes.

She was early, then. How she hated waiting. She shifted her weight from one foot to the other. Her life had been reduced to long meaningless stretches of time punctuated by excruciating episodes of waiting. This was no way to live. She must make him see they need to find another way. The indignity of hiding in the shadows must stop. She had money and power; she could assign him a permanent role within her service. A protector, guard. That would work. They could never marry - of course they couldn't. But what did that matter? As long as he was hers.

This was their second arranged liaison since her arrival in Brisbane, the last had been replayed over and over in her mind until the sweetness had begun to fade. She needed more from him.

Suddenly, the silence was shattered by a sharp crack, like the sound of a stick snapping underfoot. She froze, her heart beating in her chest. The night seemed to hold its breath.

Peering into the moonlight she made out the shape of a man approaching from the direction of Albert Street. A moment of fear was replaced by a wave of joy. She recognized the way the man carried himself, the way he walked. When he was close enough to touch, she threw herself into his arms, pressed her face against his jaw and closed her eyes while she breathed in the smell of his hair.

"How I've missed you," she whispered.

He stiffened slightly.

A rush of electricity shot through her body, a warning. She clung tighter.

"I cannot see you again, my love," he said. His voice brushed against her cheek, and she held her breath while she listened.

"The police interviewed me today. They know about my connections in Madrid, and they know I am here."

"What did they want?" she whispered.

"A policeman and two doctors were asking about the death of a servant..."

Isabella was cold. What did he mean he couldn't see her again?

Surely, he meant he couldn't see her again in Brisbane. Or did he mean more than that?

"Don't worry about the doctors," she reassured him. They're harmless. They are acquaintances of mine. I will redirect them."

His muscles relaxed a little against her skin.

This was her opportunity to introduce more permanency into their relationship. She could take care of him. She pulled away from his embrace so she could see his eyes.

"Come back to Spain with me," she said. "I can arrange a new identity for you and a place on board the ship. You won't have to worry about the police, you can return home, we can be together…" She heard the words gushing from her mouth, and the pleading tone. It was all wrong, the words were coming in a rush. But there was so little time, and she needed him to understand.

"Sail with me the day after tomorrow," she said. She tried to sound confident, but when she heard the words, they were thin and reedy.

She looked up beneath her eyelashes to see a cloud descend across Perez's face.

At the same time, cold fingers gripped her heart. She knew instantly she had overplayed her hand. She had lost him.

"I cannot return to Spain for some time," he said. "And I will not be creeping back to my own country like a rat."

His voice was deep and full of hate.

How had this happened? How had she turned his passion so completely and so darkly from love to hate in a single moment?

She desperately searched his black eyes for the affection that had once been there. There was nothing.

Perez took a step back and firmly pushed her away. The distance between them stretched and gaped until it was a chasm.

Carlos Perez stared at her for a moment, his eyes empty.

"Have a safe journey home, Countess," he said. He bowed formally before turning to disappear into the shadows.

A tear slipped down Isabella's face. Moments earlier she had anticipated the warmth of his skin against her own, the sweet taste of his lips, her voice whispering the words of longing that had been choking her since their last meeting. His voice in her ear confirming that his longing for her was as painful as her own.

The reality had been so far removed from her expectation she was breathless. It was as though the wind had been physically knocked out of her lungs. She bent over and held her arms across her chest to ease the pain. She cowered in the dak for several minutes before she regained the strength to return to the Governor's mansion.

It couldn't be true. He was over-reacting because the police were talking to him. In the morning, he would be consumed by regret, and he would get a message to her. He would reassure her of his undying love. The affair couldn't be over. It was impossible to extinguish a union such as theirs. Her thoughts carried her back to the Governor's Mansion and continued in this vein until the first fingers of dawn reached through the bay window to touch her brow. Then, she finally fell into a fitful sleep.

CHAPTER ELEVEN

The annual meeting of the Girls' Friendly Society was held yesterday when the bishop presided over a large attendance of the membership. The bishop pointed out the complete changes in the affairs of women during the last twenty years.

Women could not all stop at home and do housework now, because there were too many of them, and hence it was they had sought work abroad, and now, in some cases, were more useful than men.

He did not think that domestic service was healthy service for women. Servants, in many cases, were treated as a mere machine – to be used until broken. Many of them were put into rooms not fit for a dog to sleep in, and he did not believe this was calculated to promote health or cleanliness. It ought to be the object of society to look after the health and comfort of these girls.

Nowadays, the population was always shifting from place to place, and unless the Girls' Friendly Society looked after the girls wherever they went, they would become lost to the church.

In the matter of amusement, he thought there was no need to provide that - the girls could always find an opportunity to amuse themselves. What they were suffering from was loneliness, and he hoped the members of the society would do all in their power to bring them together and prevent this. **The Age 21 November 1889**

***

Clouds had begun to gather on the horizon when Hamish walked down the hill from his home on Wickham Terrace into the town and to the police depot. The heat of the previous days had been building to coalesce in a heavy grey sky moving sluggishly in from the sea. Rather than ease the pressure of warmth, the weight of the sky sat like a blanket over the town keeping the heat in. Until it rained there would be no respite.

Hamish met Bellamy coming from the opposite direction.

"The weather looks like it might turn," he said by way of greeting.

"Perhaps a sign," said Bellamy. "We may well have Lillian's killer in our sights."

"Perez, do you mean?"

"Who else?"

The sergeant entered the building ahead of the doctor.

Hamish still wasn't convinced. The more he thought about it the less sense it made. Why would a man on the run draw attention to himself in such a catastrophic way?

The thought hung in the air, though he had not said it out loud. There was no need, Bellamy was aware of his scepticism.

"It will be interesting to hear from Pennyweather," said Bellamy. "I can't wait to know what the Spaniard was up to after we rattled him yesterday."

Pennyweather arrived at the office to find Hamish and Bellamy waiting.

"You look like you've had a rough night," said Hamish. Dark circles had formed under the constable's eyes, and his face was unshaven. Hamish handed him a cup of coffee he'd made for himself, but it was barely warm. Pennyweather clutched it and sipped more for comfort than stimulation.

"I didn't have much sleep."

"Get him a fresh cup of hot tea," said Bellamy. "He needs tea not that American rubbish."

Hamish didn't mind being directed to fetch tea for the junior officer. Pennyweather had been unshakable in his support for both the sergeant and him, during several cases that had landed them in dicey situations.

When Pennyweather was somewhat revived, he began his account of the evening.

"I followed Perez home from the aquarium as you directed," he began. "He does reside in a house at Eagle Farm. He didn't leave the farmhouse until about Nine-thirty at which time he walked into Hamilton, to the Hamilton Hotel. From there, he stepped into an omnibus. Fortunately, I had time to jump on the same transport before it left the hotel.

We travelled along the river until we reached the terminal at Breakfast Creek, where he changed to a tram heading into town. There were several passengers who made the same exchange, so I joined them without being noticed by Perez. We travelled across the bridge and through Fortitude Valley then down Albert Street toward Alice.

Most of the passengers had left the tram by the time we reached the gardens, so when Perez stepped off on the corner of Albert and Alice, I remained on board until the tram reached the end of the line further along Alice Street.

I knew he had entered the gardens, so I came down from the top entrance. I was soon able to catch sight of him again as he approached the main promenade. He stopped at the fountain, where a woman was waiting for him."

Hamish and Bellamy sat forward in their seats.

"What woman?"

"The Countess Isabella de la Vega, sir," said Pennyweather.

Bellamy and Hamish exchanged glances. Hamish put both hands to his head and held his fringe off his face.

"Oh dear," he breathed. "Alejandro is not going to be happy about this. He asked me to keep her from finding Perez."

"It looks as though she's a step ahead of her cousin," said Bellamy. "She was clearly in contact with him all along."

"Could you hear what they said?" asked Hamish.

Pennyweather put down his cup and shook his head.

"I was too far away to hear anything. But I could see Perez become irritated by something the countess said. He removed himself from her embrace and his demeanour become somewhat chilled. He bowed and left her soon after. The countess appeared to be distressed by his departure. She was hunched over as if unwell for some time. I had to leave to follow Perez, so I didn't see what happened to her after that.

He walked briskly all the way back to Eagle Farm. I had to hurry to keep up with him. He's fit, I can tell you that. Anyway, he didn't get home until after one in the morning. Constable Bennet was waiting there to relieve me, and I had still to get home myself."

"Get some sleep," said Bellamy. "You'll need to take over from Bennet later."

Pennyweather trudged out looking miserable. It was obvious he didn't relish another evening following Perez.

"Jan could step in for an evening," suggested Hamish. "He's not got anything on at the moment."

Bellamy stared at him. "Jan is a lab assistant," he said as if he were describing something equivalent to a rodent.

"Nonetheless, he could follow a man, as easily as anyone," snapped Hamish.

Bellamy didn't bother responding. Instead, he leant back in his chair.

"Perez remains our best suspect," he said.

"Hmm," said Hamish. "I think we rattled him yesterday."

"What do you think went on with the countess last night?"

Hamish shook his head. "It must have been important whatever it was. He travelled for hours to meet her, and they spent only a few minutes together."

"Perhaps he told her their romance was over."

"That would explain why she was upset."

"But why go so far out of his way to tell her in person? Surely, he could simply not see her again. In a couple of days, she'll be sailing back home."

Bellamy tapped his pencil on the desk. "I'll wager he killed that girl," he said. "But why?"

"Perhaps she was threatening to tell the authorities about his connection to the anarchists."

Bellamy shook his head.

"I doubt the girl would have any idea what the symbol meant. She probably took it as a souvenir of her relationship with him, regardless of whether the relationship was real or in her imagination. And Lillian wasn't the one in possession of the badge, Delia was. Why kill Lillian and not Delia?"

"He certainly seems to have a habit of leading women on," said Hamish.

Bellamy agreed.

"I have arranged with the Langford's to interview George Prentice this morning, are you joining me?"

Bellamy took his hat from the hat stand and strode past the counter, while Hamish rushed to follow him. They took the police cab to Bowen Terrace rather than walk there in the humidity.

When Hamish and Bellamy arrived at the Bowen Terrace Mansion there was no need to enter the house, they made their way around the back to the stables and coach house where George Prentice lived in a two-bedroom lodging above the stable.

Prentice was outside the outbuilding, wearing a broad brimmed hat that shaded his eyes. His shirt, once white, was now a dusty beige, sleeves rolled up to his elbows, revealing tanned muscular forearms. His hands moved with practiced ease as he brushed down a sturdy chestnut horse. Occasionally, the horse flicked its tail lazily to swat a fly.

Hamish wrinkled his top lip as he breathed in the smell of leather and horse-manure. When Prentice caught sight of them out of the corner of his eye, he gave the horse a gentle pat on the neck and stood.

"Sergeant Bellamy and Dr Hamish Hart," Bellamy introduced them while holding out his hand in greeting. Prentice wiped his dusty hands on his trousers and shook Bellamy's hand with a strong grip. Hamish chose not to extend his hand, wary of the lingering dust and horsehair, but smiled and nodded instead.

"We're investigating the murder of Lillian Murphy," the sergeant explained.

Prentice clenched his large fists at his side.

"Terrible, terrible thing."

"How well did you know the young lady?"

Prentice took a breath. "Not well. I saw her only at the meetings in Alice Street."

"We've been informed you were stepping out with Miss Murphy's sister," said the sergeant. "Is that true?"

Prentice puffed out his chest.

"Yes, it is. In fact, I was ready to make a proposal of marriage...until this happened. Now it seems untimely. I'll wait until Delia and her mother have had time to recover from this terrible shock."

"Was Delia aware of your intentions?" asked Hamish.

Prentice reddened.

"Yes, I think so. We had hinted at the subject."

"What about Lillian," Bellamy cut in, "Did she show affection for a young man of her own?"

Prentice pushed his sleeves up and clenched his fists tight again. Hamish could see the whites of his knuckles.

"She was taken with the Spanish fellow running the worker's rights meetings." He shook his head. "I thought he was alright at first, talking about the value of the working man, how those of us in service should expect the same respect as other workers and share the same benefits. But when he saw Lillian's eyes shine as he spoke, he took advantage of her. I tried to speak to Delia about it, but she said Lillian knew her own mind and to let it be."

"How far did the dalliance go?" asked Hamish.

Prentice glared at him from under unruly eyebrows.

"I mean, was it relatively innocent...?"

The big man spoke through clenched teeth, his jaw tight. He said, "I haven't told Delia, but I saw Perez with Lillian behind the hall about a week ago. The cad had her pressed against a wall in the shadows. It was dark but I saw enough. My first instinct was to rush in and belt him senseless, but as I stepped closer, I could see that Lillian was very much engaged in the entanglement. She didn't look like she wanted rescuing. I didn't know what to do. The lady's honour had already been compromised - if you understand my meaning. I thought it best to walk away."

His muscles relaxed a little.

Hamish grimaced. He glanced at Bellamy who was steady, determined. It seemed to Hamish, for a moment, that the sergeant must be right. Perez probably did kill the girl. If she was putting pressure on him, perhaps she had regrets and was threatening to make claims of assault, as well as making public his affiliation with the anarchists. That might be sufficient motive for murder.

But there was still a niggling doubt. He seemed more the type of man to brazen out such claims, or to simply disappear again, than to commit rape and murder.

Prentice went on with his story, and Hamish forced himself from his thoughts to listen.

"I made up my mind to confront him the next day, make him understand it was better for his health if he stayed away from Lillian. But no one could tell me where to find him. No one seemed to know anything about him. I resolved to wait until the next meeting. That was the night of the murder. I didn't go inside. Instead, I waited for him. But he didn't come out the front door as he always had. The meeting ended and everyone filed out. Then, I saw Delia leave. I was worried about her getting home without me. I had always accompanied her, you see. I told Delia I had missed the meeting to tend to the horses, but I asked her if Perez had already left, and she told me he wasn't in the hall when she was tidying up. He must have left through the back door."

Hamish's brows knitted. "Why go out the back door that night, if he had never done so before?"

"Do you think he knew you were waiting for him?" asked Bellamy.

"I don't see how. I didn't tell anyone of my intentions. Delia was surprised to see me as I had told her the master was returning late that evening and I had to settle the horses. When I turned up unexpectedly, I told her I'd finished just in time to come along and walk her home."

"And you didn't see Lillian at all that evening?" asked Hamish.

The man shook his large head.

"She could have been waiting for Perez at the back door," suggested Bellamy.

Hamish saw a flame rise in Prentice's eyes. "I can't believe that while I waited at the front for him, he was sneaking out the back to..."

"Don't punish yourself with the thought," said Hamish. "We don't know she was out there."

Hamish and Bellamy exchanged glances.

Bellamy was thanking the horseman for his time when Hamish interrupted him.

"Why did Lillian go to the meetings in the first place?" he asked. "I mean before she became enamoured with Perez."

Both Bellamy and Prentice stared at him unsure what he was getting at.

"Lillian wasn't in service, in fact her life revolved around the care of her mother. How did she become interested in the labour movement?"

Bellamy seemed to grasp the sense in the question and turned to Prentice for an answer.

"It had to do with her mother," he said. "I don't know the details, but Mrs Murphy came from Ireland as a single female immigrant when she was only eighteen. She had a rough time of it before she met and married the girls' father. She worked in service at one of the big houses. Delia told me Lillian wanted to learn more about their mother's life back then."

Hamish nodded and thanked Prentice for the information. As they were climbing into the buggy, he suggested to Bellamy they should talk to Mrs Murphy again.

Bellamy twisted his mouth to one side.

"Hmm. I'm not convinced Mrs Murphy's past has anything to do with our investigation, but I suppose we could bring it up."

"We're no closer to knowing who stole the painting or who killed Lillian," said Hamish.

Bellamy stared out the window.

"It's Perez who did for her, alright."

Hamish leant forward to get the sergeant's attention.

"What about the tracks from the road onto the mud flats?"

"I asked Pennyweather to interview all the cab drivers working that evening. None of them admit to carrying passengers in that direction. One picked up a couple from the Hamilton Hotel, but they travelled toward Breakfast Creek, the opposite direction from the Reach. Most people leaving the Hotel do so aboard the omnibuses that run to the Breakfast Creek transit exchange."

"Pennyweather is nothing if not thorough. I presume he checked with the couple who travelled by cab?"

"He did," said Bellamy. "I still think Perez is our main suspect, but he couldn't have done it alone. Firstly, it's clear he has no transport of his own as Pennyweather watched him walk all the way from the gardens last night. He must have had assistance from someone with a horse and buggy on the night of the murder."

"Should we stop in and visit Mrs Murphy on the way?" asked Hamish.

Bellamy raised his eyebrows. Hamish knew his sergeant thought it was a waste of time, but he was determined to pursue every lead.

They arrived at the cottage in good time, hoping Mrs Murphy and her daughter would be in. Hamish was concerned that he still didn't have a true grasp of the murdered girl. He needed to know more about her, to understand her. He felt that until he did, he would not be sufficiently confidant of a conviction in her murder.

Mrs Murphy answered the door in a dishevelled state.

"Have you some news?" she asked without any greeting.

Hamish pushed aside his own disappointment that they did not

as Bellamy assured Mrs Murphy they were pursuing the investigation as quickly as possible.

"We hoped to gain some more background information about Lillian," said Hamish. "The more we know about her the more likely we will be to find her killer."

"How so?" asked Mrs Murphy.

Bellamy also looked sceptical and keen to see where Hamish was heading.

Mrs Murphy straightened and patted down her skirt. She seemed to remember she was greeting guests and needed to extend the appropriate courtesies. "Can I offer you anything?" she asked.

Hamish and Bellamy followed into a small, but comfortable drawing room.

"No," Hamish said for them both. He was eager to get on with the interview.

He leant forward and began. "We've been told that Lillian went to the workers' meetings initially in order to understand your own early life in service, Mrs Murphy."

The woman sat down with a thump in the remaining armchair. It seemed obvious to Hamish she hadn't been expecting the question, and she didn't welcome it.

Her brow furrowed. "I suppose she may have," she said, perhaps considering the possibility as she spoke. "She had been very interested in my experiences as a young woman of late. She asked a lot of questions."

"What was she interested in, particularly?" asked Hamish.

Mrs Murphy squinted. "She wanted to know about my coming to this country. And how things were for me once I arrived, I suppose."

"How old were you when you immigrated?"

"I was only eighteen," said Mrs Murphy. "I cringe when I think about it now. I would hate to think of Lillian or Delia in that situation at their ages."

Suddenly the irony of what she had said made her face break down into sorrowful sobs.

"The worst has come for Lillian just the same," she said. Tears streamed down her face.

Hamish handed her his handkerchief. "Would you mind telling us about your past?" he asked.

"I don't see how...."

"Anything might help," Hamish assured her. "There may be some questions that Lillian was asking that upset someone."

"Enough to kill her?"

Hamish nodded.

Mrs Murphy took a deep breath. "My mother died when I was six," she began. "My father was an alcoholic and while you might think that afforded me a certain amount of freedom while he was drunk, it did not. He was very strict. He had eyes and ears everywhere in the village and if I stepped out to chat with a female friend, he would hear about it and beat me when I returned home. I was suffocating in that house."

Her tears dried up and her eyes darkened with anger. "As soon as I turned eighteen, I joined the protected migration program."

She threw her head back. "I'd read about it in the newspapers. Well off women in Britain were working in partnership with the government to provide protected assistance to young single women to travel to the colonies. It's still going on now. It's more organized today though, through the Girl's Friendly Societies. But back then, it was new and quite poorly run."

She wrung her hands. "I didn't tell my father, I just signed up and left. I had a little bit of money my mother had left me which I came into on my eighteenth birthday. Not enough to pay for passage to Australia, mind. But the government was subsidizing the scheme because there weren't sufficient women in Australia to fill the vacancies in domestic service."

Mrs Murphy looked Hamish in the eye. "One of the women told me the colonial government was ordering batches of women from Britain just as they would order Manchester cottons."

Hamish felt the flush of shame he always experienced when he heard of injustices even when they had nothing directly to do with him.

"Anyway, the journey over on the ship was no less uncomfortable than I expected it to be, and there were enough of us girls to keep each other going, but when we reached the shores here in Australia the real shock came. I arrived at the government depot in Brisbane in 1862. We were herded like cattle to what was essentially a barn with a dirt floor and no windows. It contained two tables and thirty-two iron beds for one hundred and thirty-two girls. There were no mattresses or bedding on the beds and most of the women had to sleep on the bare ground without blankets or pillows. Apparently, we were supposed to bring our bedding with us from the government ship, but no one told us that."

"Good Lord," breathed Hamish. "Was there no place like Lady Musgrave's Hostel in those days?"

Mrs Murphy's face twisted into a grimace. "Girls like us couldn't afford a place like the hostel," she said. "But no, nothing like that existed back then anyhow. There was no choice but the government depot. That was part of the subsidized agreement. We had to stay at the depot until we found work."

Both Hamish and Bellamy waited silently for her to continue.

"There were no washing facilities, no stove, and we received the scantest rations, a bit of beef, stale bread and tea and sugar. We were desperate for fresh fruit and vegetables after months at sea, but there was none of that."

"How long did you have to stay in these conditions?" asked Hamish.

Hamish heard a quiet sigh as Mrs Murphy jerked back her head. "I stayed longer than most," she said. "I was offered a position by one of the women organizers of the program. But the household was miles from anywhere in the bush and I was afraid to end up somewhere like that, isolated and unable to get away. I wanted to work in town. I thought if domestic staff were as short as they said, I could get something closer, where I'd feel more secure. But when I refused the woman's offer - I was marked. The organizers closed ranks and wouldn't recommend me for work."

"The girls' were expected to take on whatever was offered, then?" Hamish said. "Even if the position didn't suit them?"

Mrs Murphy smiled at his innocence. "There were plenty of girls worse off than me," she said. "Girls who had registered in the program to join relatives in Melbourne, were sent to Brisbane, friendless and alone. They lied to the girls to coerce them into coming out here. Once here, young working-class women had little choice but to accept whatever work and conditions they could get."

A shiver crept up Hamish's spine as he remembered the Pacific Island labourers brought to Australia to work the sugar plantations. The story told by Mrs Murphy sounded hauntingly similar in some ways.

"The women who were supposed to be 'protecting' us, were just ensuring they had the first pick of the strongest girls to work in the households of themselves and their friends. They reminded me too much of the middle-class women at home. All full of 'good intentions' but really just feathering their own nests."

"But you finally found work?" asked Hamish.

"I did. As a house maid. I was glad of it. I earned eighteen pound a year, though I worked long hours for it. There was no end to the demands on my time. I don't think I had one afternoon off in all the time I was there."

"And you shared this story with Lillian."

"Yes. With both the girls. But Lillian was put out by the way I was treated. She started talking to Delia about her work. The Langford's treat Delia well but Lillian believed domestic service should be unionized. I told her not to put ideas in Delia's head. She had a good position in a respectable household and that's not easy to come by."

Mrs Murphy seemed exhausted by her memories of the past.

"We'll leave you to rest," said Bellamy. "I think that's all for now. I don't believe there is anything there that connects to the death of your daughter. We're sorry to have troubled you."

Hamish and Bellamy were silent as they left the women with her troubled memories. When they were in the buggy, Bellamy said, "You don't think there is anything there that can assist us in the investigation, do you?"

"Only that Mrs Langford is an active member of the Girls Friendly Society," said Hamish.

Bellamy's eyebrows shot up.

"The women who help the girls gain employment?"

Hamish nodded.

CHAPTER TWELVE

Only those who paid a visit to the aquarium yesterday can have any idea of the picture which this popular resort presented. And only those who went down can have any idea of the difficulties which had to be overcome when once on Campbell's Wharf, before being able to get on a steamer. Truly an hour before the first steamer left in the morning there were persons waiting to go onboard and from then until three o'clock the three steamers belonging to the company – the Alice, Woolwich and Natone – were kept as hard at it as they could go.

A specially arranged timetable for the departure of the steamers had been announced but had to be departed from for the simple reason that within a few minutes of either steamer arriving at Campbell's Wharf it was filled to overflowing and at once steamed away to return without delay for another load. On no previous occasion has any place of amusement formed such a powerful attraction as the aquarium, and it is estimated that about ten thousand persons visited the grounds during the course of the day.

At the aquarium itself, large crowds filled the halls, and the balconies were packed. Round the seal pond in front of the animals, people stood five or six deep. The swings, merry-go-rounds, flying machines and camera obscura were crowded all day, while there were numbers of people rambling around the grounds, in the bush house or watching the cricket match. There was enjoyment for all. Although the sun shone very strongly, the atmosphere at the aquarium was delightful, the odd breeze from the bay mitigating the fierceness of the sun's blaze. **The Telegraph Friday 27 December 1889**

***

The following morning Hamish again struggled out of bed feeling unrested. He and Bellamy were going round in circles interviewing the same people over and again, while still getting no closer to a solution. The only real opportunity for an arrest lay in the hope that the witness might identify their suspect. Perhaps they should bring in Carlos Perez and have the witness look at him. He could tell them whether it was Perez he saw in the cab following Lillian Murphy, or not.

As soon as Hamish set foot on the street the humidity hit him, like a slap in the face from a giant wet hand. A grey sky hung low overhead for the second day, but on this morning, he could smell the rain coming on the edge of the wind. Sweat was already gathering under his collar. It was only spring. He couldn't imagine how hot it would be in summer. A headache formed as he trudged down the hill toward the police depot. Overhead he heard a feint crackling as thunder rattled over the sea. A storm was brewing, and he was glad of it. The town needed something to break this heat.

Bringing the witness in to identify Perez as the man in the cab following Lillian seemed like a logical next step to Hamish. He rehearsed his proposal for the sergeant on his way down the hill. His reasoning was straightforward. Perez was their primary suspect, so they need only stand him before the witness and have him either identify the man, or state that he was not the person they were seeking. If he was not, they could eliminate him from their enquiries. A third option came to mind, perhaps the witness would not be able to say with certainty whether Perez was the man in the cab that night or not. But even that would be worth knowing. They would then be aware that they in fact, had no witness at all.

By the time he reached the depot, Hamish was certain: they needed Perez in front of the witness immediately. He burst toward Bellamy's office, ready to demand as much, when Pennyweather crashed through the depot's front doors, skidding into the sergeant's office and nearly toppling Hamish in his rush.

"For heaven's sake, man, what's the matter?" Bellamy barked.

Hamish steadied himself, wincing at the sharp pain in his groin from his impact with the mahogany desk corner. "That's going to leave a mark," he muttered as Pennyweather sucked in a desperate breath.

"Another body, sir!" Pennyweather gasped, barely able to speak as he struggled for air.

Hamish's pulse quickened. "Where?"

"Queensport Aquarium, sir. Just got word from Fitzpatrick, the manager. He said we're to come immediately."

Hamish's eyes flicked to the wall clock. How long had it taken the message to reach them from Hemmant? Time was slipping away. Who knows how many people had contaminated the scene already? "What's the fastest way there?" he pressed.

"The ferry's 45 minutes," Bellamy replied, "but we'll lose time waiting for it."

Hamish scowled. "By then, any evidence could be trampled beyond recognition."

"Where's the Police boat?" Bellamy demanded.

"Moored in Moreton Bay. Won't be back for at least an hour," Pennyweather responded.

Bellamy muttered under his breath. "The train to Pinkenba could work, but who knows the schedule..."

"Road it is," Hamish declared, already halfway out the door.

Bellamy shouted instructions back into the office. "Send a cart to Queensport Aquarium in Hemmant immediately—and pick up Jan on the way. Dr. Hart may need him."

He rushed after Hamish, calling to the stable boy, "Harness up! We're heading to Hemmant—no time to lose!"

The police driver was only just settling the horse after collecting Bellamy from his home. The animal wasn't eager to be going again so soon, in the heat, and neither was the driver. Both glared at the sergeant for a moment before doing as they were instructed.

Hamish, Bellamy and Pennyweather were soon hurtling along beside the river.

"Why aren't you following Perez this morning?" Bellamy asked the young constable.

"I was, sir. At least I was about to catch up with him at the aquarium. Bennet followed him there then ended his shift. I was about to leave for the aquarium to take over when word arrived from the manager that there had been a death."

"Whose dead?" asked Hamish.

"I don't know, the message didn't say. Apparently, there is a lot of confusion on site."

Hamish spent the rest of the trip imagining the damage the workers would be doing to his evidence.

"I told them not to move the body or touch anything," said Pennyweather as though reading his mind.

Hamish nodded hopefully.

It would take them three-quarters of an hour to reach the aquarium by road, and it would have taken the messenger as long to reach them. That's at the least an hour and a half the body would have been lying in the heat since being discovered.

Hamish shuddered as they rattled on beneath the darkening sky. To his left torn clouds were chasing shadows in the river, to his right, the clouds had blackened, and rain fell over the distant hills. Hamish worried about whether the body was inside the hall or out in the grounds where it would be exposed to the rain when it arrived. They seemed to be in a race against the clouds as they galloped forward through the towering trees that lined the river closer to Hemmant.

Finally, the forest opened, and they saw the arch of the aquarium entrance. They leapt from the cab almost before it had stopped, ran through the deserted hall, while large fish watched them lazily from behind glass. Then Hamish felt his heart sink. The body must be out on the grounds somewhere. They didn't need to ask where to find it, they only needed to follow the shouts of workers who had gathered at the scene. They ran past the merry-go-round, past the picnic shelters, past the yet to be completed animal cages. Then as they approached the outer paddock and saw the gaggle of onlookers, Mr Fitzpatrick rushed forward to greet them.

He pushed the curious workers aside and guided Hamish, Bellamy and Pennyweather to the body. First, they registered fence posts, and a roll of wire unravelled on the ground. Then their eyes travelled beyond the fence posts to a young man. A pool of blood stained the grass a dark crimson beneath his head. A deep gash ran across his skull where an axe had cleaved through flesh and bone. It was obvious the deceased had been working on laying the new fence.

Hamish turned the body so that the head fell loosely toward them. Dark vacant eyes stared upward, as if caught in a moment of shock.

"Perez," breathed Bellamy.

A trail of blood spatter marked the path of the lethal blow. More blood dripped along a path away from the body stopping abruptly at the murder weapon. A bloodied axe that lay still on the ground.

"There's a cart on its way to collect him," said Hamish. "In the meantime, I'll do what I can here. Get these ghouls to move away."

The sergeant was already barking orders at the workers and a handful of visitors to clear the area.

"Get a rope," he called out to Fitzpatrick, "we need to secure the area."

The manager and Bellamy secured the rope to one of the fenceposts and encircled the site with stakes, marking off an area that included the body and the bloodied weapon.

Bellamy told Fitzpatrick to remain outside the secured area and to direct workers and visitors back to the main hall where they were to wait to be questioned.

Hamish knelt beside the body carefully inspecting it. He noted the position, the head wound and several other wounds on his neck and torso.

The sergeant leant over Hamish, still crouched by the body. "He was hit over the head from the back," said the doctor quietly, as much to himself as to Bellamy. "With that axe over there."

"Considerate of the killer to leave us the weapon at the scene," said Bellamy.

Hamish looked up at him and raised one eyebrow.

"How long ago, would you say?"

Hamish felt the warmth of the body. He checked for redness indicating settling of the blood. Then he felt the blood from the wound at the man's neck between his fingers. "Perhaps two hours," he said. "He must have been discovered very soon after it happened."

Bellamy looked around. "With any luck there were enough people about to give us more information," he said.

"Hopefully we have plenty of witnesses," agreed Hamish.

An onlooker stepped forward, a young man who could have been one of the workers.

"Everyone is waiting in the main building to be interviewed. Mr Fitzpatrick told his foreman to keep them there until you two arrived," he said.

"How many workers would there have been out here?" Hamish asked.

"I don't know. Mr Fitzgerald will be able to tell you."

Hamish scanned the crowd that had gathered to watch the spectacle. "What about visitors?"

Bellamy blew air through his lips.

"We'll only know who they are if they signed the visitor's book when they came in," he said.

"If they came to murder a man, they probably didn't sign the book," Hamish pointed out.

Bellamy looked around. "We're on the edge of the property."

Hamish saw long grass and low scrub in every direction. The forest that lined the road opened into farmland skirted by marshes and waterholes inland. Tiny slivers of light in the grass gave away the waterholes. It would be a treacherous place to navigate if you were unfamiliar with the bogs and wells that hid within the grass.

"Perez was employed to install these fences," said the sergeant. "Anyone coming in to murder him would have been more likely to have done so from beyond this area, rather than coming through the main entrance. Until this fence is complete, there's nothing stopping anyone from entering the grounds from this side."

Hamish stood up and wiped his hands on his handkerchief. There was nothing more he could tell from the body in the open. The cause of death was obvious, the man's head had been cleaved by an axe. There were also several other wounds to his shoulders and torso. It had been a vicious attack. There were many more wounds than would have been necessary to kill him.

"We'll only find out more about this murder if people are prepared to talk," said Hamish.

"Stay here and guard the body with your life," Bellamy told Pennyweather.

Hamish added, "When Jan arrives tell him I need a sketch of the site, the position of the body, the axe and any footprints he can see around the site. There are some footprints in the blood there, near the axe, for a start. Stay outside the rope and don't add any of your own footprints, for heaven's sake. And tell him to wrap the axe carefully in cloth and place it in a sack to take back to the morgue with the body."

"I can wrap the axe," said Pennyweather.

"No," Hamish startled him with his sharp response. "No, leave it where it is until Jan arrives. He'll know how to do it without smudging anything."

Bellamy called to Hamish to follow him.

"We need to start the interviews before people have time to forget, or start making up stories, about what they saw."

When Hamish looked up at the sky, a heavy drop of water hit him in the face.

"The rain is coming," he called out. "Use that hessian to cover the body."

He eyed the grey clouds gathering at the tree line about three hundred yards away.

"We'll have to hope the rain holds," he said. A distant rumble confirmed that time was short before the site would be caught in a deluge. He looked out for the cart.

"Which way will they come in?"

"The best way will be to come around the side of the grounds," said Fitzpatrick, striding toward them from the direction of the main building. "I'll tell someone to meet the cart and bring it along the fence-line there." He pointed to their left, beyond the big cat enclosures.

"How many men were working with Perez on the fencing?" asked Bellamy before the manager left them to give the instruction.

"None," said Fitzpatrick. "The perimeter fence was less a priority than the enclosures for the big cats. I'm expecting arrival of a couple of specimens next week and the enclosures must be ready. I had most of the men working on that. Only Perez continued to work on the fence. I was hoping to have that complete before the Christmas holidays. Once the big cats arrive, any of the local louts could come in this way and stir them up. It could be dangerous."

Hamish glanced across at the big cat enclosures in various stages of completion. A pair of large tigers paced back and forth in the one completed cage watching them with undisguised suspicion. The enclosures were about one hundred yards from the perimeter fence where Hamish was standing. Someone might have seen something. It was also possible that if the men were intent on the work, they might not have looked out in the direction of Perez. If his assailant crept up from behind, he wouldn't necessarily have had time to call out.

Fitzpatrick ran ahead to organize someone to watch out for the cart while Pennyweather waited with the body for Jan and the cart to arrive.

Hamish glanced around the kill site praying the rain would hold off, then accompanied Bellamy back to the main building where the workers and a handful of visitors were waiting.

They reached the main hall to a barrage of questions generally summed up by one: "How long do we have to stay here?"

A man with an expensive suit and cane pushed through the visitors and staff who were all trying to talk to the sergeant at once.

"Look, sir," he said, "My wife and I have an important lunch engagement, and we'd like to leave immediately. We saw nothing."

Bellamy politely informed the man that he and his wife would be required to stay, just like everyone else, until they had provided their details and a statement to his constable.

Hamish whispered under his breath, "who is currently outside guarding the body."

Bellamy swung around as though he'd heard him and glared. "Well?" he said.

Hamish let out a deep frustrated sigh and put his hand into his breast pocket to retrieve his notebook and pencil.

"Very well," he said, turning to the man. "Your name and your wife's name?"

"Address?"

He wrote down the details in his notepad.

"And what you have said is your full statement?"

"Yes." The man looked back at his wife standing near the entrance ready to flee as soon as they received the nod.

"You and your wife can leave," said the Hamish. This brought on a chorus of cries from visitors who thought they ought to be allowed to leave as well.

"You'll have to take statements, if we are to move this lot," Bellamy said to Hamish. "We'll deal with the visitors first so they can get away. The staff will have to wait."

Bellamy spoke in his most authoritative voice. "All the visitors to the aquarium come forward, please. Staff can go upstairs and wait. No one is to leave these premises until Dr Hart, or I have spoken to you."

Hamish looked wide-eyed at the sergeant.

"Just take their names and addresses," Bellamy said. "We'll tick them off against the visitor's book later. It won't necessarily contain all their names, but it's a start. Ask if they were anywhere near the perimeter, and if so, did they see anything of note."

Hamish took a deep breath. This kind of routine interviewing did not inspire him in the least. He doubted any of these visitors had gone near the perimeter of the grounds where Perez was installing the fence. There were no amusements there to see. He understood that in the interests of thoroughness, all visitors had to be interviewed. He just didn't think it necessary they be interviewed by him. Still, he wanted Pennyweather outside guarding the body, so it fell to him to swallow his pride and take the visitor's statements.

Hamish and Bellamy gathered names and addresses from people who stated they had seen nothing while a light patter on the roof gathered force and became a din. Hamish had visions of the murder weapon being washed clean of any clue as to who had wielded it. He could only hope the cart had arrived before the full force of the rain.

Half an hour later, the only people remaining in the hall were the staff who had waited upstairs in comfort at Bellamy's instruction. Hamish and Bellamy went upstairs to join them. The rain pounding on the roof was almost deafening on the second floor.

"Those of you who were working in the main building identify yourselves," called out Bellamy. Hands shot up.

"Please come forward."

Names and addresses were taken, and workers were asked if they had seen anyone behaving in an unusual manner. No one had. They were dismissed. Many left huffing that they could have told them that an hour ago and been home by now.

"They're not supposed to finish work for hours," said Hamish. "They're getting home early as it is."

He wondered if Mr Fitzpatrick would be paying them for a full day's work, even though the aquarium had been closed for business in the wake of the murder.

When the workers from the main building left, Hamish and Bellamy looked around at the scattering of employees remaining. These were men who had been labouring in the outer areas, mostly on the big cat enclosures. They were interviewed as a group.

"Were you all aware of Perez working on the fence line this morning?" Bellamy's tone held a hint of impatience.

Most of the men shifted uncomfortably, hesitant.

"We was aware, but not so that we saw him, necessarily. We just knew he was there because that's where he always was," one of the men mumbled, barely meeting Bellamy's eyes.

They all nodded in weak agreement.

"Was he working alone?"

One burly fellow who introduced himself as the foreman of the group confirmed it. "He was."

"Were you not supervising his work as well as that of the others?" Bellamy's voice was sharper now, frustration creeping in.

"That I was," he replied defensively. "But my priority was to get the enclosures completed in time for the big cats' arrival. Perez worked well on his own."

"Did anyone see someone on the site who didn't belong?" Bellamy asked, voice tight.

They all shook their heads, looking anywhere but at him.

"The fence line isn't far from where you were working. How is it that someone could be clocked with an axe without any of you seeing anything?" Bellamy demanded, his frustration boiling over.

A crack of thunder immediately above shook them all, and some men grabbed at the table to steady themselves, eyes darting up to the roof.

"Well?" Bellamy snapped when the shock subsided.

The foreman spoke up. "The men were busy with the work. They weren't looking out for what was going on elsewhere."

"And none of you heard anything either, I suppose?" Bellamy's sarcasm was evident.

"We were making a din ourselves with the tools and all," one of the men offered.

"Can you tell us what time you last saw Perez?" Hamish's brow creased with frustration.

The men exchanged looks, their silence stretching unbearably.

"At tea break," the foreman finally said, shrugging. "The men stopped for a mug of tea around ten. Perez sat with us then."

"And no one saw him after that?"

A couple of the men shifted uncomfortably in their seats, and Bellamy's sharp gaze narrowed.

"Is there something else?" he pressed.

One of them spoke reluctantly. "We did see him a bit later than that. He was cracking the logs with that axe. The one... Anyways, it was after tea break."

"How long after?" Bellamy demanded, exasperation clear in his voice.

The man scratched his beard, glancing around helplessly. "There's no knowing the time out there."

"Oh, but you know when it's time for tea break. And lunch," Bellamy's tone was scathing.

"It's the foreman what tells us that," the man said defensively.

Bellamy's gaze shifted to the foreman, his eyes hard. "And you? You don't carry a watch either?"

The foreman looked abashed. "On jobs like this, I call a break when there's a convenient shift in the work."

Hamish's brow furrowed deeper. "So, when you say tea break is around ten, it could be anything from nine to eleven?" His voice was thin with frustration.

The men stared back at him, their expressions blank, uncomprehending.

"What difference does it make?" the foreman muttered, sounding defensive.

Hamish let out a long, frustrated breath, running a hand through his hair as he turned away to contain his irritation, while Bellamy pressed on.

"To sum up, no one saw anything, and no one heard anything out of the ordinary?" Bellamy's words were almost accusatory, his tone conveying his disbelief.

The men remained silent.

"Who found the body?" Hamish's voice cut through the silence, and he turned back to watch their faces closely.

A smaller, younger man raised his hand slowly, reluctantly.

"Tell us how that came about," Bellamy urged.

Hamish shoved his hands in his pockets to keep himself from wringing them. If they couldn't get something out of this lot who were right there at the time of the murder, he wondered if they would ever be able to find the killer.

The young man glanced around at the others, seeking silent approval. The foreman gave him an encouraging nod.

"I was heading to the rock pile to collect another barrow of rocks for the enclosure," he explained haltingly. "I happened to look toward the fence and saw no movement. At first, I thought Perez had gone and left all the fencing and tools lying about. I was annoyed if I'm honest, because it would be me cleaning it all up. But as I got closer... I saw Perez on the ground. That's when I called out to the foreman. He caught up, and we ran to the fence, thinking there'd been an accident. But when we saw Perez lying there... well, no one cuts off their own head, do they?"

Bellamy pulled at his collar, visibly agitated. "No. Indeed, they don't." He exchanged a look with Hamish, who merely shrugged, his frustration apparent.

"If there's nothing more, each of you can provide me or the doctor with your name and address, and you can go."

There was a bustle of activity as they all came forward at once.

Gradually, the men left one by one agreeing to meet at the Queensport Hotel. The younger man who had first seen the body lingered behind the others.

"I didn't want to say in front of the men," he began, speaking to both Hamish and Bellamy quietly. "And it's probably nothing, but when I was fetching a pile of stone, earlier this morning, not right before I saw Perez, but earlier, there was a man walking across the wetlands beyond the grounds. I remember thinking he was stupid going that way because the ground is boggy, and you can't see the waterholes for the long grass. No one local would be walking there."

"Interesting," said Bellamy. Hamish looked eagerly at the man. "Could you tell us what he looked like?"

The young man's face crumpled. "No. It was quite a distance. He was of slim build. And like I said, not from around here."

"But you might recognize the man if you saw him again?" Hamish asked hopefully.

"I reckon I might," he said. "He had a way of walking...I don't know but I might."

"One more question," said Bellamy. "Can you be sure when you last saw Perez alive?"

From the look on his face, the man was thinking carefully.

"I saw him just after tea break, like we told you," he said at last. "Then not again until I saw him on the ground. I suppose he must have been working out there when I noticed the fellow walking between the waterholes, but I can't say for sure that I saw him."

Bellamy thanked the man and dismissed him. As he was walking away Hamish called out to him and he turned to look back.

"Why didn't you want to share this in front of the others?"

The young man's face reddened. "There is no one hated more than a snitch," he said. "I don't know if the man had anything to do with Perez, but there is no honest reason someone would be lurking around those wetlands."

Hamish and Bellamy had a drink with Mr Fitzpatrick while they waited for the police cab to be brought to the front of the building. They suspected their driver had been at the Queensport Hotel quenching his thirst and sheltering from the rain while they conducted the interviews. Pennyweather joined them, tired and wet after waiting with the body.

"The cart arrived before the rain came down too heavily," he said. "Jan wrapped the axe like you said, and he was able to make a sketch of the scene as well, then it right pelted down."

"No one touched the axe itself, did they?" asked Hamish. "There may be fibres that will help us identify the killer."

"No one touched it," said Pennyweather. "Other than Jan. He wore gloves and he wrapped the axe in a cotton sheet straight from the morgue. The sheet would be clean, wouldn't it?"

Hamish stared at him in disbelief.

CHAPTER THIRTEEN

Ask any successful lawyer to what he ascribes his success, and he will tell you that he has taken care to have had 'evidence' to support the cases he has undertaken.

What sends a murderer to the gallows? Evidence.

What sends the thief to goal? Evidence.

What procures a divorce from a cruel husband? Evidence.

Facts can only be proved by evidence. **The Telegraph 4 October 1890.**

***

A young man they had interviewed earlier as one of the general labourers on the site brought word to Hamish and Bellamy that their cab had arrived. They turned to head down the grand staircase when Mr Fitzpatrick stopped them.

"When can I have permission to re-open?" he asked, a note of desperation in his voice.

Bellamy pulled a face that suggested he was giving the question due consideration. "Tomorrow," he said, and continued down the stairs.

"I pray this incident doesn't dampen business," Mr Fitzpatrick called out after them.

Hamish stopped and looked back at the distraught manager. "I rather fear it will have the opposite effect," he said. "It will likely prove to be a morbid attraction for visitors."

He quickened his step to catch up with Bellamy, who was already half-way to the front entrance.

Bellamy climbed into the cab first, followed by Hamish. As he was about to shut the door, Pennyweather appeared beside the cab. Bellamy blinked at him.

"What transport would you like me to take back, sir?"

Hamish and Bellamy exchanged glances. Hamish raised an eyebrow and Bellamy rolled his eyes.

"Get in," Bellamy conceded at last.

Hamish squished closer to the sergeant and the young constable tucked his long legs under his chest while Bellamy shifted about irritably.

"The alternative is to leave Pennyweather in the rain waiting for the ferry," said Hamish.

"I don't mind about that, but the lad has work to do. I'm not having him lazing by the river for the rest of the day."

It was Hamish's turn to roll his eyes.

"Jan travelled on the cart with the body. He will protect it as efficiently as I would myself," said Hamish.

"The man is dead," grumbled Bellamy. "I'm not sure what protection he needs from your lab assistant."

Hamish was about to dive into a tirade about the importance of protecting evidence, but he decided to save his breath. The worst of the downpour had passed, but it rained steadily as they rattled back into town. Hamish turned his mind to the facts of the case as they knew them. "Now we have an art theft and two murders," he said, raising his voice to be heard above the rain.

"And Perez out of the frame," added Bellamy sulkily.

Hamish raised his eyebrows. "Perez could have killed Lillian, perhaps Perez was killed as revenge for the murder of the girl."

Bellamy considered that possibility. "In that case, the most likely person for the killing of Perez might be Lillian's would be fiancé."

Hamish looked out of the window at the long grass bowed and dripping with the weight of the rain. Occasional glimpses of light flickered, and heavy dollops of water splashed into the waterholes dotted across the landscape, almost, but not entirely obscured by the grass.

"He was fuming about Perez's treatment of the girl," Hamish murmured. "But I can't help thinking about the determination on Alejandro's face when he came to see me the other night. I have no doubt he would kill to keep the countess safe."

Bellamy sighed. "That takes us back to Perez as probably responsible for the murder of Lillian. And Perez killed by Alejandro for a motive totally unconnected to the first murder."

"Could be," said Hamish.

The marshlands gave way to tall trees choked with thick green vines that threatened to obliterate them. The smell of bat excrement smouldering in the heat and the rain overwhelmed them while they travelled in silence for ten minutes.

Hamish was chewing over an idea. "Then there is the fact that Lillian was looking into her mother's past..."

"What of it?" snapped Bellamy.

"I think it's odd that Lillian was using the Langford's studio to paint. She wasn't even very good. She said so herself the night her painting was stolen. Could she have inserted herself at the house for another reason?"

"Like what?"

"Perhaps there's a link between her interest in her mother's past and the Langfords. Mrs Langford is a director of the Girl's Friendly Society, perhaps she had something to do with Mrs Murphy's placement when she first arrived in Moreton Bay."

Bellamy's brow knitted.

"That's a leap, isn't it? If Mrs Murphy had been mistreated by the Langfords, she would hardly allow one daughter to work there and the other to paint in the conservatory."

Hamish watched the river pass them by, thinking as he spoke. "I know it's not an obvious connection. And I'm not saying Mrs Murphy was mistreated by the Langford's directly, but there was no love lost in her story for the women who were supposed to provide support and protection for the girls immigrating to the colony to go into service."

"If someone killed Lillian because she knew something about the past that the Langford's wanted kept quiet, then who killed Perez?"

"I still think Alejandro killed Perez."

Bellamy took a deep breath. "We have to prioritise," he said. "I like Prentice for the murder of Perez, and you think it is Alejandro. We'll talk to each of them, see where that gets us."

"I'll conduct a full autopsy on the body of Perez this evening," said Hamish.

"Be sure to complete the paperwork smartly," said Bellamy.

Hamish sent a sideways glance toward the sergeant. "Who was the last person to see Perez alive and at what time?"

Bellamy rolled his eyes. "At this stage, we list the young fellow who found the body."

"But Perez was dead when he found him," cried Hamish.

"What does it matter for the purpose of the form? You can leave a window for the time, can't you? Say 9.00 am – 10-00 am."

"But..."

Bellamy shot him a silencing glare and Hamish closed his mouth without voicing another objection. He was uncomfortable with estimates and assumptions. He knew that precision and certainty would be necessary to effectively develop any semblance of 'forensic science'.

"Good," said Bellamy. "We'll interview Prentice and Alejandro tomorrow."

"We'll need to be quick if we hope to build a case against Alejandro," warned Hamish. "He is sailing the day after tomorrow."

CHAPTER FOURTEEN

It's the neighbour no-one wanted, and for plenty of good reasons. Brisbane city's morgue has a long history of floods, rotting corpses, and concrete slabs.

The 'house of the dead' had numerous homes over more than 100 years. Brisbane's first public morgue was built on the grounds of the old convict hospital between North Quay and today's George Street in 1863. A detached one-room brick building with a hipped roof and fireplace it was called a 'house for the dead.' But the putrefaction and stench from the unrefrigerated corpses made it hard for patients to recuperate. So, when the city's main hospital moved to its current site at Bowen Hills three years later, the morgue stayed.

The continual stench, however, drew even more complaints, this time from the judges at the nearby Supreme Court. Various sites were offered, but then rejected by the city engineer who wrote in 1878: 'The depositing of dead human bodies frequently in an advanced state of decomposition would be a horror and a nuisance...'

So, in 1879 the public morgue was moved to the riverbank on the old Queen's Wharf Road. The single-story timber building was a suitable distance from people and residences.

The river was a convenient place for the morgue as quite a lot of bodies they were doing post-mortems on were ones that had been drowned in the river either accidentally or through suicide.

Just nine years on in 1887, the public morgue was flooded, then two years later it was damaged by a landslip. The landslip was not the only problem. Without insect screens, rats were able to enter the building to feed on decaying corpses. It was repaired only to be washed away by floods again in 1893.

Abc.net.au/news/brisbanes-old-morgue-how-the-house-for-the-dead-survived (2018)

***

The gaslight in the autopsy room sent a yellow glow across the corpse of Carlos Perez on the table. Hamish disliked conducting autopsies in the evenings because of this light. So much of his examination depended upon subtle changes in skin tone. And the heaviness of the clouds outside had not helped, causing a dullness to fall over the small room like a blanket. If there was a room in Brisbane that held the humidity more effectively, Hamish did not know of it. The atmosphere in the morgue was suffocating and the dull drip of rain into the river outside was like a hammer tapping against his head. That the deceased citizens of Brisbane were subjected to disintegration and degradation within this oven-like structure was more than he could bear on some days. He kept the place as clean as was humanly possible, but there were still days when he would open the doors to find that rats had found their way in. Changes needed to be made. He'd written letters to the Chief Magistrate and the Governor about the risks the morgue presented to the health of the living if nothing were done. The location by the river, almost at the level of the river's surface may well be handy for hauling in bodies drowned in the water, but it simultaneously meant that the morgue was regularly flooded, even at a significant high tide. Recently, a landslip behind the morgue meant that the back wall was halfway submerged into the cliff face. A new purpose-built building was sorely needed, to be located at a more suitable site. If decision makers were not concerned about the disrespect the conditions afforded the dead, or the threat to the health of the medical examiner, they would surely respond to the health risks to the public.

Jan was already in the morgue when Hamish entered, standing in the corner as always, his pencil poised. He had removed the clothing from Perez's body and laid him out ready for Hamish's examination.

"Thank-you for staying late," said Hamish as he perused the body.

Jan didn't answer. Hamish knew the lad would be available at whatever hour he was needed. He leaned over the body and placed one hand on the man's head, tipping it slightly so that he could see the major wound clearly.

"There's deformation of the right side of the head," he began. "The immediate cause of death is an extensive brain contusion following fragmentation of the neurocranium."

Hamish carefully examined the head, shoulders and chest, mumbling to himself as he did so.

"There's a total of twenty-three slash, stab and cut wounds as well as contused lacerations on the scalp, face and neck," he said.

There was silence other than the small sound of Jan's pencil sailing across the page.

"This was a vicious attack."

Hamish looked across at Jan.

"Why so violent? The cleave to the head finished him, and it appears to be the first strike taken."

Jan's face showed no emotion. He knew the comment was not intended for the notes, so he waited, his ice-blue eyes never shifting from Hamish.

The doctor shook his head slowly.

"The injuries resulting in the death of the victim were sustained during an assault on the head with an axe, which was used both as a slashing tool and a blunt instrument."

Jan copied each word carefully.

"That's it. There's no need to open him up. I'll leave you to clean him," said Hamish.

Hamish stepped back and stared at the man on his autopsy table.

"I have to think these two murders have been carried out by the same killer," he spoke quietly, as though only to himself. "The level of violence in each of the deaths is too severe. It suggests someone with a violent disposition. Someone who enjoyed the killings."

Jan had begun methodically cleaning the body.

Hamish turned his attention to the sketch Jan had made of the crime scene. He could see that the killer had walked two or three yards carrying the bloodied axe before dropping it on the grass. There was one clear footprint in the blood where the killer had taken a step back toward the body. He'd taken one last look before he rushed off the way he'd come. On the next page, Jan had drawn a life-size image of the footprint. Hamish could see that it came from a large boot. Apart from the pool of blood under the head and the blood splatter around the body, there were no other disturbances to the ground.

Turning his attention to the axe that lay on the table alongside the sketch book, Hamish carefully unwrapped the cloth and examined the handle. He noted incomplete finger marks in the blood. They clearly came from a large hand.

"We're looking for a male perpetrator, working alone," he said.

"Bellamy will want the notes first thing in the morning. Just give him the notebook if you don't have time to type them."

As he said it Hamish knew Jan would type out the notes and present them in the neat file, he always used to hand his work to the Sergeant. Hamish would need to complete the remaining particulars, such as 'last person to see the deceased alive." It irked him to write down a name that may not reflect the precise truth. Had any of the other men seen Perez after the time they all agreed, just past the tea break? It seemed unlikely they were going to admit to it, if they did. He supposed they were lucky the young man had come forward to tell them about the figure crossing the marshes. And what time exactly was the tea break?

He looked around the room, little more than a cell and took a breath of fetid air. Is this really where he would spend the next years of his life? A restlessness had overtaken him. He wasn't sure whether it was this case that became more frustrating by the day, or his compulsion with taking forensic investigation seriously, of developing a discipline that could be followed consistently and be more effective in accurately identifying those guilty of violent crimes. He seemed to be the only one who thought such a thing necessary, the only one who could see the potential in it. He sighed and promised himself he would at least follow up on the letters he had written recommending a new morgue be built, preferably near the hospital at Bowen Hills.

Hamish walked home slowly, losing himself in the darkness of the night as he turned to climb the hill to Wickham Terrace. There were no gas lights this far out of town. The old convict-built windmill stood as no more than a shadow against the sky at the top of the hill, it served as his guide on moonless nights such as this. He could still hear feint rumblings in the distance telling him the storm had circled round and was travelling west past the mountain range and on to the downs. He tried to give himself a rest from thinking about the investigation, but his mind kept recoiling back to the vicious wounds he had examined on the corpse of Carlos Perez. He thought Alejandro capable of killing Perez in duty to his cousin, but he couldn't understand why he would do so with such unnecessary violence.

His mind then went to George Prentice. The horseman may well be intent on revenge for his fiancé's sister, but the same question applied. Why would he strike with such violence? Hamish couldn't imagine him wielding the axe and slashing him over and again in such a way. In addition, George Prentice makes sense as a killer, only if Perez killed Lillian in the first place. Why would Perez abduct her and take her to the mudflats on Hamilton Reach? Every indication was that she would have joined him willingly, and there were far more comfortable places to go for an assignation than the mudflats. And what about the second man? If Perez were alone, he would have to be driving. Lillian could have jumped out and run when the cab turned off the road. It must have been obvious to her that she was in danger by then, regardless of how willingly she might get into a cab at the suggestion of Perez. No. There were two men. He was sure of it. Would Perez include another man in the assault and increase the risk of exposure? It didn't make sense any way Hamish twisted it. What if there were two completely unrelated murders? He couldn't believe that either.

Stopping before the door to his home, Hamish took a deep breath, hoping that tomorrow would reveal a new lead in the case. He unlocked the door and as he opened it, a small ball of wiry energy pushed through and leapt into his arms. The tiny body trembled with life, extinguishing all thoughts of death and murder, with a rough, wet tongue to his face.

CHAPTER FIFTEEN

The spring sun shows me your shadow,
The spring wind bears me your breath,
You are mine for a passing moment,
But I am yours to the death.
"Chimaera" by Rosamund Marriot Watson (1860–1911)

***

Isabella de la Vega

The countess paced like a lioness in a cage. She hadn't slept since her last meeting with Perez. The coldness in him stayed with her, chilled her, despite the tropical heat of the colony.

He meant what he said. She would see him no more. A suffocating pain gripped her chest and the world around her dulled to a muted grey. In the echo of his final words, she felt a desolate emptiness.

She hadn't left her room all day, knowing full well her hostess would be worried. She told her maid to inform the Lady Governess she had correspondence to attend to and would join the family for dinner. But as the sun bled pink into the evening sky, she knew she couldn't face them. She would have to feign illness, not altogether a lie, for indeed she was ill. More than ill, she was broken.

As the time drew nearer, and she anticipated the knock from her maid notifying her that dinner was about to be served, Isabella took a deep breath and shook herself. As much as she hated the thought of interacting with people, it would not do to pine like this. The doctor would be called, and she would have to face her hosts anyway, as well as a physician who wouldn't be able to find anything wrong with her.

Better to dry her tears and join her hosts for dinner. Afterall, she'd spent her entire life pretending to be present when she was no such thing. She recalled the endless chatter, people with nothing meaningful to say, but saying it anyway and earnestly expecting her to respond. She had learned how to sound interested even without hearing them. She would need all her skills this evening.

She had decided to ring for her maid to help her dress, when there was a timid knock at the door and her footman Mateo, stepped in at her call. His face was white, and the countess's heart immediately skipped a beat. He stood stiff before her and resolute in his intent to follow through with the task that had fallen upon him.

The blood drained from Isabella's face. A sound caught in her throat, and she couldn't allow it to escape. Her eyes were wide.

Mateo held out a hand that trembled. In it he clasped a worn leather glove. Unable to force herself to take it, Isabella swallowed and looked from the glove to Mateo's face.

"He promised he would find a way to get a sign to me," she murmured.

The footman opened his mouth to speak but Isabella put her fingers to her lips.

"I don't want to hear how it happened," she said. "The sign has reached me, as he promised it would."

She fell to the floor in a heap of fabric. Mateo left the room quietly and slipped out of the house without being seen.

When her maid found her a few moments later, she was lying on her side on the bed, her feet tucked up against her chest. The maid left her alone and informed Lady Musgrave that her guest was unwell.

CHAPTER SIXTEEN

To understand the antipathy to service which exists among the masses, and why so many girls who would be better off in service become ill paid and overworked seamstresses or shop assistants; it is only necessary to look at the cardinal point in this democratic creed. "Liberty at any cost" is the watch word of the social and political reformer, and the chief ground of discontent among servants is their deprivation of liberty.

The degree of labour expected from servants varies in different households but in all the labour is exacting and protracted. Servants, as a rule rise at six and go to bed at whatever time suits the convenience of their employers. They are at work before the master or mistress is awake and during the fifteen or sixteen hours that follow, they are at their post and ready to do their bidding. They are the last to go to bed at night.

Let a lady or gentleman try to realise how rigorous are the laws which govern the actions of servants, and it will be seen that the intractability of their retainers is not entirely unjustified. Has it ever occurred to the master or mistress what humiliation and distress attach to the circumstance that the footman or housemaid, the cook or the butler, dare not stir beyond the four walls of the house without permission? **The Colonist 28 April 1888**

***

Pennyweather was using the electric pen for the first time to create fliers advertising the Policeman's Ball. He was instructed to make fifty copies and distribute them in shop windows and on public notice boards. Hamish peered over his shoulder with great interest. They were both so intent on the process, they didn't notice Anne-Marie Langford enter.

When they did look up, she was approaching the front desk with an anxious, yet determined expression.

Pennyweather's face registered his surprise.

"Good morning, Anne-Marie," said Hamish, equally pleased to see her, and startled. "How can we help you?"

Brown eyes looked up at him through fine long lashes. Tiny lines wrinkled on her forehead, and he wanted to smooth them with his fingers. "I need to speak with you and Sergeant Bellamy," she said, her voice barely above a whisper.

Hamish stepped forward and took her hands in his. "What can be wrong?" he asked seeking the answer in her eyes.

Pennyweather nodded back to Bellamy's office. Hamish put his arm around her waist and led her behind the counter and through the open door.

The sergeant looked up as they both entered. Hamish still had his hand at Anne-Marie's back both protecting and guiding her. Pennyweather followed, bowed to Miss Langford and closed the door behind them.

The young woman was looking from Hamish to the sergeant, wringing her hands and trembling.

"I've heard, that is, we've all heard...it's all over town, that Carlos Perez was found murdered at the aquarium yesterday," she began. "Is it true?"

Her large brown eyes stared. Hamish thought of a gentle wallaby, startled by noisy ramblers in the bush.

"It is true," said Bellamy in a measured tone. Anne-Marie gave a nod in recognition, but her shoulders remained tight as though she carried a heavy burden.

"I should have said something earlier," she hesitated. "I know I should have..."

She gazed at Hamish.

He reached out to take her hand and it lay limp and light in his. He gestured for her to continue.

"Relax, he said gently, "and tell us what's on your mind."

Anne-Marie took a deep breath. "Lillian was seeing the Spaniard, Perez," she said.

When Bellamy's face remained unmoved, she hesitated.

Hamish squeezed her hand with reassurance and urged her to go on. She seemed confused.

"I didn't think anyone knew of this apart from myself and Delia," she said. "I saw him once, waiting at the side gate for Lillian. She ran into his arms. I wasn't sure what to do, so I spoke with Delia about it."

Anne-Marie shook her head in frustration.

"Delia said she was already aware of their relationship. She was angry with Lillian but said her sister wouldn't listen to reason."

Desperate eyes willed Hamish and the sergeant to understand. The next sentence came in a gush.

"Now they are both murdered and poor Mrs Murphy not knowing..." Tears broke through and ran down Anne-Marie's cheeks.

Hamish wiped her face gently with his handkerchief.

Anne-Marie summoned all the courage she had to confess the real dilemma that had brought her to the Police Station.

"Do you think poor Lillian was killed because of her connection with Perez? I feel responsible..."

"No," whispered Hamish. "How could you be?"

Anne-Marie straightened her shoulders.

"Perhaps if I'd spoken sooner...I know I should have done something...but I didn't want to interfere...and I suppose I valued our friendship..."

Hamish drew her to him in a soothing embrace.

"You cannot blame yourself," he said. Her face was turned up to his, her eyes moist from crying and her lips red from biting at them. A new wave of emotion came over him. He checked himself for being soft on a pretty woman in despair. But it didn't help.

"We do believe there is a connection between the two murders but there's nothing you could have done to prevent these evil deeds."

He spoke gently, hoping he could soothe her shame.

Anne-Marie's face was wet, and Hamish's handkerchief soaked.

"I kept it from her mother. I knew what was going on, and I failed to keep her safe..."

"Lillian knew her own mind," said Hamish. "No one is responsible for her death other than the men who killed her."

"Men?" cried Anne-Marie. She looked to Bellamy for confirmation.

It was evident from his face that Bellamy had been watching the interaction between Hamish and Anne-Marie with more than professional interest. He couldn't hide a small upturn of his lip, and a raised eyebrow directed at Hamish.

"We have evidence to suggest two men were involved," he confirmed in an even tone.

Anne-Marie sighed deeply and wiped her eyes. "Do you think Perez a man capable of murder?" asked Bellamy.

"I couldn't say, I've never met him, but I know from both Delia and Lillian he had great charisma. He seemed to be the type to shy away from people like me and mother. He was a champion of the working classes." She blew her nose. "Do you think Perez killed Lillian?"

"We don't know yet," said Bellamy. "It's an idea, that's all."

Hamish helped Anne-Marie up and walked her out of the building. Her arm wound naturally through his and she leaned into him.

"Did you walk?" he asked when he saw no vehicle waiting. "Do you want me to send a message for someone to come and collect you?"

Anne-Marie shook her head.

"I'll take you home," he said. "I'm not leaving you to walk home alone."

Anne-Marie had put up a hand to resist when they caught sight of Rita strolling across the road toward them.

"Hello, I didn't expect to find you here," she said cheerfully. As she drew closer, she noticed the tears and the red cheeks. Hamish's crumpled handkerchief was curled up in her friend's hand.

Rita's smile immediately fell to concern.

"Oh Anne-Mare, what is it, my darling?" She scooped the woman into her arms, and her sympathy started Anne-Marie crying again with all the previous gusto.

"What's happened?" she whispered to Hamish over Anne-Marie's head.

His lips stretched tight, then he mouthed the word, "later".

Rita nodded. "I'll see her home," she said.

She winked at Hamish and started moving her friend gently down the street.

Hamish watched their backs, slightly jealous that he was not the one with Anne-Marie's head on his shoulder as they walked.

When he returned to Bellamy's office, he ran his hand across the scar under his fringe and slumped into a chair.

"That explains why she seemed nervous," he said. "She was holding back the information about Lillian's affair with Perez."

"I suppose she thought she was helping, at the time," said Bellamy. "I'm more convinced than ever that Perez is our killer, in the case of Lillian Murphy's death."

"Maybe so," said Hamish.

He noticed the ridiculous boyish grin on the sergeant's face.

"What are you smirking about?"

"Nothing," said Bellamy quickly. "Is there something you wish to tell me?" His eyes were glittering.

"Only that I believe Alejandro killed Perez to protect Isabella," said Hamish, brushing back his fringe. "From the level of violence inflicted in both murders, it feels to me like the same killer," he said. "But if we assume Alejandro killed Perez, it's difficult to see why he would have killed Lillian."

"I told you, Perez killed Lillian," said Bellamy. "I still think George Prentice the more likely suspect for the murder of Perez. He could have killed him to revenge the death of Lillian."

"I need to talk to Alejandro," said Hamish. "I need to gauge his reaction to the death of the Spaniard for myself. You didn't see how desperate he was to keep Isabella away from him. He truly believed him to be dangerous."

"Alejandro must be our next call, then," agreed Bellamy. "But we need to be discrete. Any hint of trouble that might involve the guests of the Governor will be a political nightmare. Both you and I may find ourselves with our jobs on the line."

Hamish put on his coat slowly and sipped at the tea Pennyweather had delivered to him.

He wasn't looking forward to confronting Alejandro about the death of Perez. As a Spanish nobleman, Alejandro would see it as his duty to rid his cousin of an unsuitable lover. But if Alejandro did kill Perez, he had to be held accountable. Hamish wondered if the governor would agree. Bellamy was right, it would be quite a scandal to accuse his houseguest of murder. And the associated implication that his motive was the preservation of his cousin's honour would be equally disturbing.

Bellamy put his head around the door and said, "the Police cab is waiting."

Hamish took one last mouthful of his tea and stood up. He and Bellamy stepped into the morning air.

"Did you find out anything new at the autopsy?" said Bellamy as he climbed into the cab.

"Didn't Jan leave the notes for you?"

Bellamy hastened to assure him that the notes had been on his desk when he came in. He hadn't had time to open them before Hamish arrived, followed by Anne-Marie.

"No," he said. "Perez was an exceptionally healthy man, until his head was crashed in by an axe."

Bellamy's tone became earnest. "We need to tread carefully at Government House. We're only seeking information," he warned, his voice low but edged with caution. "If there's even a hint of accusation against one of the Governor's guests, all hell will break loose."

Hamish swallowed, a knot of unease tightening in his stomach. "I know."

"Best leave the questions to me," Bellamy added, casting a glance that brooked no argument.

"Gladly."

The cab rattled on toward Government House, every jolt and sway matching Hamish's growing sense of dread. He couldn't shake the image of Alejandro's cold, aristocratic composure cracking under pressure, of anger flashing in his eyes. How far would Alejandro go to defend his honour, or his secrets?

When they arrived, a stern-faced manservant met them at the door, his expression as immovable as stone. He led them in silence through the echoing halls to the library, where they were left to wait. Ten minutes of oppressive silence crept by while each tick of the clock made Hamish more nervous. He tried to distract himself, his eyes tracing the rows of leather-bound volumes on the shelves, but his mind kept drifting to the red cedar desk at one end of the room. Whoever sat there would have an unsettling command of the space, with a sweeping view of the gardens outside, a watchful perch that saw everything.

The room itself seemed cut off from the world, isolated, as though even the sounds of life were forbidden to intrude. Seated in green velvet armchairs, Hamish and Bellamy exchanged wary glances. A thought crossed Hamish's mind, what if Alejandro had slipped away during the night?

When Alejandro finally appeared, he carried an air of resignation, his expression haunted. He knew about the death of Carlos Perez. That much was clear. But what else did he know? And what was he hiding?

"How is the countess?" Hamish asked, his voice uncharacteristically blunt, dispensing with any pretence of courtesy.

Alejandro's gaze flicked up, his face drawn. "I assume... not well. She won't let anyone near her."

"I assume then, she has heard about the death of Carlos Perez. How did she find out about the incident?" Bellamy's tone was neutral yet probing.

Alejandro hesitated, "I don't know," he admitted. "I assume Mateo informed her. He despised Perez. He'd have relished delivering such news."

Hamish watched Alejandro closely, noting the shadows beneath his eyes, the uncharacteristic slump of his posture. Here was a man frayed, unravelling.

The conversation shifted, and Hamish asked, "Where were you yesterday between nine and midday?"

Alejandro's eyes narrowed and suspicion flared.

"My whereabouts?" he repeated. He looked from Hamish to Bellamy, measuring their intentions. After a taut pause, he spoke, voice clipped. "I was here, in my room, occupied with correspondence. I sent a letter with my servant to the ship bound for Sydney and London."

Alejandro's eyes flicked between the two of them, searching for hidden meanings. Hamish made a note, though his gut told him Alejandro wasn't lying. Still, it was too soon to trust instinct alone.

"Were you aware that Countess Isabella met with Carlos Perez the night before last?" Bellamy asked, his tone deceptively calm.

Alejandro's face froze and his jaw tightened as shock registered. He leaned forward, his voice dropping to a venomous hiss. "How do you know this?"

The words hung in the air, thick with menace. Bellamy held Alejandro's gaze, unflinching. "I had Perez followed. Unfortunately, no one was watching him at the aquarium yesterday, or perhaps we might have prevented... certain events."

Alejandro's eyes flickered with something dark, something dangerous, as he processed the revelation. Hamish could feel the shift in the room, a palpable tension that settled like a weight on his shoulders. In that instant, he knew Alejandro was grappling with something, some private agony, some terrible realization. And just as quickly, he dismissed the thought that Alejandro was the killer. If he didn't know about the meeting, then he had no motive. Yet, that didn't mean he wasn't hiding something.

"What happened to him?" Alejandro's tone was neutral, but his eyes were alive with unspoken questions.

"Someone took an axe to his head," Hamish replied, his words sharp. "Quite savagely."

Alejandro's expression hardened, his eyes darting as he considered his own theories. But when he finally spoke, his voice was measured, concealing whatever secrets lay beneath.

"I don't know anyone here who'd want to kill him," he said, each word precise. "But in Spain... well, he had no shortage of enemies. Perhaps one of his enemies found him here."

Hamish exchanged a final look with Bellamy, both feeling the unspoken tension simmering beneath Alejandro's carefully controlled facade. There was more to this man, to his secrets and his scars, than they could yet fathom.

Hamish was convinced the Spaniard had come to his own conclusion. He believed that if Alejandro didn't kill Perez himself, he knew who did.

"What kind of enemies did Perez have in Spain?" asked Hamish.

"Political enemies, mostly. I suppose you know by now that Perez was a member of the Spanish Anarchists? Police in my country have been searching for him for months in connection with the bombing of the Palace in Madrid."

"We did know. And word of his demise has been sent to the Policia in Spain by telegraph," said Bellamy.

Hamish squinted. "Are there agents of your country looking for Perez here in the colony?"

Alejandro appeared to consider his answer. "There may well be," he said.

Hamish and Bellamy exchanged glances.

"You realize we'll need to interview the countess," said Bellamy.

"Not today, surely?"

"Perhaps not now, but we will return later. This must be cleared up before we can allow you to sail."

The Spaniard shot up from his armchair. "You are not serious!" he cried. "The countess and I sail for our homeland the day after tomorrow. We have nothing to do with these deaths you are investigating, and you cannot detain us. It will mean diplomatic disaster if you attempt it."

"Let's hope the matter is resolved expeditiously," said Bellamy. "If there is any more you can add to help us with that don't hesitate to contact myself or the doctor at the station."

Alejandro's face reflected both shock and defiance as Hamish and Bellamy left the library the way they had come in. Hamish saw from the corner of his eyes that the nobleman was pacing the floor of the library. They found their own way to the door where the man servant rushed to meet them, obviously disturbed by the breech of protocol in their leaving the library unaccompanied. He opened the door for them and closed it again behind them.

"What do you think of that?" asked Bellamy when they were on their way back to the station.

"He knows something he is not sharing," said Hamish.

"I had that feeling too."

"It's odd that he said, 'the investigation of these deaths.' We were only questioning him about the murder of Perez. Do you think he is linking them in his own mind?"

"It seems that way," says Bellamy. "In which case, if the death of Perez was a political killing as he suggested, why would the same killer have murdered Lillian?"

"They wouldn't," said Hamish. "It may be a case of misdirection on Alejandro's part. I have to say though, Alejandro seemed truly shocked when we mentioned that Isabella and Perez had met. If he didn't know about the meeting, he didn't really have a reason to kill Perez. When he spoke to me, he was only concerned that they be kept apart until their ship sailed for Spain."

Bellamy agreed. "Our time is limited by the fact that Isabella and Alejandro are leaving the country."

Hamish reflected on the interview and decided he knew two things. Firstly, something changed in Alejandro's thinking the moment he learned that Isabella and Perez met in Brisbane. Secondly, he still felt that, from a forensic point of view, the two murders seemed linked.

He was thinking aloud when he said, "I can't see Alejandro traipsing through the wetlands of Hemmant in his white stockings."

Bellamy stroked his chin.

"He might have been dressed to blend in. He wouldn't wear his best stockings to commit murder."

"His gait alone would give him away," said Hamish. "He walks like a spoiled cat."

Bellamy laughed. "It is difficult to imagine those silky hands wielding an axe."

"Just so," agreed Hamish.

Bellamy turned to the doctor, "But you still consider him the most likely suspect for the killing of Perez?"

Hamish shrugged his shoulders. "I think I do," he said. "Though I don't know how I would prove it, or whether we could ever bring him to trial. Although, we have the witness, the young fellow working at the aquarium. He may be able to identify the killer."

"I would want to have more to tie him to the murder than the eyewitness alone," said Bellamy. "He was quite a distance from the man he claimed to have seen. Let's not get ahead of ourselves. We still have George Prentice to speak with."

CHAPTER SEVENTEEN

Regarding the deterioration of domestic servants, 'the cry is everywhere the same – the badness of our modern servants.' But who is to blame? The mistresses or the maids? The masters, or the employed? The one class are educated, the other comparatively ignorant – and influence filters downwards – it does not permeate the social classes from below. We cast longing looks backwards to the bygone times when servants were the humble friends of the family, ready to serve for love and bare maintenance if bad times came. And identifying themselves with the fortunes of their masters.

But we forget that we ourselves have changed even more than they since the days when mistresses overloaded their maids in closer companionship than is warranted now by the conditions of society. When daily details were ordered by the Lady, and the execution of her orders were personally supervised, when housekeeping was at once an act and a pleasure, a science and a source of pride. The young servants were trained immediately under the eye of the mistress and by her direct influence, as now they are trained under the head servant of their special department.

Through change of teachers alone, if no other cause was wanting, we could trace the source of the deterioration complained of. The Lady who, two generations ago, taught the stillroom and the mysteries of syrups and confections, of jams and jellies and dainty sweetmeats; who knew the prime joints, and the signs of good meat, tender poultry and fresh fish, as well as the cook herself; who could go blind-fold to her linen press and pick out the best sheets from the ordinary; who could check as well as instruct the housemaid at every turn – such a mistress as this, for her own part diligent, refined, truthful, God-fearing, was likely to give a higher tone, infuse a more faithful and dutiful spirit into her servants than is possible now, when the thing is reduced to a profession like any other, and the teacher is only technically, not morally, in advance of the pupil. It is the mistresses that have let the reigns slip from their hands, not the maids. **The Sydney Mail 29 May 1886**

***

It was close to lunchtime when they left Government House. The day was getting away from them and they were keenly aware that the Countess and Alejandro would be sailing in a little more than forty-eight hours. If Alejandro was involved in either killing or both, they had scant time to find evidence of it. They climbed back into the cab and Bellamy instructed the driver to take them to the Langford's House on Bowen Terrace.

"We've narrowed the field to two suspects for the murder of Perez, I think," said Bellamy. "George Prentice had reason to kill Perez if he believes him to have murdered Lillian Murphy."

"Let's hope he has some knowledge of Lillian's murder that we do not, because it is going to be the devil's job to prove that Perez killed her now that he's dead himself."

"It matters only that Prentice believes it to be so, for our purposes."

When they arrived at the gate of the big house, Bellamy climbed from the cab with renewed energy.

"It will be a whole lot easier for us if George Prentice is the killer, rather than Don Alejandro, that is for certain."

They found George Prentice at the stable, his arms wrapped around the saddle he'd just pulled from a large roan. When he saw them coming, he lifted his chin defiantly, his lips set in a hard line.

"We need to ask you some more questions," said Bellamy.

The horseman stood with the saddle tapping against his legs. It would have weighed heavily, but Prentice held it with one hand as if it were nothing.

"Questions about what?"

"I suppose you've heard of the death of the Spaniard," Bellamy said, watching him closely.

Prentice's jaw clenched. "Good riddance," he spat. "The world's better off without him."

Bellamy's gaze sharpened. "We need to know where you were yesterday, between nine and noon."

"I was here, with the horses," Prentice replied, turning his back on them to hang the saddle from an iron hook. His movements were abrupt, his posture showing his irritation.

"Was anyone else around?" Bellamy persisted.

"No. I work alone most days," Prentice said, running a calming hand down the horse's neck, though his expression showed anything but calm.

"Did any of the family members come down to speak with you?"

"No."

"Did you go up to the house?"

"I did not," he replied, voice flat.

Bellamy let out an exaggerated sigh, trying to get a reaction. "Mr. Prentice, you realize you're a man of interest in this case? You've made no secret of your hatred for Carlos Perez, and now he's dead."

Prentice's eyes narrowed, and his muscles tensed visibly as he clenched his hands. The horse sidestepped, sensing his agitation. He grabbed a handful of hay and held it out to the animal, who settled quickly, munching on the offering. "So, what if I hated him?" he shot back. "What are you trying to say?"

Bellamy didn't back down. "There's an argument to be made that you killed Perez because you believe he murdered your fiancée's sister."

Prentice fixed Bellamy with a stare that could cut through iron. "And don't you believe he killed Lillian?" he asked, challenging the sergeant to admit it.

Bellamy looked down, scuffing the dirt with his shoe. "It doesn't matter what I believe," he said. "It's whether you believed it enough to act upon the idea."

Prentice snorted, an edge of mockery in his voice. "Then go on. Tell the magistrate what you think I did."

He turned away dismissively and led the horse into its stall, moving with a rigid anger.

Bellamy shared a look with Hamish before pushing forward. "Do you think Carlos Perez killed Lillian Murphy?" he asked directly.

Prentice came out of the stall, wiping his hands on a cloth with exaggerated casualness. "I believe he was more than capable of it," he said, voice low and simmering with resentment. "But do I know he did it? No. And that's the truth."

His face was set, his gaze unflinching. To Hamish, Prentice seemed too blunt, too forthright to be hiding anything. If he'd killed Perez, Hamish had the feeling he'd be declaring it to their faces.

With a final look, Prentice turned his attention to a chestnut horse, making it clear that as far as he was concerned, the conversation was over.

Left without any certain direction to take, Hamish and Bellamy were looking around the yard for any sign of potential witnesses who could attest to the whereabouts of George Prentice at the time of the murder at the aquarium. They noticed a stableboy shovelling hay in the adjoining outbuilding.

"Why don't you talk to him," said Bellamy. "I'll go inside and speak with Mrs Langford. We should be able to establish whether Prentice was here yesterday or not."

They both nodded to Prentice before leaving the front of the stable, but the man remained intent on the horses and ignored them.

Hamish strolled over to where the boy was shovelling huge forkfuls of hay from a stack in the corner, scattering it thick and even across the dirt floor. The lad couldn't have been more than sixteen, wiry but stubborn looking, with a perpetual scowl etched on his young face.

Hamish introduced himself, but the boy barely acknowledged him, continuing his work as though the doctor wasn't there.

"Been here long?" Hamish asked, trying to break the ice.

"Six months or thereabouts," the boy replied without looking up, his rhythm steady and uninterested.

"How do you find working with Prentice?"

At this, the boy stopped, leaning heavily on his fork. He glanced up, his expression blank, eyes narrowed. "He's alright," he said flatly, like he was daring Hamish to argue.

"Would you say he has a temper?" Hamish probed.

The boy snorted. "A temper?" He rolled his eyes. "He's steady, like. Don't take no nonsense, but he don't fly off like some."

Hamish could feel the boy's irritation simmering. "What were you doing yesterday in the morning?"

The boy's face hardened, his eyes darting with suspicion. "Why d'you wanna know?" he shot back.

Hamish shrugged casually, keeping his tone light. "Just making conversation."

The boy's scowl deepened. "I was here, wasn't I? Haulin' hay, like every other day."

"Did you see Mr. Prentice? Was he here with you?"

The boy scoffed. "I dunno, do I? I ain't his keeper. He's off doin' his thing, and I'm doin' mine."

Before Hamish could press further, the boy turned away, jamming his fork back into the haystack as if to signal the conversation was over.

"So, you can't say for sure if you saw him here in the morning?" Hamish persisted.

The boy huffed loudly, tossing down the fork with exaggerated irritation. "No," he drawled, voice dripping with sarcasm. "I can't say one way or the other, alright?"

Without waiting for a response, he hefted a heavy bale of hay, slamming it onto the pile against the wall, then grabbed a straw broom and began sweeping with a fierceness that made it clear he wanted Hamish and his questions gone.

Hamish watched him manipulate hay from one place to another for a few moments hoping Bellamy was having better luck with Mrs Langford and Anne-Marie.

Then he headed away from the stables and back toward the house. He met Bellamy on the gravel path that joined the house to the stone entry gate.

"Anything?" he asked.

Bellamy shook his head. "Nothing. They both insist Prentice would have been in the stables dressing the horses as he did every morning, but neither could say they had seen him."

"Did you ask Mrs Langford if she'd ever known him to be violent?"

"I did."

"And...?"

"She laughed," said Bellamy.

Hamish puffed air through his lips. "That's what the stableboy said as well."

Hamish wondered if the sergeant was yet ready to put Prentice before the witness. "Any chance the worker at Hemmant would be able to identify him?"

"He may be able to," said Bellamy, "but I doubt he will. Prentice is a local and is probably known to the men. If the young fellow who saw the man outside the grounds of the aquarium pointed the finger at a local man, his colleagues would vilify him for it.

In any case, we only have one shot at witness identification. I'd like to have additional evidence before we take that shot."

Bellamy turned to Hamish. The doctor shook his head. If they were not ready to call the witnesses in, he had no ideas.

As there seemed no more could be gained at the Langford House, they headed down the gravel path toward the gate.

They hadn't taken more than a few strides when they heard a woman's voice. Hamish turned to see Delia slip from behind the washroom to the right of the stables. She was watching fretfully, looking to the left and the right.

"Is she calling to us?" asked Bellamy.

Hamish scanned the yard. "There's no one else around."

Delia gestured with her hand for them to join her, then she ducked quickly back into the laundry building.

They left the gravel path and picked their way through the grass, skirting away from the stable, hoping no one noticed them. Bellamy stopped some distance from the washroom and suggested Hamish go on.

"She'll be less intimidated if you speak to her alone," he said. "I'll wait for you at the cab."

Hamish watched him turn back toward the gate then strode on to catch up with Delia.

"I need to talk to you," she whispered when he was by her side at the entrance to the laundry.

"Go on," said Hamish.

"Not here," she said looking about. "Come to my mother's cottage this evening, at seven. I'll talk to you there."

With that she slipped into the building and ducked between a large copper boiler and several wicker baskets of linen. Presumably she continued through the back walkway into the house.

Hamish stood stunned. What was it that she couldn't tell him right away? He strode across the grass back to the gate to join the sergeant.

"What's that all about then?" asked Bellamy.

"We won't know until tonight. She wants us to come to the cottage at seven."

Bellamy looked back toward the spot where the girl had disappeared. "She's skittish about something."

"She's positively terrified. I think we should take Rita. Her presence might calm her."

CHAPTER EIGHTEEN

Sir, one careful and capable housewife (my wife) believes that ample consideration is already given to the welfare of domestic servants and that those of them who are able and willing can make themselves, and others, very comfortable by simply conforming to the existing conditions of life, if they were not, as they certainly are, SO extremely desirous of indulging in personal, and in most cases injurious gratification. The letter from 'Housemistress' published in your columns some days since, will not tend to make the young persons more satisfied with their occupations. This is one of the class of mistresses who spoils girls for employment. Respectable women should not want to be out several nights in the week. If they perform their household duties faithfully, they could reasonably be expected to expend a portion of some of their evenings in reading or sewing, not walking about the streets or visiting dancing saloons. The inordinate desire for freedom has overstocked the seamstress and tailoress market, and necessarily those who are seeking for domestic servants seek in vain.

If the baker's strike (and strikes seem to be altogether the proper thing, just now) and domestic servants decline domestic service, the ladies of this country will be upon their mettle indeed. I really do not see why girls in this colony should be unwilling to perform as servants where I believe they are well treated. They are permitted reasonable time for recreation, and if they desire anything beyond, they are altogether unfit for respectable houses and will certainly never make good housewives themselves. **The Argus Melbourne 18 January 1883**

***

Hamish, Bellamy and Rita arrived at the Murphy's cottage promptly at seven. The night was cool and clear. The recent storm had cleaned the town and taken the oppressive humidity with it. Hamish was hopeful that whatever Delia had on her mind would move them forward in the case. He disliked the feeling that they had been travelling in circles for days.

When Mrs. Murphy opened the door, a flicker of relief crossed her face upon seeing Rita with Bellamy and Hamish. But as she ushered them inside, a shadow of hesitation crept into her gaze, and her voice carried an edge of uncertainty. She led them into the drawing room, her eyes darting anxiously between Delia and the guests, as though steeling herself for what lay ahead.

Delia sat waiting, a tray of tea and cake set before her, though only two cups had been arranged. Mrs. Murphy's hands fluttered nervously over the tray, as if unsure what to do next. "I'll just... fetch another cup and saucer," she murmured, her voice barely a whisper. She disappeared into the kitchen, leaving a tense silence in her wake.

When she returned, Hamish noticed her hands were trembling as she placed the extra china on the tray. She poured each of them a cup of tea, her fingers visibly shaking as she held the teapot, and Hamish reached out instinctively, ready to steady it should it slip from her grasp.

Bellamy could feel the air thickening with unease, his impatience gnawing at him. Unable to bear the suspense any longer, he leaned forward, his voice pressing. "Mrs. Murphy, please. What is it you wanted to tell us?"

Mrs. Murphy froze, her gaze flickering toward Delia as if seeking reassurance. For a moment, she looked as though she might retreat, the words caught in her throat. Then she drew a shaky breath, her fingers twisting the edge of her apron. She glanced at each of them, her lips parting and closing as though the secret itself were weighing her down. Hamish's pulse quickened in anticipation, feeling that they were on the brink of revelation.

The silence stretched, thick and heavy, as they waited, their gazes locked on Mrs. Murphy, each of them sensing that whatever she was holding back had the power to change everything.

Mrs Murphy and her daughter exchanged glances, and Delia took a sip of tea before she began.

"I think you know that Lillian had become interested in mother's early life in this country."

"Yes," said Bellamy, waiting for her to go on.

"Mother had a difficult time finding work, as she has herself told you, and when she did find a position, she was determined to make a go of it."

Mrs Murphy was pulling at her handkerchief.

"Lillian found out something at the Langford's that upset her."

Hamish, Bellamy and Rita leant forward.

"She found an old letter written by Mrs Langford to a friend and the letter included a reference for a young servant. This is the reference."

She held out a yellowed sheet of quality paper. Hamish took it and read it out to the others.

"Meg Murphy has been in my service as cook and laundress for six months. I have found her to be strictly honest, sober, clean and tidy in her kitchen and in herself. She is a good plain cook and quick in learning a new dish. Meg leaves me by her own desire, and I am sorry to part with her. Patricia Langford."

"This refers to you, Mrs Murphy?" asked Bellamy.

The older woman wrung her hands and nodded, avoiding the sergeant's eyes.

"Yes," she said quietly. "I have an exact copy that I used to gain subsequent employment.

Delia continued. "Obviously, Lillian was shocked that mother had not told us she worked for the Langford's. She asked if I had known, and I told her I had not. She was terribly worried about how mother had been treated when she came here under the assisted migration program, and she wanted to know if she had been treated poorly by the Langford's in her first position."

"This letter suggests Mrs Langford was very happy with your work, Mrs Murphy. Why was Lillian suspicious?"

"I told her Mrs Langford and Anne-Marie had been nothing but kind to me," Delia burst out. "But Lillian wouldn't let it go." She looked across at her mother tearfully.

Mrs Murphy's chin trembled. "She insisted on knowing why I stayed there only six months," she said. "She was spurred on by the lectures that Carlos Perez was giving." The older woman glanced from Hamish to Bellamy and settled her eyes on Rita.

"I suppose I could have lied to her," she said, "but how could I have known?"

Rita held Mrs Murphy's gaze and spoke gently. "Why did you leave after six months?"

Tears welled in the older woman's eyes and her face flushed. "Mr Langford came into my room one night," she said simply. Tears rolled down her cheeks and her shoulders slumped as if a burden long held had unexpectedly slipped.

Rita's eyes widened and she gripped the seat. Hamish saw that her knuckles were white.

Mrs Murphy raised her eyes to the ceiling then dropped them again. "He...well... I think you know my meaning..."

"He assaulted you?" asked Rita.

Mrs Murphy nodded, her attention now on the rug at her feet. "I thought I would die from shame. I had to get out of that house. I told Mrs Langford I had to move to the other side of Brisbane to look after an elderly relative in the evenings. She accepted my excuse without question and wrote to a friend who lived out that way to see if she might employ me as a day girl. I didn't take the position with her friend. I found something else. But I didn't tell anyone what had happened. It was too shameful. No one would have employed me, and I would never have been able to marry..."

Rita put her hand on Mrs Murphy's arm.

Hamish felt his heart pounding in his chest. He felt the woman's shame, if not difficult enough at the time, it seemed she was reliving the experience now.

"Do you think Mrs Langford knew?" Rita asked.

Mrs Murphy shook her head vigorously. "She can't have known. She would never have stood for something like that."

"And you told Lillian about this?" asked Bellamy.

"I didn't at first. But she kept asking questions. She wouldn't let it go. I thought if I told the girls, that would be the end of it. It was so long ago, and Mr Langford has been dead these last ten years."

"How did Lillian respond?" asked Rita.

Delia jumped in. "She was furious. She wanted to tell Mrs Langford. She repeated something she'd read about the mistress of the house being responsible for everything that goes on under her roof and that Mrs Langford had been negligent in her duties by not being aware and not keeping her servants safe. She was terribly worked up about it."

"Do you believe Lillian told Carlos Perez this story?"

"Yes, I believe so," said Delia.

Rita's brow furrowed. "Why did you allow Delia to work for the Langford's, and Lillian to use their studio?"

"I must admit that when Delia came home and told me she had secured a position in that house I was shocked for a moment, but the trouble was mine, not hers. And as I said, the man has been dead ten years. Mrs Langford has been kind to both the girls."

Delia added, "Mother didn't want Lillian to tell Mrs Langford. It would have been upsetting and shameful for both her and Anne-Marie. I told Lillian it wasn't her story to tell. It was mothers. But she remained determined."

"Who else knows about this?" asked Bellamy.

"No one, other than Perez, as far as we know."

"What about George?" asked Bellamy.

Delia blushed. "I didn't tell him."

"The stable manager?" asked Mrs Murphy. "Why would you tell him?"

The redness on Delia's cheeks deepened.

Mrs Murphy blinked as awareness scratched at her eyes. "Oh dear, I have not known either of my daughters," she cried.

Mother and daughter fidgeted in their chairs. They took great effort to not look one another in the eye.

"And Lillian hadn't spoken to Mrs Langford before she was killed?" said Bellamy, unwilling to slow progress in the interview, but waiting for the women to come to terms with the secrets they kept from each other.

"I don't believe so."

Bellamy looked at the ceiling for a moment, then asked, "Why are you telling us this now?"

Delia's eyes widened, tears pricking at the corners. "In case it has something to do with her death," she said.

"Do you think it might?" asked Bellamy.

"No!" Delia cried. She stood up and turned away from them. Then sat again at the edge of her seat. "It didn't seem right not saying anything."

"Who were you afraid might see you talking to us today?" asked Bellamy.

"No one." The tears began to pour freely. "I don't know," she murmured.

"You have done the right thing," said Rita gently.

"You won't say anything to Mrs Langford?" she sniffed. "I don't want to lose my job."

Bellamy watched both Delia and her mother closely. "I can't make any promises," he said. "If it is relevant to our enquiries, we will have to question both Mrs Langford and Anne-Marie about it. But at this stage, we have other lines of enquiry. It might not come to that."

They took their leave immediately, so as not to prolong the embarrassment for the two women any longer than necessary. As the weather was pleasant, they had told the driver not to wait, and they set off across the hill towards Hamish's terrace house sharing their thoughts on what this new information added to their enquiry.

"I don't know that what Delia told us changes anything," began Bellamy. "I still think that Perez killed Lillian because she was threatening to 'out' him, and Delia's fiancé, Prentice killed Perez out of revenge."

"That remains a possibility," said Hamish.

Bellamy shot him a frustrated glance, but Hamish didn't see it in the dark.

"It's not just a possibility," he said. "It's the simplest explanation, and the simple explanation is more often than not the correct one."

"Plenty of people have cause to want Perez dead," countered Hamish. "What if Perez did kill Lillian and quite separately, Alejandro killed Perez to prevent him from seeing Isabella?"

Bellamy shook his head. "I don't believe it," he said. "Alejandro only had to wait two days and he and Isabella would have been on their way to Spain. The anarchist would be well and truly out of Isabella's life."

Rita stumbled on the uneven ground and Hamish shot his arm out to support her.

"I don't think we can ignore the fact that Lillian was looking into her mother's past and uncovered a terrible secret," she said tentatively. "I'd hate to think it, but maybe Mrs Langford did know about the letter Lillian found, and she couldn't bear the idea of disgrace if the secret got out."

Hamish let go of her arm and looked at her in disbelief.

"You think Mrs Langford murdered Lillian?" he said.

"Not herself," said Rita. "We know from your forensic examination that the actual killer was male."

"Then who killed Perez?" asked Bellamy.

Rita threw her head back.

"I don't know, do I? Perhaps the same person. Maybe Mrs Langford thought Lillian told Perez about her mother's past."

"This is ludicrous," said Hamish. "There is no way Anne-Marie would be a party to anything like this."

Rita snorted. "No one said anything about Anne-Marie being involved. But really, Hamish you must remain objective about the possibilities. Just because you are infatuated..."

"I'm not infatuated..."

Rita and Bellamy both stopped. They took one look at the bewilderment in Hamish's face and burst out laughing.

"I'm not," he repeated.

Rita and Bellamy exchanged sceptical glances before they continued walking in silence each nursing their own theories. Finally, the convict-built windmill opposite Hamish's house came into view.

"We have a lot of people with motives to kill, and we can't be sure the same person committed both murders," he said. "What if we separate them and treat each as a single case. Let's start with Lillian. We know she left the exhibition at around ten, or soon after and was seen heading toward the Oddfellows, either to meet up with her sister or with Carlos Perez. Both deny seeing her. She didn't make it to the hall."

Bellamy and Rita nodded in agreement.

"At some point between Alice Street and Charlotte Street, we can assume the killer picked her up in a cab."

"We've interviewed everyone we can find who was on the streets that night, or in the pubs. No one remembers seeing her get into a cab, willingly or otherwise," said Bellamy.

"Nonetheless, that is what must have happened. We do have the fellow who saw the cab pass the hotel soon after Lillian did."

Bellamy agreed.

"Who has access to a cab?" asked Rita.

Bellamy pursed his lips. "Mrs Langford?"

"Presumably Perez could lay his hands on one should he desire it," said Hamish.

"Prentice is in charge of the stable, it wouldn't be too difficult for him to take out a rig without his employers being aware of it," added Rita.

"Of course, Alejandro could use one from Government House, although perhaps it would be more likely to be noticed."

"I've been thinking," said Rita, "Could one man have both driven the cab and kept Lillian captive all the way from Alice Street to Hamilton Reach?"

"No," said Bellamy. "He could not. We know we are looking for two people. One may have been the killer and the other simply taken along to drive."

"So, the killer had to be in a position to coerce another man to assist him," said Rita.

"That doesn't really narrow the field," said Hamish.

"Why don't we move on to Perez. Prentice is the most likely candidate there," said Bellamy.

"Unless Mrs Langford had him killed as well, to preserve her secret," put in Rita.

"That murder was more daring," said Hamish thinking aloud. "It was carried out in daylight."

They had reached the point at which Hamish was in front of his home and Bellamy and Rita needed to walk on down the hill into town. They all stopped and stood still. No one was willing to move on until they had teased out the knot they had created around the murders.

"There was a significant risk he might be seen. I wonder if someone local, who might risk being recognized would take that chance?" Bellamy said.

They all considered that.

"What links the murders?" asked Rita, "apart from the fact they occurred within two days of one another."

"Perez," said Hamish immediately.

"The Langfords," said Bellamy.

Rita's eyes grew wide. "The painting," she said.

They all recalled the theft of the painting.

"It seems obvious the painting was taken because it linked Perez to the anarchists. Who, other than Perez himself would have wanted to hide that?"

"Perez stole the painting and killed Lillian," said Bellamy. "Then Prentice murdered Perez."

"But we know Perez was at the Oddfellows, he couldn't have stolen the painting."

"He had one of his cronies do it, the one who drove the cab, no doubt. It all fits. He arranged for his friend to take the painting then pick him up in Alice Street, where they enticed the girl into the cab and drove her to the mudflats at Hamilton Reach."

"I don't know," said Hamish.

"You're always looking for the most complicated scenario, rather than the simplest one. This is what they mean about wasted resources. I think we can call the first murder closed, with Perez the killer, and concentrate on finding out who murdered Perez. Not that anyone cares much that he is dead."

"That's nothing more than conjecture on your part," said Hamish. "You have no evidence that Perez murdered Lillian."

"I have motive," said the sergeant defiantly.

"Plenty of people had motive," objected Hamish, as we have discussed ample times. Also, even if it was Perez, what about the driver who assisted him?"

"We have no chance of finding him and proving his involvement," said Bellamy. "It could be anyone."

Bellamy looked hopefully down the hill toward home. Hamish knew he had made up his mind about Lillian's murder, but Hamish wasn't sure, and by the look on Rita's face she wasn't convinced either.

"Are you ready to head home?" Bellamy asked Rita.

She shook her head.

"I might stay with Hamish a while longer and see if we can make any progress," she said.

Bellamy hesitated. He didn't relish the idea of Rita and Hamish chewing over the details of the case until late and then Rita walking home alone, but he knew better than to say so. Reluctantly he bid them good night.

"I hate suspecting Mrs Langford of involvement in this mess," Rita said when he was gone.

Hamish nodded. "The only way to exclude her is to find out if she was aware that Lillian had uncovered her mother's past in the Langford household."

"And if she knew about the abuse beforehand," added Rita. "But we promised Mrs Murphy we wouldn't tell her unless it was absolutely necessary."

Hamish shook his head.

"We didn't promise. Bellamy did."

"It is likely to cause Mrs Langford and her daughter some anguish if we bring this up," Rita warned.

"I think it's necessary if we are to eliminate Mrs Langford as a suspect in two murders. Mrs Langford is a highly respected woman in Brisbane society. If she was aware Lillian had uncovered a secret that could sully the family name and her husband's memory, she might be moved to take drastic measures. Perhaps she only intended for Lillian to be frightened, and things went too far. And I suppose it's possible Lillian told Perez the secret, so he had to go as well. Someone like Perez would not be beyond blackmail, either."

"I just can't imagine Mrs Langford doing something like that," said Rita. "But I can't discount it for sure. And I agree with you that Anne-Marie can't have known anything about any of this."

She was silent for a few minutes, then said. "We need to talk to them both. Do you want to go tomorrow?"

"First thing," said Hamish. "We're running out of time."

CHAPTER NINETEEN

A great deal has been said recently in regard to the scarcity and inferiority of female domestic servants. It is my opinion that good servants will remain scarce until mistresses alter their harsh treatment of servants. I wish to make an appeal through your valuable paper to those gentlemen who are heads of families. I would ask them to use their influence with their wives to see that their servants have proper meals at proper times and not, as is invariably the custom, for them to partake of bread and weak tea for breakfast and a few odd scraps for dinner. I would also suggest that mistresses should not speak in the loud and abusive manner they do when having occasion to find fault with their servants. If mistresses will use kindness it will make a great difference in the way they will be served in return. **The South Australia Advertiser 13 March 1889.**

***

Hamish picked up Rita the next morning at eight and they sat in the cab in a sombre mood. Neither of them relished the task they had set themselves and it felt like there was no scenario in which it wouldn't work out badly for them. Either they would deepen their suspicions that a friend arranged murder, or they would reveal a painful secret and cause untold distress to the family unnecessarily.

In addition, Hamish was acutely aware that Alejandro and Isabella would be sailing the next day, and they were running out of time if they hoped to solve the murders before they left.

Outside the cab, the sun was shining on a string of houses that stretched like beads along the crest of the hills. The brilliance of light reflecting from the corrugated iron roofing made the mood inside the cab feel worse by comparison.

"I've sent a message on to Mrs Langford to let her know we're coming," said Rita.

When Hamish didn't respond she went on.

"I think as a friend of the family, I should break the news. It will also absolve you somewhat, in Bellamy's eyes – if I am the one to break his promise to Mrs Murphy."

"I don't think it will," said Hamish slowly, still watching the people of Brisbane going about their business out of his window, "but I agree that you should do the talking." He had no wish to inform Mrs Langford of her husband's indiscretion, or to scratch a sore, if she already knew.

The housekeeper opened the door and led them into the drawing room without saying a word.

Mrs Langford and her daughter were alert and apprehensive when Hamish and Rita entered. Rita smiled at each of the women and greeted them warmly while she slipped onto the couch beside the two women, who caught one another's eye nervously as they shuffled to make room for her.

"I have something to share with you," she said.

"Have you identified Lillian's killer?" asked Anne-Marie breathlessly.

"No," said Rita. She glanced at Hamish, and he nodded for her to continue.

"But we did find out something that might be relevant, so we have to ask you about it, as unpleasant as that might be."

Both women paled and beads of sweat formed on Mrs Langford's brow.

Rita took a deep breath and went on. "Lillian discovered that her mother had once worked for you and your late husband, Mrs Langford."

Anne-Marie swung her head around to face her mother. The older woman's face was blank.

"It was when she was young, when she arrived in Australia on the assisted migration program."

Mrs Langford's eyebrows furrowed. She seemed to be searching deep into her mind for some fragment of the past she had long since put away.

Suddenly, a flicker of her eyes indicated a memory had surfaced.

"Catherine Murphy," she murmured, looking up at Rita. "Catherine Murphy is Lillian's mother?" she said incredulously.

"And Delia's."

"You didn't know mother?" cried Anne-Marie, her face flushed. Hamish wondered if Anne-Marie was hearing this for the first time.

Mrs Langford shook her head slowly, staring into space as if she were trying to see into the past.

"Catherine was a lovely girl," she said slowly, the lass still nineteen in her mind's eye. "She was a good worker and I liked her. But a relative was ill, I think. She said she had to leave. It came very suddenly."

Mrs Langford looked anxiously from Hamish to Rita. "I wrote her a reference and I tried to secure her a job in a friend's household. Day work so she could take care of her relative."

The older women searched Rita's face for some hint at what was to come. As if foreshadowing bad news she added, "She didn't accept the position with my friend. And I didn't hear of her again..."

They all sat silently for a few moments until Anne-Marie could remain quiet no longer.

"You mean to say that Lillian and Delia are this woman Catherine's, daughters? Why didn't they say anything?"

A knot formed in Hamish's throat at the confusion in Anne-Marie's voice. The news was about to become much worse, and he would've given anything not to be there when Rita shared it.

"They didn't know of the connection until quite recently," said Rita. "Lillian found an old letter, a reference you had written for her mother."

"In the letter Lillian found you refer to the servant as Meg Murphy?" Bellamy pointed out.

"Yes, that's right. Her full name is Catherine Margaret, but in those days, she went by the name Meg. She asked me to use that name on her letter of recommendation." Mrs Langford blinked. "It was so long ago."

Rita spoke gently but firmly, directing her story toward Anne-Marie, who listened eyes wide open and mouth slightly ajar.

"Lillian became curious about her mother's migration to this country and her early life in service. She persisted with her questions until her mother, reluctantly, I believe, revealed the full story."

Mrs Langford wriggled in her seat and stretched her neck, so she was gazing over Rita's head.

"Please don't," she said in a cracked whisper.

Rita sat upright so she could meet Mrs Langford's eye. But the older woman was looking somewhere beyond the room.

"Catherine left your employment suddenly because your husband sexually assaulted her," Rita said.

A gruff sound, guttural, straight from the soul made Hamish and Rita jump. Anne-Marie's hands had covered her face with a slap as the sound escaped. Her chest was heaving, but there were no sobs. Hamish thought she was struggling to breathe and gazed in panic at Rita. Consumed with his own shame at simply being a man in these circumstances, he wasn't sure he was the best person to offer comfort.

Rita put her hand on her friend's shoulder, but she shook it off immediately and stood up facing away from them.

Mrs Langford remained very still, her mouth stretched into a thin line and her hands clasped tightly in her lap. She suddenly looked old and frail.

"Sit down," she told her daughter.

Anne-Marie sat, careful to allow distance between herself and Rita on the crowded couch. Hamish noticed that she was shivering as she studied the pattern on the rug.

Mrs Langford's voice might have existed somewhere outside herself, it was so thin as she spoke. "I didn't know that happened to Catherine," she said. "But it happened to other girls. At first, I suspected, but I didn't know for sure. One girl left suddenly, as Catherine had, and it made me wonder why. But I couldn't allow myself to think...that. Friends were having difficulty keeping domestic staff as well. It wasn't just me."

She wrung her hands and her face flushed pink.

"Then, the third girl, was louder, more brash. She had an odd attitude whenever I asked her to perform a task. It was as though she was no longer an employee but had taken on some special role in the household."

She turned to Anne-Marie who was visibly shaking.

"When I spoke to your father about it, he said nothing. "Then one night I woke up and heard them together, and I knew."

"There was a hell of a row, and your father dismissed the girl claiming she had seduced him. I wasn't fooled. Your father moved into the study and slept there for the rest of his days."

Anne-Marie peered at her mother from beneath swollen eyelids. "I thought that was because father was ill," she said.

"He was ill," replied Mrs Langford. "And he passed less than twelve months later. That's why I didn't pursue the matter. We both knew he wasn't long for this world. For the sake of the family, I made sure he had a comfortable death and you and I have been able to continue our lives without scandal."

She closed her eyes.

"But I suppose such things catch up with one sooner or later. If I had known what happened to Catherine, I might have acted sooner. But then, maybe I wouldn't have. What would you and I have done? Where would we have gone?"

She looked at Anne-Marie as though waiting for acknowledgement. Some nod that would validate her choices. "My decisions were based in love," she whispered. "For you...and, if I'm to be honest, for myself."

Anne-Marie took a deep breath and looked Hamish in the eye. "So, what does this have to do with your investigation?" she demanded in a cracked voice.

Hamish struggled to remind himself of why it had seemed so necessary to harm the peace of these women in this way. He forced himself to own up to the truth. He spoke quietly but firmly.

"If you or your mother had known about this, you may have had reason to silence Lillian."

He almost choked on the words as he formed them and braced himself.

But only silence followed. Both women seemed caught in their own thoughts.

"Did you know?" asked Rita in little more than a whisper.

Anne-Marie looked like a rabbit caught in a snare. She opened her mouth to object -but closed it again before any sound escaped.

"Lillian told you, didn't she?" said Hamish.

Anne-Marie shot a glance at her mother who had crumpled into the couch in defeat.

"She confronted me in the afternoon, before the art exhibition," she said. "She was angry that mother had not done more to ensure her mother's safety. I tried to reassure her. I wanted to say she was lying but somehow the words wouldn't come out of my mouth. I felt ashamed, like maybe I had known even when I was little but didn't want to face it. She said that there was wickedness in this house, and I believed her – at least there was when Father was alive."

"What happened after the argument?" asked Hamish.

Anne-Marie looked up stunned.

"Nothing happened. We all went to the exhibition that evening."

"Did you speak with your mother about the argument?"

Anne-Marie looked across at her mother who seemed to have physically shrunk in size since they arrived. Her eyes were blank.

"No," said Anne-Marie. "The truth is, there was something about the story that rang true. I remember being little and noticing my father tugging at the girls' skirts, playfully, you know? I remember hearing sounds I didn't understand coming from the parlour, and the maid's rooms. As an only child, I was always wandering the house, pretending, telling stories in my head."

She looked at Rita directly.

"I just needed to calm down. We had all worked so hard for the exhibition, and despite everything I think Lillian was excited to see her painting among the others. I was going to talk to Lillian the next day. But then..."

Hamish watched her closely. Then his eyes shifted to Mrs Langford, slumped in the chair, her face blank. He believed that Mrs Langford hadn't known about Catherine at the time, whatever she may have suspected later. And he believed Anne-Marie when she said she intended to talk to Lillian the next day. He was deeply sorry for the pain the interview had caused, but he was adamant the story had to be told. He wondered if the news would quell any romantic feelings

Anne-Marie had for him, just when he was beginning to feel his chest flutter when he was around her.

"We'll leave you alone," said Rita.

She stood and put a hand-out to place on Anne-Marie's shoulder. Her friend didn't shrug her hand away this time. Instead, she placed her own hand, palm down on top of it. Neither woman looked at them as they left the house. They passed the housekeeper, who had clearly been listening from the adjoining room, and deflected her icy glare as they went.

"I hope I haven't lost a friend," said Rita while they waited on the road for the cab to return.

Hamish sighed, unable to articulate his feelings for Anne-Marie, especially not to Rita.

"She may come round," said Rita. She looked at him as though she understood without him telling her and smiled. She took his arm and squeezed.

"At least we can be reasonably certain they didn't know about Catherine, at least not until the eve of her death. There wouldn't have been time to arrange her murder."

"I can't believe I ever thought it possible," said Rita. "Neither of those women are capable of murder - or of arranging a murder."

"Anyone is capable, under the right circumstances," said Hamish.

When the cab arrived, Hamish directed the driver to let Rita off at the Lady Bowen Lying-In Hospital, then he travelled on to the police station. He wasn't looking forward to telling Bellamy what he'd done.

CHAPTER TWENTY

If I had the selection of a corps of detectives, I should pick out men who are known as lucky. Certain men are thus characterized. I have worked alongside officers who were as sharp and keen as men ever become, who were persevering and tireless, who had the pluck of a warrior and the patience of a dove, and yet they were "down on their luck," as the saying goes; that is the big things passed them by and fell into the hands of others. In detective work one must have courage and judgement. One must be shrewd and sharp. But if a detective is working a blind trail, the rest must be left to luck. And the luck and ill-luck of detective life is something wonderful. The luck we hear of everyday. The ill-luck is suppressed as much as possible. **Murray Advertiser Saturday 13 July 1889.**

***

When he walked in, Bellamy looked up from a mountain of paperwork.

"I need your report on the autopsy of Carlos Perez," he said.

Hamish was in no mood to argue about paperwork. "Didn't Jan leave it on your desk?"

"He left his notes typed up. What I want from you is the Statement of Particulars completed and with your signature."

"I told you he was attacked with an axe to his skull. Nothing challenging in it."

"Yes, but I need the paperwork just the same, with all the details complete. Anyway, where have you been?"

Hamish moved a pile of folders off a seat so he could sit down.

"That's something I need to talk to you about," he said.

Bellamy pushed his chair back, so it rested against the wall balancing on two legs. His pencil went instinctively to his mouth while he waited.

"Rita and I went to see the Langford's," he said.

Bellamy's eyes narrowed.

"Rita thought...that is, we thought..."

Bellamy's jaw tightened.

"We thought it essential to the case to ascertain whether or not Mrs Langford or Anne-Marie had known about Catherine's connection to their family, and the...secret...as it were."

Bellamy crashed his chair forward on all four legs.

"You did what?"

Hamish bit his lip.

"I made a promise to the Murphy women," he hissed through clenched teeth.

Hamish continued to chew his lip.

Bellamy let out a frustrated groan. "You've made me look a fool." He threw his shoulders back and threw his pencil down so hard onto the table, it ricocheted off and hurtled toward the door. He sat seething for several minutes while Hamish waited. Then he spoke. "And did they?" he barked.

Hamish blinked. "What?"

"Did they know?" Bellamy barked louder, as though Hamish's difficulty in understanding the question resided in impaired hearing.

Having come to terms with the change in direction the conversation was taking, and grateful for it, he said, "Anne-Marie did. Mrs Langford didn't."

Bellamy took a few more deep breaths and spoke in a calmer tone.

"How did Anne-Marie find out?"

"Lillian confronted her, Friday afternoon before the art exhibition. They argued, but Anne-Marie says she knew in her heart it was true and was going to tell Lillian so on Saturday. But, of course, she didn't get that chance."

"You believe her?"

"I do."

"That takes us around a merry-go-round and back again, doesn't it," he huffed. "You two can tell Mrs Murphy and Delia what you've done," he said. "I hope that girl doesn't lose her job over it."

Bellamy took the next pile of papers waiting in a box at the edge of his desk and slammed them down in front of him. He put his head down and purposefully ignored Hamish.

Back in his own office, Hamish settled into completing the Statement of Particulars in relation to the death of Carlos Perez. The cause of death was simple. The identity of the latest person to see him alive was not. It could have been any of the workers present that day, or it could have been all of them. He wished he had been more precise in his questioning at the time. He knew it mattered little to the outcome of the investigation because most of the workers said they had seen Perez after their tea break. But partly because he was irritable with Bellamy and partly because he needed to know exactly who the last person was, he went to the front counter and asked Pennyweather to return to the aquarium. He told him he needed to stay until he identified exactly which of the workers had seen Carlos Perez working on the fence line prior to his death. He wanted the name of the absolute last person to see him alive. He told the constable he refused to fudge the paperwork simply to appease Bellamy and the administrators. Pennyweather blinked a few times in rapid succession but left for the aquarium to carry out the instruction.

After that, Hamish felt there was nothing more he could accomplish hanging around the office where Bellamy's bad mood might return at any moment. He was uncomfortable about going behind his friend's back, but he wasn't sorry. At some level the sergeant must know he was right. While Hamish may have been wrong to break the sergeant's promise, Bellamy was wrong to have made it in the first place. Hamish knew that when it came down to it, the sergeant knew as well as he did that every lead had to be explored in a murder enquiry. Perhaps he'd even done Bellamy a favour in revealing the secret without him having to be there for the unpleasant conversation. Deciding this was the best way to view the situation, he headed home early to think through his next steps.

Wallace poured them both a sherry and they sat companionably in the drawing room. "I removed the scuff from the settee today," he said.

Hamish glanced across at the blue velvet seat in the bay window. "Rita's boots?"

Wallace nodded.

They both rolled their eyes, but there was a wide grin on Wallace's face. Hamish managed to lift his mouth at one corner as Red climbed onto his lap. He twirled his fingers in the coppery hair and thought about how much he missed being in the house. When he was running the general practice, he was at home most of the time. There was a dreariness about going into an office every-day that weighed on him. There had been a comradery between himself and Bellamy when he'd been a consultant assisting him in investigations that wasn't the same when he worked with the sergeant as his boss.

Hamish was wallowing in the peace and quiet of his home when a knock on the door shook Red out of a blissful sleep and made him sit upright, sniffing the air. Hamish glanced across at Wallace with resignation.

Red seemed to know who was at the door before Wallace reached it, because his tail was wagging in spirals.

Footsteps clattered up the stairs and the cheerful voice of Rita chatting with Wallace echoed in the stairwell. But the footsteps told of more than one visitor. As they turned into the drawing room, Hamish was surprised to see Bellamy.

Wallace darted about getting glasses and another bottle of sherry while the guests settled. Rita flopped onto the velvet settee and raised her feet. A glare from Wallace stopped her mid-movement. She placed her feet back on the floor with a prim glance at Hamish.

"Staying for dinner?" asked Wallace.

Red scurried about greeting the visitors and then ran back and forth between Hamish and Wallace. Rita called him over and plucked his little body up, bundling him onto the settee. Hamish went to object but closed his mouth and huffed instead. Red, who knew full well he wasn't allowed on the velvet couch, turned in several circles before curling himself into a self-satisfied ball of wiry hair.

"Why not?" said Bellamy. "With Agatha away I haven't been eating well. A home cooked meal might be just the ticket."

Rita didn't need to answer. She was such a regular fixture in the house, particularly for meals, there was no doubt she was staying. Wallace went downstairs to prepare their dinner.

"I think we need to focus the investigation," said Bellamy. "It's clear to me that Perez murdered Lillian and then Prentice killed Perez."

"It remains a possibility," said Rita, "but hardly the only one."

"It's the simplest solution," said Bellamy.

Hamish was carefully formulating a response in his mind. He wasn't convinced, but he didn't want to offend Bellamy while their relationship was sensitive. As he was about to speak, there was another knock at the door. This time Red flew from the couch and shot down the stairs barking.

Wallace was in the kitchen downstairs, behind the practice rooms. They heard him go to the door and a few minutes later he appeared at the top of the stairs with the guest.

"Delia!" Hamish cried.

Both Hamish and Bellamy stood up to take her hand in greeting. Rita smiled.

"Sit down," said Hamish. "Will you have a drink with us?"

Delia took the glass from Wallace shyly.

"How may we help you?" Hamish asked.

Delia held the glass with two hands. "I wanted to let you know that mother and I met with Mrs Langford and Anne-Marie for tea this afternoon."

Hamish blushed to the roots of his sandy hair.

"They were lovely," Delia rushed to reassure him. "Mrs Langford apologized profusely for what had happened to mother and for not doing more to protect her. Both women were terribly upset about it all. But we all agreed that the past was best left in the past and we are all stronger women now. The best part is – I still have my job."

"That's wonderful news," said Rita.

"Splendid," agreed Hamish.

Bellamy smiled, with what looked to be both genuine delight and relief.

"The loss of Lillian has hit us terribly," Delia went on. "Something that happened thirty years ago, as vile as it was, seems less significant in the light of our loss. We all cried at the thought of what my poor sister went through. She must have been terrified."

Everyone was silent.

"Are you feeling up to answering some more questions that might help us with the investigation?" asked Bellamy.

Delia wiped a single tear from her cheek.

"Of course, if it means finding out who did this awful thing."

"We were wondering what your fiancé thought of Perez."

Delia's eyes were moist and glassy.

"He admired him in the beginning. He talked me into joining the meetings because he thought so highly of him."

"Then?"

Delia stared over Rita's head and out of the bay window.

"Then, he saw that Lillian was taken with Perez. He wanted me to intervene, convince Lillian to stop seeing him. But it wouldn't have done any good. She was obsessed with him. And she thought he could help her find out more about what it was like for mother all those years ago.

She used her time at the Langford home to sneak around. I don't even think she enjoyed painting, and she wasn't very good. Anne-Marie encouraged her because she's kind. I told Lillian that Anne-Marie and her mother were good to me. I like working there."

Rita gave the girl a sympathetic smile.

"Where did you get the silver badge that belonged to Perez?" She asked gently.

"I found it in Lillian's purse. I was looking for a clean handkerchief and I knew she always carried one in her purse. When I pulled it out the badge fell to the floor. I immediately recognized it, I'd seen Perez wearing it on his cap, but only at the meetings. He always removed the cap when he went outside. Anyway, I didn't want mother to see it. And I suppose I resented Lillian's obsession with the man. So, I took it and threw it in my drawer at the Langford house. I'd forgotten it was there."

"Did you recognize the symbolism?" Rita said.

"No. But I showed it to Prentice, and he told me. He'd read about the Spanish Anarchists, and he thought Perez must be running from the authorities in his country."

"Where was Prentice when Perez was killed?"

Delia's eyes grew wide. Her voice was shaking when she answered. "He was working," she said croakily. "But I didn't see him. You would have to check with Mrs Langford, or the stableboys."

Her eyes shifted from Hamish to Rita to Bellamy. Her face twisted in sudden, overwhelming terror, her eyes wide and unblinking as though she'd seen something beyond comprehension.

"You don't think he killed Perez, do you?" she whispered.

No one spoke at first, then Hamish said, "Do you think he could have killed him?"

Her face was as white as a sheet.

"I have to go," she said, putting down the glass of sherry. She hurried downstairs with Hamish struggling to keep pace. He opened the door for her, and she rushed from the house like she was being chased by wild horses.

"No prizes for guessing where she's headed," said Rita.

Hamish slowly shook his head.

"We'll have to interview Prentice more formally, no one can give him a firm alibi for the morning of Perez's death. And we need to speak again with Alejandro," he said. "He and the countess sail tomorrow afternoon. They'll be boarding by lunchtime."

Bellamy whistled through pursed lips.

"We can't prevent them from sailing," he said. "Even if we suspect Alejandro of murder, it would be a difficult thing to bring charges. He and the countess are members of the Spanish Royal family, for God's sake. And guests of the Governor and Lady Musgrave!"

"Even so," said Hamish.

"For all our sakes, I hope you're wrong, Hamish."

The sergeant shook his head vigorously and placed his empty glass on the occasional table.

"It's late and we have a busy morning ahead of us," he said. "I'll see you first thing."

Wallace led the sergeant to the door.

When the old man returned, Hamish was staring into his glass.

He cleaned away the glasses and carefully removed the one Hamish was holding.

Hamish didn't move. He listened to the clanking of glass as Wallace stacked their dinner plates and glasses downstairs.

Without really knowing how he got there, Hamish found himself at the door pulling on his coat.

"You're not going out at this time, are you?"

Hamish started at the sound of Wallace's voice.

"It's not that late, is it?"

"Where are you going that can't be left until morning?"

Hamish sighed.

"I feel terrible about the pain I caused Anne-Marie and her mother," he said watching the clear blue eyes of his friend.

"But Delia said they had settled their differences, and she has still had her job."

"I know, but the pain will still be there. And I caused it."

The older man's eyes softened. "You're worried about how Anne-Marie feels about you, now."

Hamish opened his mouth to deny it, but no sound came. He thought about taking off his coat and going back upstairs to bed.

"There won't be time to see her tomorrow," he said. "We need to bring this investigation to a conclusion, at least in relation to the countess and her cousin, before they sail. I fear that leaving it another day or two might cement any ill feeling..."

"Go," said Wallace. He smiled and his eyes crinkled at the corners. "It's never too late in the evening for an apology. But beware of that old dragon housekeeper at the Langford House. She'll not be happy about having to open the door to suitors in her nightgown and slippers."

Again, Hamish opened his mouth to protest but didn't bother. He stepped out into the night. The walk to Bowen Terrace took him past row upon row of worker's cottages. Most of them were dark and lifeless at this time of night. The absence of gas streetlamps left the path dim, with only the pale light of a full moon overhead casting long shadows before him. He calculated that it must be at least ten by the time he was crunching his way up the gravel driveway. He wondered whether he was on a fool's errand turning up at this time of night to apologize. He would be more likely to make things worse than find himself forgiven. They would probably send him away. But he wouldn't be able to sleep if he didn't see Anne-Marie that night. He recognized the desire as irrational and berated himself for it. But there was no chance of him turning back.

Several windows were lit with gaslighting when he crunched up the gravel pathway to the big house. At least some members of the household must still be awake. He knocked on the door several times before he saw the foyer light blink on. The housekeeper did, indeed, open the door in her nightgown with a nightcap covering her hair. A look of thunder met Hamish. The woman appeared even more terrifying backlit from behind.

"I was hoping to speak with Miss Langford," said Hamish with all the courage he could muster.

"I was hoping to marry the Duke of Wellington," barked the housekeeper. "But that's not going to happen either."

She stepped back to slam the door, but Hamish grabbed the edge and held it.

"It's urgent," he said. He could hear the rush of his heart pounding in his ears. His inexplicable desperation to see Anne-Marie gripping him like a vice. He saw the flicker of resolve melt in the housekeeper's eyes, and he hoped she mistook his anxiety for professional zeal and assumed he had something urgent to convey about the murder investigation.

She opened the door and stood aside.

"Wait there," she ordered as he stepped into the foyer.

Hamish waited, shifting nervously from one foot to the other while the housekeeper scurried off.

It was at least ten minutes before she came back down the stairs alone. His heart skipped a beat while he braced himself for the inevitable send off.

But the housekeeper didn't send him packing, she led him to the library and told him to sit. "Miss Langford is not used to taking visitors at this hour," she said gruffly. "You'll need to wait."

With that, she left the room, grumbling that she was returning to bed and to hell with the lot of them if they were going to encourage visitors at this hour of the night.

Hamish waited. He usually rehearsed what he was going to say in situations that were awkward, but in this instance, he had no idea what he would say at all. That he had turned up at this time of night surprised him as much as it would have done anyone else. What the poor girl would say was anyone's guess. She would expect him to have news of the murders, and he had none. He had only a half thought out apology for the pain he had caused.

Anne-Marie finally appeared at the top of the stairs clad in a house gown that flowed softly from her shoulders in folds. She stopped for a moment watching him, before she walked down, her back straight, head held high, slowly, gracefully. The pale blue silk of her gown shimmered in the dim light. When she stood before him, he couldn't shift his eyes from the way her hair, neatly pinned back, accentuated the contours of her face. Her eyes, expressive and brown, met his with a gaze that was both frail and resolute. Her skin was like porcelain and a quiet strength shone from within her. But there was a subtle tension in her frame. Hamish searched her face, and a flicker of uncertainty passed over her features.

She motioned for him to sit, and she sat opposite. He waited a moment for her to speak, to ask him why he had come, to object to the lateness of the hour. But she was silent. Her hands were held calmly in her lap, while she watched him. They might have sat there like that all night if Hamish hadn't finally taken the initiative.

"I'm so sorry," he began.

Anne-Marie tilted her head to one side.

"For what?"

"For hurting you, and your mother, for causing pain, for making you cry..."

He realized he was babbling and stopped.

Anne-Marie watched him carefully for a moment and then her lip curled into a small smile.

"Hamish, you didn't cause us pain. You revealed a truth that caused us shame and unhappiness, but the cause of that pain wasn't you. It was my father, and it was a lifetime of pretending something awful wasn't happening, didn't happen."

A knot formed in his throat. "I came because I couldn't sleep without knowing...without asking if what I said changed...our friendship..."

Anne-Marie's face opened into a broad smile. Her eyes glistened. Soft brown curls, pulled back from her face, fell onto her shoulders.

"Nothing you could say could change our...friendship," she said. She was laughing at him now. Small, sweet chuckles that warmed his heart. Suddenly, her lips seemed irresistible to him. He leant forward to kiss away the quiet laughter.

She leant into him, and Hamish felt the anxiety melt away.

They settled into the couch, his arm around her shoulders, and her head resting against his chest. Hamish listened to her soft breathing. He smelt the lavender oil in her hair. He would have believed himself intoxicated if any alcohol had passed his lips. She reached out and took his hand, holding it in her hers. Warmth flooded through him, and he wanted to stay forever on that couch, her body curled into his.

But with a jolt, his senses returned and reminded him he was in a woman's arms, in her home, late at night. This wasn't acceptable, no matter how willingly the woman held him.

"I must leave you now," he said.

"Will you be able to sleep?" she whispered.

He kissed her head. "I will sleep," he said.

She uncurled herself and stood up. "Catch the killer tomorrow, my darling doctor."

She stood on her toes and kissed his cheek. "Good night."

Back in his own bed, in his own home, Hamish couldn't believe he had done something so rash as to turn up to a woman's house at ten o'clock in the evening. He thought about the kiss, about the way it made his head spin, about the way he felt safe with her. There was a split second in which his brain whispered, "What about Rita?" But he smiled. Rita would be happy. She loved them both.

CHAPTER TWENTY-ONE

A voyage to the Antipodes is in the present day not the terrible undertaking it was 30 years ago. From London, Liverpool, Glasgow and other British ports numerous vessels sail at regular and short intervals both to Australia and New Zealand. There are also three district lines of subsidized steamers, which carry Her Majesty's Mails and keep up monthly communication with the different colonies. Each of these lines conveys passengers. The oldest established, and perhaps favourite of the three is that of the Peninsula and Oriental Company, whose contract time to Melbourne from Southampton is about 54 days and from London via Brindisi is about 46 days. Of late the service has generally been performed several days under the contract time.

Sailing ships have occasionally done the distance in 70 days or less; but the smartest clipper cannot make any progress in the teeth of adverse winds and enjoys no immunity against the possibility of being becalmed in the tropics for a fortnight. No one should embark for Australia in a sailing vessel without being fully resigned to the prospect of not getting there in less than three calendar months, and he may be a month longer without any fault on the part of the ship or crew. A good steamship is greatly preferred to a sailing vessel for a long voyage. **Australian Town and Country Journal Saturday 16 August 1879.**

***

Friday brought one of those crisp mornings when the sky dazzles, but the air is still cool. Anticipation vibrated in the air as Hamish hurried to the police station to meet Bellamy. It was almost as if the events of the night before hadn't happened, but he felt more focused than he had in a long time. He was acutely aware that he only had a couple of hours to determine, to his own satisfaction, whether Alejandro had been involved in either the murder of Lillian or of Carlos Perez. He doubted his involvement in the first but was almost certain of his involvement in the second. Once the ship sailed with the noble family aboard, he may never get to the truth.

Bellamy was already in his office when Hamish arrived.

"Meet us at the wharf in three hours," he told Pennyweather. "Isabella and Alejandro will be boarding by then, and regardless of what we find out in the next couple of hours, we will all be there to see them off."

Hamish caught the sergeant's eye.

"I pray there's nothing to your theory," Bellamy says. "This could become a political nightmare."

"I hope it isn't as bad as that," said Hamish.

"I don't think you comprehend the ramifications. I haven't even told the commissioner we are going to interview Alejandro and Isabella. If the Governor takes offence, both you and I will be out of a job."

A thought occurred to Hamish. "What if you're not involved?"

Bellamy frowned and stared at Hamish as though he'd gone mad.

Hamish felt the idea grow. "What if Rita and I go to Government House alone?"

Bellamy continued to stare.

"You don't need to be there. In fact, Alejandro is more likely to be open if I speak with him alone. You needn't know anything about it, officially. Rita has a friendship with the countess. Nothing would be more natural than a woman visiting her friend to bid her farewell."

Bellamy turned the plan over in his mind. "If it goes wrong, you'll lose your job," he says. "I won't hold enough sway to save it."

"I know," said Hamish. He knew as he said it that he didn't care.

Bellamy was about to voice further misgivings when Rita arrived.

"It's just us," Hamish said as he bundled her out before Bellamy could stop them. They caught a cab rather than the Police vehicle so as not to implicate the sergeant.

Hamish felt a tickle up his spine as he realized Rita was staring at him. He shuffled in his seat and turned to her.

"Why are you looking at me like that?"

She was grinning from ear to ear and shoved her shoulder into his.

"Ouch! What are we, children?" he cried.

"I heard from Anne-Marie this morning," she said, her smile morphing into a cheeky grin.

"How did you hear so soon?"

"Don't worry. I'm thrilled. I think she'll be good for you."

Hamish drew his fingers around his collar in an attempt to address the prickling feeling.

"We need to focus on the investigation this morning," he said abruptly. "We've almost run out of time to get to the bottom of these murders."

Rita neatened her skirt and sat up straight.

"Right. Focus."

Then she broke out into another broad grin, which he caught in the corner of his eye, unwilling as he was to look directly at her again.

When their knock was answered at Government House, the housekeeper was red faced and flustered.

"The household is at sixes and sevens with preparations for the departure of the countess," she told them. She directed Hamish to the library to wait for Alejandro, while she sent the house maid to the countess' chamber to ask if she would receive the lady doctor. Hamish left Rita waiting in the hall, confident the countess would see her.

The library was no less grand and imposing than the first time he had been there, but he was less nervous this time and took the time to take in the opulence. High arched windows allowed streams of natural light to filter in casting a warm glow across the walls. Floor to ceiling bookshelves were filled with volumes bound in rich burgundy, green and brown leather, their spines worn from use. The desk, polished to a deep shine, was adorned with an ornate brass lamp, a quill and inkwell, and the scent of aged leather hung in the air. Hamish pressed his boots into a thick Persian rug, its colours muted by time, while in sat in one of the two overstuffed armchairs flanked by a fireplace that looked like it had never been used. Portraits of colonial men, officers in bright uniforms, looked down upon him with disdain as he braced himself for the conversation he would have to have with Don Alejandro.

Soon the Spaniard joined Hamish in the library with more cheer and enthusiasm than Hamish had seen from him yet. His high spirits may well have been linked to his anticipated departure, but Hamish couldn't help thinking that the death of Carlos Perez had contributed, regardless of whether he had a hand in his demise or not.

"Good morning to you, my friend," he said.

"Good day to you," said Hamish. "There is a spring in your step this morning. I'm sorry to disturb preparations for your departure."

"Not at all, doctor. While I am looking forward to the voyage, I can honestly say that making your acquaintance was a highlight of my stay in this budding colony."

He smiled showing the whitest teeth Hamish had ever seen and he realized he had not seen Alejandro properly smile before.

Hamish decided the only way to proceed was to come to the point. "I'm glad your problem with the countess has been resolved," he said, his throat dry.

Alejandro lifted an eyebrow. "It is indeed fortunate, in one way," he said. "Although, less so for Carlos Perez I think."

"Indeed," agreed Hamish.

"I have the sense there is something you wish to ask." Alejandro sat down opposite Hamish as he spoke.

Hamish looked into his dark eyes for a long while.

"It's perfectly alright," Alejandro prompted. "Naturally you would suspect me of removing the anarchist. It improves all our lives to be rid of him. He is merely vermin in the eyes of the Spanish Royal Family."

Hamish spoke quietly but firmly. "I trust you understand the seriousness of the matter at hand."

A smirk spread across the nobleman's handsome face. "Oh, doctor, I must commend your tenacity in this matter. It is refreshing to see someone as committed to their duty, even when the task is...impossible."

Hamish leant forward, his voice steady. "I don't believe in impossibilities. I believe in justice. And justice does not discriminate."

Alejandro chuckled. "Justice? How quaint. Tell me, what does justice mean to a man of your station when it comes to a man of mine? Even if I had lifted a finger against Carlos Perez there would be nothing you could do about it."

The colour drained from Hamish's face, but he persisted. "You speak as though you are above the law. But every man, regardless of birth, answers to it."

He sounded far more confident in his words than he felt.

Alejandro laughed openly. "Above the law? No, no, my friend. Not above it, merely protected by it. Your government would not cause a diplomatic rift between England and Spain over something as trivial as the death of an anarchist. The King of England himself would intervene."

Hamish watched him closely. "Did you kill Perez?" he said calmly.

Alejandro spun his face away from Hamish, lit up a cigarette and turned back to him holding out an engraved silver cigarette box.

Hamish shook his head.

Alejandro drew in a long breath of tobacco. "I did not," he said.

"Do you know who did kill Perez?" asked Hamish.

At this, Alejandro hesitated. "Not with any certainty," he said.

"If you know anything, you are obliged to share the information with us, so we can put this matter to rest."

The Spanish nobleman stood up and strode to the window to look out over the lawn. Turning slowly back toward Hamish, he said, "let it go, my friend. There is nothing more you can do."

He stubbed the cigarette in the lid of the silver case. "I wish you well," he said and left the room.

Hamish watched him leave, wondering what if anything, he had learned. Alejandro knew, or at least suspected, something. Of that he was certain. He didn't believe he had any hand in the death of Lillian Murphy. It was entirely beyond a man of his breeding to rape and murder a woman at the edge of a river, in a foot of mud. He may have his own set of moral standards based on entitlement, but he couldn't even see him ordering the death of a young woman. But Perez? He was convinced Alejandro had some involvement in the killing of the anarchist.

Were the two murders necessarily linked? He couldn't count the number of times he had asked himself that question in the last week. Yet, it seemed impossible to believe that they were not. As for Alejandro, he was right, Hamish had no evidence to charge him with any crime, and even if he did, it is unlikely the authorities would pursue a charge. If the death of the anarchist had been the only consideration, he may well have accepted that this was one case in which the killer had gotten away. But he could not let the death of Lillian go without punishment. If only he could see precisely how they were linked.

CHAPTER TWENTY-TWO

One of the first duties of a woman is to be beautiful. She may not possess beauty of form or face, but she may charm by her graceful appearance, her daily accessories and well-chosen toilet, which will enhance the good points and conceal the defects. She may be attractively and becomingly attired so that she will gain more admiration than one who possess the charm of natural beauty without the advantages of dress.

A woman who dresses well and suitably does not necessarily spend all her time and thought on the subject; it does not occupy more time to select a becoming gown than an unbecoming one. What is strictly required is careful attention to form and colour and the exercise of that taste and judgement which in some women is innate. **Fitzroy Press Friday 10 May 1889**

***

Isabella de la Vega

Isabella glanced around the room that had been her sanctuary for the past week. The high ceilings, the delicate plasterwork, the soft range of creams in the damask wallpaper. Above her head hung a crystal chandelier that threw a soft light across the room. She was sitting on the grand four poster bed, on the delicately embroidered coverlet in navy and gold. There was a large gold leaf framed mirror above the dresser, and a matching wardrobe against the wall, its doors inlaid with fine marquetry. A writing desk sat in the corner, but rather than her notes so full of desire and anticipation, on top of it sat a vase of bulbous hydrangeas. Pretty though they were, they felt like an insult in her present mood.

The last of her personal items had been carefully packed and a mountain of cases stood by the door. Soon it would be as though she had never been in the room. All the swirling emotions of ecstatic love, expectation and hope, mingled with the deep lows of loss, defeat and hopelessness, all caught in this room, as if they would live there forever. But they wouldn't remain, she knew they wouldn't. The minute she left the room, it would revert to being nothing more than a space in which the next visitor could deposit the fruits of their soul. Emptiness is all the room contained.

Suddenly, a sense of freedom she'd not experienced in more than a year came over her. She rose from the depths of grief to feel stronger, lighter. It occurred to her that the man had never been what she'd made of him. It was her who had created the figure of heroic proportions in her mind. In reality, he was nothing more than a man, weak and stupid. While the affair was passionate to the point of consuming her, her feelings had proven to be superficial. Such passion had weighed her down, dulled her thoughts, impaired her ability to function. She was glad to be leaving this place. She looked up and stared at the plaster rose on the ceiling. She was tired of travelling and didn't relish the idea of the long journey home by sea, but she couldn't help thinking it may yet bring new adventures now that she was free of her infatuation with the anarchist.

She barely noticed the knock on the door, so engrossed was she in her reflections. A small maid with a white cap peeped in. It wasn't her own maid, she was at the ship already, checking that everything was ready for her arrival.

"There's a lady doctor what wishes to speak with you m'am," said the maid. "Says 'er name is Rita Cartwright."

Isabella sat up and thought about whether to accept the visitor. She was bored waiting for it to be time to board the vessel, so she ran her fingers through her hair and said, "See her up."

A few moments later, the lady doctor joined her in the chamber.

"How kind of you to come," said Isabella with a politeness that lacked warmth. She'd spent her entire life training to be pleasant toward company. She would do her duty, but in her heart, she had already departed this place. Everything that happened now was an inconvenient formality until she was on the ship and on her way home.

"I couldn't allow you to leave without conveying my best wishes for your journey," said Rita.

Isabella smiled a tight smile.

At that moment the doctor's eyes turned cold.

"I'm sorry for your loss," said Rita quietly, "I believe the anarchist meant something to you."

Isabella's eyes flickered. A dark cloud descended over them. How dare this colonial woman presume to know her emotions, her secrets. But she maintained her composure. That was, after all, her greatest skill.

"It seems our little affair has become more well-known than I thought," she said steadily. "I suppose it will be the talk of the colony."

She looked up under her long eyelashes at Rita.

"It is so much ado about nothing, I'm afraid. A mere dalliance, a flutter." Isabella held her thin white hand up before her face and examined her impeccably manicured nails. "It is of no importance."

She watched Rita closely from the corner of her eye. Did the doctor believe her? What if she didn't? It was of no consequence what that woman thought of her. The interaction had become tiresome, and she wished she had not agreed to see her.

"I apologise," said Rita. "I should not have presumed..."

The countess stood up from the bed and went to her dressing table. "I have so much to do prior to my departure," she said. "Thank-you again for your kindness, but you do understand?" She waved at the door with a dismissive gesture.

Rita didn't stand. "I believe he died in a most brutal way."

The countess turned to face her. She felt the tears welling in her eyes and her hands shaking. Damn this woman for forcing the rise of these emotions she had held in check so carefully. She didn't trust herself to speak. She simply willed that the woman would leave her alone.

The doctor was observing her carefully, she would have surely noted the slackening of the jaw, the lips that trembled. The physical signs that betrayed her words. She swallowed several times in succession before she trusted her vocal cords to work.

"Get out," she said in a dry whisper.

This time the woman rose and left, but not without an infuriating glance backward, full of knowing...

CHAPTER TWENTY-THREE

Most flattered and least trusted of the race,
Dropped for a whim and followed for a face,
Loved for their follies, their devotion scorned,
In presence slighted and in absence mourned,
Their hearts, their characters by men abused,
Who never think help should be refused,
Presented by Kings and trampled in the mire,
The best and worst they equally inspire.
Cursed for their weaknesses, hated when they're strong,
Whatever happens, always in the wrong.
Tact is their genius. And yet one thing more,
Woman is lost when woman is a bore.
The Week Brisbane Saturday 27 October 1888

***

When Hamish left the mansion, Rita was already standing by the cab waiting for him. The people of Brisbane were rushing by on their way to work and to shop at the many stores opening their doors for the day. The sunlight stung Hamish's eyes as he stepped out. He put on his hat and tipped it low to shade his eyes. He was glad he didn't have to wait for Rita.

"Did you find anything out from Alejandro?

"He is an arrogant man, that's for sure," he began. He may have had Perez killed, but if he didn't, I think he has a good idea who did. How did your farewell with Isabella go?"

Rita looked puzzled.

"I'm not sure," she said. "She threw me out."

Hamish gestured for Rita to climb into the cab first. He assisted her up the step and then climbed in after her.

"She seemed like a different person," Rita went on. "The Isabella we met at the exhibition was warm and open. But today she was cold and dismissive. I can't decide which version is the real Isabella. I have to say, though that this morning's version gave me a chill. There is a dark soul behind that beauty. I suspect, the more I think about it, that today I met the Countess Isabella de la Vega for the first time."

"We should head to the wharf," said Hamish. "This ship is going to sail and there's not going to be anything we can do to stop it.

The wharf was as busy as Hamish had ever seen it. Three ships edged against the wooden barrier, greenish water lapping irritably between hull and dock. Workers bustled back and forth loading and unloading cargo, as crates, barrels and various goods were transported on and off the ships. The air was filled with the sounds of shouting workers, creaking ropes and seagulls. The steamer that would carry the countess was at the front of the row. It had several decks and three towering smokestacks.

Hamish and Rita found Bellamy standing toward the bow of the steamer watching. They filled him in on their visit with Alejandro and the countess. There was nothing concrete to add to the investigation.

Bellamy nodded.

"I didn't think we would find out much," he said. "They have no incentive to open up to us now, even if they are involved."

Hamish thought the sergeant looked somewhat relieved.

Passenger's luggage was beginning to appear in a tall stack to the left of the gangway.

As they stood there watching the crew gather bags to be transported onto the ship, Mateo appeared, shuffling luggage from the carriageway to the wharf.

"Those boxes belong to Isabella," said Rita. "I saw them in her chambers."

Hamish and Bellamy watched the pile grow as if in a trance. Mateo hadn't noticed them standing there when he picked up the first of the boxes. He gathered up two expensive suitcases and tucked a small parcel wrapped in paper and string under his arm.

Suddenly, Hamish left the others and rushed forward.

"Mateo," he cried.

The footman stopped and turned to see Hamish coming at him like he had seen a fire. Mateo stopped and stood struggling to keep hold of the luggage.

"The package," Hamish said, a little too urgently, his hand held out toward the wrapped parcel.

Immediately Mateo's eyes went dark, and he dropped one of the suitcases.

"What of it?" he said taking a firmer hold of the parcel.

"May I see what's inside?"

Mateo tucked the parcel firmly under his arm and retrieved the suitcase.

"Certainly not." He stepped forward to continue toward the gangway.

Desperate to stop him, Hamish made a grab for his arm, but Mateo pushed him away.

Hamish looked back at Bellamy who was still waiting with Rita.

"Stop him," he called back to the sergeant.

Bellamy took several long rapid strides toward Mateo.

"Stop. Police." He called.

At the same time Hamish rushed forward. As he approached, Mateo threw his arm back to punch Hamish in the jaw, but the doctor ducked, and Mateo was sent off-balance. He dropped the parcel, and both Hamish and Mateo swept in to retrieve it. Mateo had almost taken hold of the package when Bellamy came from behind, grabbed him by the shoulders and drew him back to a standing position, his arms held firmly behind his back.

Rita swept in and plucked the parcel from the wooden dock tearing away the paper. Lillian's Still Life was revealed.

Hamish, Rita, Bellamy and Mateo stared at it. Everyone was still, as if caught in a moment that had more weight than any moment before or after. Then Mateo began to struggle like a feral cat, his body tense and his eyes wild. Bellamy placed his feet wide to give himself as much stability as possible as he held on to the wreathing, stretching, cursing man. Hamish stepped in to assist and together they pushed the writhing creature forward.

"You'll hurt yourself struggling like this," said Hamish, gripping the man's shoulders in his attempt to contain him.

No one had noticed the arrival of the coach from Government House conveying Alejandro and the countess.

Alejandro jumped from the coach as it pulled up and ran toward the scene with Bellamy still holding Mateo captive and Rita holding up the missing painting.

"What's going on?" cried Alejandro. "Let him go," you will have the Governor to answer to."

Hamish looked up at the coach where Isabella was watching them sullenly.

"This man is being taken to the station for questioning," said Bellamy, "in relation to the rape and murder of Lillian Murphy, and the killing of Carlos Perez."

"What are you talking about?" cried the Spanish nobleman.

Bellamy called out to Pennyweather to wait for them at the police vehicle. Mateo slowly stopped struggling. He watched Alejandro closely, daring him to allow the process to continue.

Alejandro looked from the painting to Mateo and then at Bellamy. He stepped back.

"We sail in two hours," he said, and stood aside to allow Bellamy to drag Mateo past him. Mateo's muscles tensed again, and he kicked upward with one leg after the other, almost setting Hamish off-balance. It was all he could do to maintain his grip and keep himself from falling. He threw himself to one side and shook free of Hamish's grip. Bellamy allowed his body to fall to one side with the Spaniard and retained his hold on his wrists, still behind his back. Mateo wasn't able to shake the sergeant, and he couldn't gain traction with his feet. Bellamy regained control and continued to force him toward the cab. Mateo hissed something at Alejandro as they passed, but it was unintelligible to Hamish or Rita.

Pennyweather had waited at the cab as instructed and assisted Bellamy to bundle the footman, still putting all his energy into trying to free himself, into the vehicle. Bellamy and Pennyweather sat on each side of him keeping him contained while Rita and Hamish moved off to find another cab to transport them back to the station.

Rita, Hamish and Bellamy were soon reunited in the interview room at the police station. Mateo sat opposite them, staring straight ahead. His energy had been spent but his eyes were still wild. His jaw was set. He ignored Bellamy's questions and maintained the look of someone expecting to be plucked out of the situation at any moment.

Bellamy was asking Mateo how the stolen painting had come to be among the countess' suitcases. The footman stared into space with a fiercely determined expression.

Bellamy exchanged glances with Hamish and Rita then called for Pennyweather to watch their suspect, checking first that the man was well and truly handcuffed, with a chain around his feet. The three of them stepped out of the room and spoke in quiet tones.

"I'm not sure exactly how this all fits together, but I'm now certain this man was responsible for the deaths. He was probably sent by Alejandro to carry out the killings," said Bellamy.

Hamish pursed his lips.

"That certainly rings true in the case of Perez, but I still can't see why Alejandro would bother to have Lillian killed."

Rita was listening to both sides. "Send for the witnesses," she said. "One, or both of them, might recognize Mateo if he is the killer."

They all agreed. It wasn't certain the man who had seen the cab drive past the hotel after Lillian walked by on the evening of her murder, or the worker from the aquarium who had seen a man crossing the paddocks beyond the fence prior to the discovery of Carlos Perez's dead body, would recognize Mateo, even if he was the killer. But they were running out of time, and it was worth a try.

Pennyweather was sent to retrieve them.

Meanwhile, Hamish, Bellamy and Rita made themselves a cup of tea and waited. The prisoner had no interest in talking, so they left him alone, securely locked in the interview room.

"He must be wondering by now why the countess and Alejandro haven't sent someone to rescue him," said Hamish as they sipped their tea.

"I have to admit I'm wondering the same thing myself," said Bellamy.

"I think they've decided to sacrifice him," said Rita.

Ten minutes later, the first man stood outside the interview room and looked through the glass.

"It's not the driver," he said. "I had a clear view of him." He stared at Mateo for some time before speaking again. "He was in the cab," he said.

"Are you sure?" asked Bellamy.

The man nodded. "I'm sure, it's the colour of his skin. I remember wondering what a half-caste was doing riding about in a cab. But he's not, is he? He's a Spaniard."

Bellamy nodded slightly to Hamish who had gone into the interview room to keep an eye on Mateo. The footman kept his eyes firmly ahead refusing to face the window or look at Hamish. Hamish thought he remained confident his employers would come for him before the boat sailed.

The worker from the aquarium stepped before the window next. "Can you get him to stand up and walk?" he asked.

"His legs are in irons," said Bellamy. "He won't be able to walk, but he can stand."

Bellamy spoke to Hamish through the door and Hamish told Mateo to stand up. The man mistakenly assumed his employers had come to retrieve him, so he stood up without hesitation.

"That's him," said the workman. "He's the one I saw striding across the wetlands just beyond the fence line. He was even wearing those trousers."

Hamish put his hand on Mateo's shoulder to push him down into the chair, but he kicked out and sent the chair flying into the wall. He threw himself forward and caught his right shoulder under the table then threw himself upward sending the table over as well. Hamish moved out of the way and pressed himself against the wall, while Bellamy rushed into the room and gathered Mateo with the full force of his body against his chest and forced him to the floor. Hamish righted the chair as Bellamy lifted their captive by one arm and forced him back into it. Hamish lifted the table and returned it to its usual position.

Hamish left the room to retrieve a second chair then he and Bellamy sat opposite their suspect. Blood was dripping down his cheek from a cut beneath his eye from impact with the corner of the table as he upset it.

"I think your employers may have abandoned you," said Hamish watching him closely. "Do you not wonder why they have not sent for you by now?"

Mateo's jaw muscles tightened.

"You are in possession of a painting that belonged to the murdered girl, and two witnesses have attested to seeing you in the vicinity of the victims around the time of the murders," he said. "Do those seem like coincidences to you?"

Still, Mateo remained mute.

"You don't believe we can charge you," said Hamish. "You still believe they're coming for you."

The Spaniard's eyes flickered for a split second.

"We're holding you for further questioning," Bellamy told the prisoner. "You can talk to us now, or after the ship has sailed, suit yourself."

Bellamy nodded toward Pennyweather through the window and the young constable entered the interview room. He took one arm while Bellamy took the other and they lifted the man to his feet. They forced him through the door and toward the cells. Mateo let his legs go limp so that they had to drag him all the way.

"He still believes Alejandro is going to sweep in any minute and save him," Hamish repeated.

"He might, at that," said Bellamy. "I'm half expecting a call from the Governor at any moment myself."

"And I still don't understand why Mateo would kill Lillian. Was he out drinking and came upon her, an innocent young woman alone? It doesn't quite make sense. And why keep the painting?"

Rita looked on quietly thinking.

"I'm going back to the wharf," she said. "I need to speak with Isabella again."

"What will that achieve?" asked Bellamy.

"I'm not sure," she said. "But the Countess is the key to this, not Alejandro."

CHAPTER TWENTY-FOUR

I was born at San Sadurni de Noya, Province of Barcelona in 1859, where I was brought up as a carpenter. As such, I was the president of the Carpenter's Trade Union and a member of the Republican Party.

I was arrested on June 25 on the pretence that I was to answer questions at the Palace of the Civil Government. They searched my house and found a book on Republicanism. They then took me to prison where I was kept in a cell with seventeen others. Two weeks later I was called out with two others, and we were placed in three separate subterranean cells. Two gendarmes bound my wrists together with spiked iron chains tightened by a key and ordered me to run up and down the cell which was twelve paces long. If I stopped running, I was whipped. This lasted twenty-two hours with nothing to eat or drink. They then offered me salt-cod, but said I would eat vermin if I did not confess to throwing the bomb on June 7. I lost consciousness and on recovery found that the nails of both my big toes had been forced back by spikes.

I have sworn that I do not have any association with the Spanish Anarchists.
Evening Journal Saturday 11 September. 1897.

***

Isabella de la Vega

The Countess Isabella and her maid were unpacking a gown of the most exquisite pink silk and lace and laying it out on the bed when there was a knock at the door.

Isabella looked up cheerfully as her maid answered the knock. When she saw Rita's face her own smile faded but she quickly composed herself and welcomed the doctor in.

What did it matter if the infernal woman had worked it out? They would soon be on their way across the ocean toward the other side of the world. The real world. The only world that mattered. Europe.

"Doctor Cartwright?" she said. "I didn't expect to see you again."

Rita noted the formality of the greeting. Isabella had never referred to her by her title. Rita entered smiling broadly.

"Nor did I expect to see you," she said.

Rita ran her hands across the beautiful fabric draped over the bed and looked around. The cabin is small compared to your chambers at Government House," she said.

Isabella watched warily. The doctor is no fool. But what is it she is playing at? Isabella chose to let her come to the point of her visit in her own time.

Rita perched herself at the edge of the bed. The maid looked horrified and went to speak, but Isabella silenced her with a look.

"You loved him," Rita said at last.

Isabella threw her head back and laughed. Her eyes were cold when she looked back at Rita.

"I thought I did," she said. "But I was mistaken. He was not the man I had imagined him to be."

Rita nodded.

"Mateo has been identified by witnesses as the killer of both Lillian Murphy and Carlos Perez."

Isabella blinked but offered no response beyond that.

"There you are then," she said softly. "You have your man."

"I thought you ought to know," said Rita. "I had the impression he was a loyal servant to you."

"He was...loyal," said Isabella, the first sign of a crack in her armour. She quickly regained composure. "Nonetheless."

"I expected you to be surprised," Rita suggested.

Isabella wanted this infuriating woman to leave her alone. Now that she had boarded the ship her mind was elsewhere. Why had she ever accepted the invitation to visit this backwater in the antipodes? She couldn't get away from the place soon enough. The whole sorry saga with the anarchist had been beneath her. But she was young. She had learned from it. And no harm done.

"Mateo will hang," of course, said Rita matter-of-factly.

Isabella's eyes narrowed.

"And so, he should, if he committed these crimes." She turned to the dresser and placed her pearl backed hairbrush and comb in order.

"What I don't understand is why Mateo killed Lillian, surely he wasn't so evil as to attack an innocent woman in that way, in a random act of violence?"

Isabella sat on the stool in front of the dresser and looked at Rita's reflection in the mirror.

She spoke slowly and quietly.

"I knew about the dalliance with the serving girl," she said. "Perez was weak, as are most men."

She paused to catch Rita's eye in the mirror.

"But when I saw the little painting depicting the anarchist symbol – I knew how foolish he had been. That painting would have confirmed his presence at Moreton Bay. I had Mateo steal it to protect him." She shook her head. "Perez was an idiot."

"You instructed Mateo to eliminate the girl, didn't you?" Rita spoke in equally measured tones.

Isabella lifted her head and held it high like a pedigreed pony.

"I have no interest in how it was done, but the servant girl was dealt with."

"Then Perez rejected you, didn't he?"

Isabella felt the blood rush up her neck. She hated that her emotions were being displayed in this way. Who did this woman think she was, coming to her cabin and needling at her. She wanted to lash out, she wanted to slap her across the face. But her aristocratic arms lay limp in her lap. No. She would not debase herself. Afterall what could the doctor do? In an hour they would be away from this godforsaken place.

"I must prepare myself for afternoon tea with the captain," she said, "before we sail. "Thank-you for bringing me news of Mateo. I hope his conviction brings peace to the family of the servant girl. There is no one who will miss Carlos Perez."

With this, she stood, and her maid opened the door for Rita to leave.

"Before I go," said Rita, "Why keep the painting?"

The blood rushed to Isabella's face. That had been a mistake, wrapped at the last minute, a token, a memory...

"I should have burned it," she said matter-of-factly.

When Rita left her, she was patting her cheeks with powder, unconcerned by the train of events she had put in play.

***

Hamish

Rita hurried back to the police depot and crashed into Bellamy's office, out of breath and flushed.

"I know how the events of the past week unfolded," she said. "The full story."

Hamish and Bellamy waited for her to catch her breath then handed her a mug of hot tea. As she sipped on the brew, Rita relayed every detail of her conversation with the countess, then the three of them joined Mateo in his cell.

"I've spoken to the countess," said Rita. "No one will be coming to collect you."

The Spaniard's eyes grew wide.

"It's true," confirmed Bellamy.

Rita went on.

"In fact, Isabella's exact words when I told her you would hang, were... and so, he should, if he committed these crimes."

Mateo lurched to his feet and drew his arm back as if ready to lash out at Rita, but Hamish caught his arm mid-flight and held it in a vice-like grip. The man summoned all the tension in his muscles to force himself free, but Hamish was used to his reactions now and his hold was firm. Bellamy nodded to Pennyweather who was watching alarmed. The constable disappeared and returned in less than a second with handcuffs that Bellamy quickly applied to the prisoner, both arms pulled tightly behind his back.

"Sit down," he instructed in a voice that demanded instant compliance. Mateo sat.

His muscular body bent low over his knees, and he remained hunched over that way for some minutes. Hamish thought he might vomit. So much tension had been stored in the muscles of his body, and now the energy seemed to be released, gradually, reluctantly. His head swayed from side to side on his neck, his large hands covered his face.

At last, the movements in his muscles subsided and he brought up his head.

"This is all about Isabella," he said with some venom. "Everything is always about Isabella."

Hamish took a deep breath. He knew with certainty Rita had read the situation accurately.

"Isabella met the anarchist three years ago, when he was an officer. He was involved in an incursion, innocent villagers were killed. He said he'd been made a scapegoat for the deaths, regardless of the truth of it - he left the military disillusioned. That's when he joined the anarchists. Isabella was obsessed with him. I helped them meet in secret. After the bombing in Madrid, Perez ran to Australia, like the coward that he was. But Isabella could not let him go. She instructed me to seek him out and keep track of him."

"You told her he was in Brisbane?" said Rita.

"I did. She then arranged for her party to travel to Brisbane to stay as guests at the Governor's mansion. It was as much to show Perez that he could not escape her, as anything else," he said.

Rita and Hamish exchanged glances.

"I reported to Isabella her lover's interest in the servant girl."

"Lillian was not a servant girl," objected Rita.

Mateo ignored her.

"At the art exhibition, when she saw the painting, she asked me to bring her shawl, and she told me to steal the painting. She also told me to do away with the girl."

Hamish and Rita suppressed a gasp.

"Then, when Perez rejected her, she told you to kill Perez," said Rita.

"I did my duty," he said.

Hamish wanted to ask if it was his duty to rape young women as well, but he kept silent.

Bellamy asked for the name of the driver who had assisted him to rape and kill Lillian Murphy.

Mateo couldn't wait to tell them the name of the local man who had been more than willing to assist for what was a laughably small amount of money. Pennyweather was immediately dispatched to bring the man in, while Bellamy formally charged Mateo with the murder of both Lillian Murphy and Carlos Perez.

They left him sitting on the edge of the wooden bench provided for prisoners to sleep on, again curled over with his head in his hands his face twisted with anguish.

Bellamy glanced through the door of his office at the clock on the wall. "The boat sails in less than an hour," he said.

Rita blew air through her lips, "the countess is taking afternoon tea with the captain right now."

"Isn't there anything we can do to hold her to account?" Hamish asked.

Bellamy shook his head. "She'll feign all knowledge of the events and there's no evidence of her direct involvement in these killings. The authorities won't allow it to become a political nightmare. We'll have to be satisfied that we've charged the men who carried out the deeds."

Hamish considered it a hollow victory. "The violence perpetrated by Mateo is terrifying," he said. "He is a severely troubled man. I'm glad, at least that he has been taken off the streets."

"Nonetheless, the countess used him as a weapon," said Rita. "It irks me to see her get away with it."

"I'll provide the Chief Magistrate with the full story, and we'll notify the authorities in Spain. But I'm afraid the countess will not face accountability. At the most, her family will keep a closer eye on her to ensure she doesn't do anything else to cause the family scandal.

Hamish, Bellamy and Rita stood on the wharf and watched the ship sail down river. It would pass the spot where Lillian's body was found before reaching the mouth and heading out to sea. The Countess Isabella de la Vegas had the decency not to stand on the balcony and wave to well-wishers on the shore with the other passengers.

CHAPTER TWENTY-FIVE

The execution of a murderer recently was the occasion of another of the revolting scenes which have been so disgracefully common. In his anxiety to avoid all chance of the strangulation of which a certain sentimental class keep a morbidly keen outlook, the executioner went to the other extreme and so arranged matters so as not only to dislocate the neck, but to sever the head from the body. **Tasmanian News 21 January 1886.**

***

The trial of Mateo was carried out over two weeks in November. His accomplice was to be tried separately. For most of the days Hamish sat in the gallery between Rita and Anne-Marie. While Anne-Marie clung to his arm, Rita sat on the other side of him, with her hands held firmly in her lap. He knew Anne-Marie required his support, she was deeply troubled by what had happened to Lillian, and by the trial. He also knew that while Rita would normally have been glued to his arm through such an ordeal, that she was keeping her distance in respect for his blossoming relationship with Anne-Marie.

Rita had an emergency at work and was unable to attend Mateo's trial in its final day, so he listened carefully, committing every detail to memory for the account he knew she would require that evening.

It took no time at all to hear from a very weak defence. The representative for the defence made a great deal of the fact that, in both cases, the witnesses were quite a distance from the accused and could not therefore have seen clearly enough to identify anyone. But, in truth, no one in Brisbane thought the Spaniard anything but guilty and no sympathy was lost on him.

Rita had been ready to testify to the words spoken by the countess, but no one wanted to hear them. The Spanish Court had been advised of the full story and had agreed readily not to seek any form of diplomatic immunity. From the perspective of the Colonial Government, the Governor of Queensland and the Magistrate, the individuals directly responsible for the killings were being charged and that was all that was needed to end the matter. The information about Isabella instructing Mateo to kill both Lillian Murphy and Carlos Perez was never presented to the jury.

Hamish sat with Bellamy as the final words were spoken by the judge. Death by Hanging. The courtroom abrupted in shouts of hooray! Mateo was to be hanged for his crimes, the fellow who had assisted him in Lillian's murder, was committed to life in prison, the first two years of which he would serve in irons. Hamish wondered why he didn't also receive the death penalty, but he was a local man, born and bred in Brisbane and Bellamy said this was enough to spare him.

Hamish and Bellamy were enjoying a good sherry at Hamish's house by six in the evening on this last day of the trial. It was a relief it was over, but it didn't hold the satisfaction that other investigation outcomes had in the past. They both felt that somehow, they had allowed one of the killers to get away.

Rita ran up the stairs at six-thirty, having picked up Anne-Marie on her way.

"I heard it is the death penalty for Mateo," she said as she caught her breath. "The paper boys are already shouting about it."

"True enough," said Hamish.

Rita sat on the blue chair but kept her feet on the ground while Wallace poured her a glass of the sherry and sat down with one himself. Anne-Marie went immediately to Hamish who placed a gentle kiss on her head before she sat down, and Red took a single leap into her lap.

"He will hang," said Bellamy. "I wish there had been a way to bring charges against Isabella, but there was not. I suppose she's back in Spain by now, with barely a thought for the man she ordered to carry out these heinous crimes."

"The nobility are not held to the same account as the rest of us," said Rita. "It's regrettable, nonetheless."

"Some days I wonder why I bother," said Bellamy. "It's the system. As soon as someone titled is involved, the rules go out the window."

Hamish nodded in agreement. "The law is supposed to be the great equalizer, but it isn't so in reality. It makes a mockery of what we do."

"What I hate the most is that the countess had no doubt at all that her money and status would shield her," said Rita. "She didn't give a jot for the lives she left trampled in her wake."

A few moments later, Anne-Marie met Wallace at the top of the stairs where he was delivering an evening supper of crumpets and honey. She took the platter from him and placed it on the occasional table. "I think you are all too hard on yourselves," she said. "The individuals who put poor Lillian through that terrifying ordeal have been brought to justice and Mateo will hang. That he is not sailing comfortably back to Spain with the others is the result of your excellent work and persistence."

Hamish shook his head. "It doesn't feel like enough."

"It is gratifying that the man will hang," offered Bellamy.

Hamish felt conflicted. "Even that doesn't sit well," he said. "I don't hold with capital punishment."

"Nor do I," agreed Anne-Marie. "Although in this case..."

"Surely, if it is justified..." cut in Bellamy.

Hamish sipped his sherry. "I can't believe taking a man's life in that way is ever justified."

Bellamy appeared astonished at such an idea.

"Of course it's justified. Guilt has been proven beyond any doubt. There have been cases where innocent men were hanged, but in this instance, there is no doubt whatsoever.

Regardless of the countess and her orders, the man chose to rape and torment poor Lillian, as well as kill her in a most violent fashion. For that matter, twenty-three slashes at Carlos Perez neck were hardly necessary to dispatch him either. Mateo was an extremely violent man."

"Nonetheless, I can't help thinking that violence begets violence. Hanging a man is such a considered procedure, carried out by so-called civilized men..."

"Hanging is a barbaric practice," agreed Rita. "In Europe many courts rely upon death by electricity. Most papers find it a more humane method of producing death."

Hamish felt encouraged. "The rope and gallows serve more as theatre for the audience than a way to combat violent crime," he said.

"You'd have us living in anarchy," scoffed Bellamy. "Your resolve is altogether too weak."

Rita's eyes softened as she watched her friend. "Actually, there's no evidence that the use of capital punishment does anything at all to minimize the number of deaths caused by violence. Indeed, the number of murders in our colony seem to increase by the year."

Wallace had clearly had enough of this topic of conversation. "This is a morbid debate," he said.

He addressed a question to Anne-Marie who had been sitting through the debate about capital punishment at a loss for what to say. "How is Delia faring? Did neither she nor her mother attend the trial?"

Anne-Marie sighed. "They couldn't face it," she said. "They want to move on with their lives. In fact, they have done just that. George Prentice has officially proposed, and Delia has accepted. Mrs Murphy says she couldn't be happier with the match."

"I'm so glad to hear it," said Rita, clapping her hands.

Anne-Marie hesitated, then added, "Of course they won't be married until they can afford a place their own. We have a horse stud out past Ipswich with a cottage and stables. It has been vacant on and off since father's death, so it is a bit run down. But mother has offered Prentice a position as caretaker. As soon as it is habitable the couple can marry and move in. Mother and I are going to reignite the business, breeding and training horses."

"That's wonderful news," said Hamish.

Rita leant over and gave Anne-Marie a firm hug. "Congratulations to you and your mother as well," she said. "The business is a wonderful idea. Prentice and Delia will make a go of it. I know they will."

"I've never met a man more suited to breeding and training horses," agreed Bellamy.

Everyone raised their glasses and drank to the happy couple and the new business, while Red wriggled irritably in Anne-Marie's lap. He put up a paw to touch her chin. He had taken a liking to the new guest in their house and wanted all her attention.

"It looks as though I've lost my friend," laughed Rita.

Everyone was suddenly silent.

Rita's eyes darted across the room toward Hamish. "No. I meant..." she began.

"I know what you meant," said Hamish quietly. He took Anne-Marie's hand and squeezed.

There was tension for a moment as everyone stared at their glasses, then it lifted, and the chatter began again.

"Delia and Mrs Murphy have become good friends to Mother and me as a result of this ugly business," said Anne-Marie. "If anything good can come of murder."

"It gives me hope to know that attitudes toward domestic service are changing for the better," said Hamish.

"I think attitudes are changing on a range of societal issues," said Rita. "We live in changing times."

"Let's drink to that," said Wallace.

Hamish, Anne-Marie, Rita, Bellamy and Wallace clinked their glasses. "To changing times!" they said.

CHAPTER TWENTY-SIX

Streets and stores put on their best appearance on Tuesday last, and our residents were not behind those of other towns in making the occasion one of liberal patronage to the shopkeepers. Early in the afternoon people from the country commenced to come in, and quite a good business was then done at all the stores and shops. But it was not until after dark that the throng really set in.

As is known by every parent, the long looked for pleasure of the children is to walk around town on Christmas Eve and see the shops. Shortly after dark, fathers and mothers with, in many cases, troops of youngsters behind them – from the dashing seventeen-year-old down to the little toddler were to be seen winding their way down the main streets and stopping at each window to gaze upon the tempting articles displayed for sale.

As the night drew on the streets were crowded and presented as lively an appeal as we have ever seen. The business done must have been great. All the stores were full of people waiting to be served. Fruit shops were thronged, and light drinks were in great demand. But the windows with the toys displayed had the greatest number of admirers.

Our mystic old friend Santa Claus must have had his work cut out if he undertook to dispose of all the toys that were purchased and visit all the stockings that were hung up for them. The hotels in the line of march did a good business, and many were the groups of friends who pledged their best wishes in long glasses of beer, or with a sip of something in a more concentrated form than colonial beer.

The many brilliantly lit shops and the numbers of Chinese lanterns swinging about above the footpaths, or amongst the green boughs with which most of the veranda posts were adorned, gave the streets a very lively appearance. The first shop to attract attention was Brown and Wilson's. On viewing the windows was to be seen a sprig of mistletoe and sprays of English holly with a barrel of dried apples in the centre. Sugars of excellent quality, also raisins, pickles, currants and plums, bottled fruits, lemons (candied), lollies and nuts.

In the drapery windows of the Reliance Stores were to be seen an innumerable supply of silk handkerchiefs and articles of all sorts, to fit all classes; umbrellas, ladies dress materials, and on the other side of the door were arranged to effect, tweeds, scents, fans, children's toys, fancy goods and musical instruments.

On approaching the stationary store, the first windows showed a magnificent array of Christmas cards, enough to draw the customer at first sight. In the next windows were vases of various shapes, and inside musical instruments, books, novels and albums and every other requisite to the literary table. **Warwick Examiner Saturday 28 December 1889.**

***

Christmas came around more quickly than anyone had expected, what with the anticipation of the trial and the tension of the execution. There were also the heady days of new love as Hamish found his feet in the first serious relationship he'd entered since leaving Melbourne. He found Anne-Marie's devotion to him intoxicating, and her down to earth intelligence grounded him. She had slipped into his life easily. Rita admired and respected her, Wallace found her charming and even Red trembled with excitement whenever she was around. She was easy to love, and Hamish wondered whether he did, in fact, love her. He wondered if one day he would wake up and find the dizzy height of emotion had passed, and he would again be alone and unsure of himself.

But it was the Christmas season, and he was bathed in the joy of it. He decided to entertain his friends with a lavish Christmas meal, the first he had ever hosted in his home. At first, he was nervous about raising the topic with Wallace in case the cook felt it was asking too much of him. But when he did make the suggestion, Wallace was delighted. He said he looked forward to giving the new gas oven Hamish had purchased for him, a decent workout.

Diamonds skipped along the river and glittered in the sun, while Hamish walked hand in hand with Anne-Marie a few days before Christmas. The air was warm on their heads and there was excitement in the voices of the children playing.

"I'm going to host my first Christmas dinner this year," announced Hamish. "I've spoken to Wallace and he's as excited about it as I am. He's been running ideas for the menu by me all week." Hamish laughed at the memory. "And Rita has taken on the task of decorations. She fancies creating some form of table centre piece from native flowers. I only hope there's room left on the table for food as well..."

Hamish took two or three steps before he realized that Anne-Marie had stopped. He turned to see if she was hurt.

"Is there something wrong?" he asked.

"No." she replied. She looked confused.

"Your plans sound wonderful, Hamish. But mother and I always have Christmas together," she said quietly.

A wave of relief passed over him.

"Of course," he said. "Your mother must join us..."

But Anne-Marie was shaking her head slowly. She took his hands in hers. "I don't know that she'll want to have Christmas dinner away from home. She and cook plan the dinner for weeks, we invite local business owners and officers. I was expecting that you would join us."

It was his turn to be confused. "I apologise," he said, "I shouldn't have presumed you'd be free on Christmas Day."

"I'm sorry, Hamish."

"No. Not at all. It is entirely my fault. It's just a lunch. We'll go ahead with our plans just the same."

Hamish smiled broadly to cover his disappointment. But she didn't return his smile.

"Are you not coming to mother's dinner, then?"

Hamish blinked. He could have said he would cancel his plans, or that he would have his dinner on Boxing Day. But he had already invited Bellamy and Agatha, and Rita and Wallace were also looking forward to it. He couldn't believe he hadn't asked Anne-Marie sooner. But he'd only come up with the plan this last week and he hadn't seen her since.

"I'm sorry," he said. "But I can't disappoint our friends."

While he was saying it, he knew that it wasn't the only reason he couldn't cancel. He was looking forward to the dinner, excited about Christmas for the first time in years. He also knew that Anne-Marie was a big part of that renewed excitement.

"I understand," said Anne-Marie as she turned to walk back the way they had come. "I think we should head home," she said.

Hamish took her hand in his and held it loosely as he walked her back up the hill to the mansion on Bowen Terrace. Somehow a bubble had burst. The world in which only he and her existed and no one else mattered had deflated, leaving them both feeling lost and unsure. Hamish kissed her gently before leaving her safely at her door. He took long strides toward home in the hope of expelling his disappointment through physical exertion.

How had neither of them mentioned their plans for Christmas before this? Hamish acknowledged he had assumed that Anne-Marie would fit into his plans, and he felt ashamed. But Anne-Marie had made the same assumption about him. A small misunderstanding, he thought, we'll each enjoy Christmas in our separate ways and spend the following day together. He couldn't understand why such a small thing had deflated him. He had heard that emotions were amplified where romantic relationships were concerned.

***

The racket coming up the stairs was enough to wake the dead. Hamish and Rita crashed into the drawing room first, closely followed by Bellamy and Agatha. Wallace was putting the finishing touches to his table and wasn't quite ready for them to pile in on him.

"It was so hot in the church," said Rita, removing her gloves. She slumped into the blue velvet chair and caught a warning glance from Wallace. With the smallest of smiles she lifted her skirt a few inches to show him that her boots were firmly planted on the floor.

"The carolling was splendid though, don't you think?" said Agatha. She had her arm linked firmly through her husband's. Hamish thought how lovely it was to see her and Bellamy together and so evidently happy with one another's company. But the thought turned immediately to the fact that Anne-Marie was not with him, and his fear that she was disappointed in him. He hadn't even been able to see her at church because she and her mother attended the catholic service at the large stone Cathedral on the hill.

"Just marvellous," said Bellamy. "You should have joined us," he turned to Wallace.

The old cook was busily pouring sherry from a crystal decanter and serving drinks from an engraved silver tray.

"I see we have the good glasses out," said Hamish.

"It is Christmas, after all." Wallace handed Hamish his sherry first.

"To Christmas!" said Hamish lifting his glass in a toast.

"To Christmas!" They all lifted their glasses.

Agatha walked over to the tree where it stood from floor to ceiling in the bay window, behind Rita on the blue chair. "This is a wonderful tree," she said. "Where on Earth did you find these charming shell decorations?"

Hamish beamed. "I collected the shells when I was on Stradbroke Island a few years ago. An Islander woman I know through the surgery, the maid of a patient of mine, was able to weave them into stars for me. She's incredibly talented. She weaves small items and sells them for extra income."

The tree consisted of a section of Norfolk Pine cut off and standing in an ornate ceramic pot filled with small stones. It was decorated with the woven shell stars, a rope of cranberries, and tiny wax candles. It wasn't crowded or ostentatious, it was simple and smart. Like the table laid out beautifully by Wallace while they were all in church. Elegant white plates decorated with a slim single silver ring around the edges sat on red embroidered placemats with sparkling silver cutlery alongside. The settings shone in contrast to the white damask tablecloth. In the middle of the table was a centrepiece – a crystal bowl of oranges with golden boughs of wattle and scattered cinnamon sticks. The aroma wafted through the room in subtle waves that reminded everyone of Christmas.

Wallace motioned for everyone to take their seats at the table and went downstairs to bring up the first course, delicate pink prawns tucked into champagne glasses with just a squeeze of lemon. They used tiny silver forks to pluck out each morsel and soak in the flavour.

"Perfect, in this heat," sighed Rita.

"I love the way you have arranged your home," began Agatha, "with the kitchen downstairs and well away from the drawing room. That means we don't need to contend with the heat from the kitchen. Our house, as you know, is all on one level and the heat can be stifling when the stove is on."

"It's mostly arranged to accommodate the clinical rooms downstairs," said Hamish. "But it does work well, as you say."

"Speaking of clinic rooms, it's been a full year since you left general medical practice to take on your new role as medical examiner," said Bellamy. "It seems like it was yesterday."

Hamish put his fork down and considered the past year. "In some ways it doesn't seem like a year, but in others it seems like a lifetime ago that I was struggling to sustain the practice."

"Do you enjoy your new role?" asked Agatha.

The question was innocent enough, but asked as it was in front of Bellamy, it was difficult for Hamish to answer.

"I enjoy the investigative role," he said slowly.

Bellamy swallowed the last fat prawn. "He doesn't like the bureaucracy," he said.

Rita wiped lemon from her lips with a napkin. "I think we all knew he wasn't going to like that," she said.

Hamish was struggling to find an appropriate response when Wallace appeared at the top of the stairs with a piping hot roast lamb surrounded by baked potatoes, sweet potato and onions. He placed the platter at the centre of the table and returned to the kitchen to retrieve beans and a gravy boat.

"That new range you purchased for him is a godsend," said Bellamy.

They all laughed and served themselves ample portions of everything on offer.

Lively conversation continued throughout the main course and the rich fruit pudding that came up the stairs next along with boats of custard oozing with brandy.

No one returned to the topic of Hamish's work with the police department.

When no one could eat another thing, Hamish, Bellamy and Agatha moved back into the drawing room and slumped into the comfortable chairs. Hamish stood behind the velvet chair looking out of the window, while Rita went downstairs to help Wallace. Dishes clanked and glasses tinkled as they moved about the kitchen.

With the meal over and the excitement of the day waning, Hamish's thoughts returned to Anne-Marie. He wondered how her party was going and whether she had thought of him at all. He sipped more sherry and stared into space while his mind took him through a range of scenarios, each one worse than the last, in which Anne-Marie was falling in love with some officer in a fine uniform.

Suddenly, he became aware of hushed voices on the staircase. He glanced up to see Rita and Anne-Marie struggling to the top of the stairs giggling as they worked together carrying a large package tied in brown paper and string, with a sprig of wattle tucked into the bow.

Hamish leapt from his seat to greet Anne-Marie with a kiss. The emotion swelled in his chest like a rising sea. The two women thrust the package into his arms.

They both stared at him with gigantic grins.

"This is for you," Anne-Marie said. "From both of us." She glanced at Rita and they both laughed.

Hamish slipped the string from the package carefully and began to tear the paper then he held his present up and examined it.

"It's a Jenner," cried Rita. Hamish smiled at the image. It was a picture of the Hamilton Reach, much like the one he had been admiring at the Exhibition.

"But this must have cost a fortune," he said.

Anne-Marie smiled.

"Actually, it's a sketch by the artist in preparation for the final work. It's still an original piece – but not worth nearly what the finished painting is worth."

"I love it," declared Hamish. "All the more for it being not quite the completed thing. Just like me, not quite complete, still wondering what I'm going to be when I'm finished."

Rita hugged him, then Hamish reached for Anne-Marie and kissed her on the lips.

AUTHOR NOTES

Others will see the islands large and small,

Fifty years hence, others will see them as they cross, the sun half an hour high,

A hundred years hence, or ever so many hundred years hence, others will see them,

Will enjoy the sunset, the pouring of the floodtide, the falling back to the sea of the ebb tide.

It avails not time nor place – distance avails not,

I am with you, you men and women of a generation, or ever so many generations hence,

Just as you feel when you look on the river and sky, so I felt,

Just as any of you is one of a living crowd, I was one of a crowd,

Just as you are refresh'd by the gladness of the river and the bright flow, I was refresh'd,

Just as you stand and lean on the rail, yet hurry with the swift current, I stood yet was hurried,

Just as you look on the numberless masts of ships and the thick-stemm'd pipes of steamboats, I look'd.

I too many and many a time cross'd the river of old.

From Crossing the Brooklyn Ferry, Walt Whitman

***

Anyone who has read this far through the Dr Hamish Hart Mysteries will know that I have a fascination for rivers. Rivers play a major role in each of the stories, partly because of my fascination with them, and partly because of the essential part they play in life in the early days of settlement. But most importantly, rivers link people across generations, as Walt Whitman so beautifully reminds us in his poem. From the convicts building a hard-fought settlement to modern city cats ferrying busy commuters, the river carries both progress and memories in its currents.

The Brisbane River is a mirror, reflecting the city's past and present, a living thread connecting generations. And finally, the river is beautiful. As I look out of my window now, I see the water shimmering beneath the summer sun. On rainy days, the dancing drops of rain on the river's surface make me feel calm. The river moves. It moves past histories both seen and unseen. It moves beneath bridges and over memories, always moving, always present.

The Brisbane River traces its origins to about 40 million years ago, according to geologists. Ten million years later, the riverbed took shape as we know today. Stretching nearly 300 kilometres from Mount Stanley in the rugged eastern ranges to the salty embrace of Moreton Bay, it is neither the mightiest nor the eldest of rivers. But when joined by the veins of the Stanley and Bremer Rivers plus 22 creeks, its reach becomes a catchment sprawling over 13,500 square kilometres.

People have always settled along rivers. For over 40,000 years, the Turrbal and the Yuggera people lived around the banks of the Brisbane River. According to Tom Petrie, the First Peoples had no single name for the river but gave sections of it different names. The Hamilton Reach, significant to this story, was once known as Yurrol—a place named for the thick rainforest vine used to weave huts, sheltering lives intertwined with the land. Dense rainforest pressed close to the river's edge, a green, tangled fringe sheltering countless forms of life and echoing with stories lost to all but memory.

Westward along the Reach, what we know as Breakfast Creek diverges from the river. Here, a series of weirs and traps, woven from stakes, saplings, and branches, waited patiently for fish. With the rhythms of the tides, fish would swim into these snares at high tide and become trapped when the waters receded. After the establishment of the convict settlement, to the First Peoples, these fish were far more than a meal; they were sustenance for their families and a source of trade with the communities of Brisbane—a testament to a complex, living culture in harmony with the water.

By the 1850s, however, this harmony was shattered. The First Peoples were forced by police across Breakfast Creek, marking a harsh boundary line for European settlement—a cruel erasure of connection to a place that had sustained generations.

The first bridge over Breakfast Creek was built in 1836 to transfer female prisoners to the stockade at Eagle Farm. The women's farm on the alluvial soils alongside the river provided grains and vegetables for the main settlement. The farm was worked entirely by female convicts who were kept well away from the men at North Quay.

Brisbane's oldest surviving house sits on a hill at the junction between the Brisbane River and Breakfast Creek. Newstead House was built in 1846 and the residents enjoyed sweeping views of the river both up and downstream. At that time there were 483 Europeans living on the North side of the river. It was already, by far the most expensive land in the new settlement. Land in North Brisbane cost one hundred pounds per block. (In South Brisbane land was one pound an acre). The area was growing so rapidly, newspaper articles in the 1850's declared "there is a sweeping destruction of trees and bushes lately growing along the river and if no care is taken, soon nothing in the shape of a native tree will be discoverable in the environs of Brisbane." By the 1860's most of Hamilton east of Racecourse Road was noted for its fine villas and 'gentlemen's estates.'

In 1885, 'The Hamilton Reach Estate' was advertised for auction with estate frontages along the Brisbane River. In addition, the Wickham Estate was auctioned with lots situated on the bank of the Brisbane River, immediately below the Hamilton Hotel and intersected by Eagle Farm Road (Kingsford Smith Drive) and Nudgee Road. In 1886, horse-drawn wagons were added as feeders between the horse tram terminus at Breakfast Creek and the Hamilton Hotel.

The Body on Hamilton Reach opens with a visit to the first exhibition of the Art Society in Brisbane and Hamish is surprised that so few paintings depicted local scenery. This was common in the era. Local artists tended to paint scenes from their country of origin. But he was taken with the work of Isaac Walter

Jenner who produced superb works of art depicting scenes around Moreton Bay, and some of his best, in my opinion, are his works centred on the Brisbane River.

The prominence of the river in these paintings reflected it's economic, geographic, aesthetic, and symbolic significance for early settlers. It was both a literal lifeline and a potent symbol in the evolving story of the settlement. There were many reasons to paint scenes focusing on the river. It served as a major geographic landmark that helped to orient early maps. Including it in paintings helped to contextualize the burgeoning township within its natural environment and provide a focal point for depicting the settlement's growth.

As a vital transport route, the river facilitated trade and communication, playing a critical economic role. Jenner's paintings often captured shipping activity, docks, ferries, and riverside commerce, symbolizing progress and prosperity.

The Brisbane River, with its meandering curves and lush banks, provided artists with an attractive subject for landscape painting. The river's beauty and changing light offered a dynamic scene that was both aesthetically pleasing and emblematic of the region's natural appeal.

For settlers, depicting the river in art was often a way to assert their presence, documenting the taming of the landscape and transformation of what was perceived as a 'wild' environment into a settlement. The inclusion of the river underscored their influence over nature, reflecting a colonial narrative.

In line with Romantic artistic traditions prevalent in Europe during the 18th and 19th centuries, rivers symbolized the sublime power of nature, life, and renewal. By placing the river in their works, artists could evoke grandeur, growth, and promise, weaving it into the cultural narrative of Brisbane as a place of opportunity and potential.

The river often served as a boundary between what settlers saw as the "wilderness" and areas being developed for European use. This contrast was depicted to illustrate the tension between nature and the emerging colonial town. The ultimate victory of 'civilisation' over 'wilderness', of control over the natural world.